What other fiction write
Tribulation

– – –

"Quirky and fun...a book you don't want to put down... Delivers deep truths with a twist and a smile, with a wink and a grin—and with that straight-to-the-heart arrow of conviction that will make you think."

—**Wanda Dyson,** author of the Shefford Files novels
and coauthor of *Why I Jumped*

"An innovative, refreshing look at the old 'too-heavenly-minded-no-earthly-good' dilemma, but with plenty of spunk and satire."

—**Susan Meissner,** author of the Rachel Flynn Mysteries

"A refreshingly different take on single-minded obsession and the pursuit of selfish pleasure. Chris Wells provides a wacky romp through this tale of end-times-prediction-gone-wrong."

—**Mindy Starns Clark,** bestselling author of the
Smart Chick Mysteries and the Million Dollar Mysteries

"Packed with...humor, pop culture, theology, and organized crime. The result is as thought-provoking as it is seriously funny. Don't get left behind on this one."

—**Jason Boyett,** author of *Pocket Guide to the Apocalypse*
and *Pocket Guide to the Bible*

"Laugh-out-loud humor full of fast-paced mystery, gangsters, pop culture, and spiritual insight. The antidote to end-times hysteria. Not only is *Tribulation House* an easy pill to swallow, it should be prescribed for everyone."

—**Eric Wilson,** author of the Aramis Black Mysteries

It started badly.

As the luxury car pulled up, mobsters Ross Cleaver and Bill Lamb got out of the sedan and walked across the gravel. The back window lowered and cigar smoke curled out. Sun in his eyes, the boss squinted at them. "What you boys got for me?"

Cleaver gave the boss his most serious face. "Everything is on schedule, Mr. Massey."

Lamb blurted, "We tried to press the drugstore guy, but he scared us off."

The boss puffed a few moments on his cigar. Then he squinted from one man to the other, then straight at Cleaver. "Was he a big fella? Real bruiser?"

"Sure, he—"

Lamb added, "Little old man. Kinda shaky."

The boss glared at Cleaver. "Shaky old man, huh?"

Cleaver pretended to ignore his associate, was trying to think of the best way to kill the dummy. "You see, it's like—"

The boss smiled helpfully again. "He was packing, right? Shotgun or something? The guy got the drop on you?"

"Of course, boss—"

"Naw," Lamb blurted. "Just this old man shaking his finger."

Massey gritted his teeth, trembling. "Some harmless old man scared you off? All by himself?"

Cleaver had nothing to say.

Lamb did. "He wasn't by himself. He had the armies of God hanging over him."

The boss almost spit out his cigar. "You gotta be kiddin' me."

━ ⁓ ━

TRIBULATION HOUSE

CHRIS WELL

HARVEST HOUSE PUBLISHERS

EUGENE, OREGON

TRIBULATION HOUSE
Copyright © 2007 by Chris Well
Published by Harvest House Publishers
Eugene, Oregon 97402
www.harvesthousepublishers.com

Library of Congress Cataloging-in-Publication Data
Well, Chris, 1966-
  Tribulation house / Chris Well.
      p. cm.
  ISBN-13: 978-0-7369-1741-4 (pbk.)
  ISBN-10: 0-7369-1741-1
  1. Swindlers and swindling—Fiction. 2. Gangsters—Fiction. 3. Rapture (Christian eschatology)—Fiction. I. Title.
  PS3623.E4657K56 2007
  813.'6—dc22
                                                              2006030647

Printed in the United States of America

  07 08 09 10 11 12 13 14 / LB-CF / 10 9 8 7 6 5 4 3 2 1

To Pastor Ray McCollum, Pastor Rice Broocks,
Pastor Tim Johnson, and my church family
at Bethel World Outreach Center

ACKNOWLEDGMENTS

The author wishes to offer thanks to the members of Well-Organized: Chris Mikesell, Daniel Dawson, Tracey Bumpus, C.J. Darlington, Katie Hart, Kristi Henson, David Meigs, Roberta Croteau, Matt Mikalatos, Bonnie Calhoun, Mimi Pearson, Linda Gilmore, Mirtika Schultz. Your support and friendship is amazing.

Also, many thanks go out to Ruth E. Anderson, Robert Bealmear, Matt Bronlewee, Carole Brown, Susan Browne, Joyce Bumpus, Janet Butler, Jerry Charles, Gloria Clover, Troy and Stacie Collins, Jacob Custer, Linda Dawson, Sue Dawson, Kathleen Emigh, Joe & Marie Endres, Tricia Goyer, Sherry Gray, Toby Hancock, Jean Jaeger, Jason Joyner, Jamie Kunzmann, Beth Lewis, Carolyn McCready, Julie Mikesell, Nick Mikesell, William M. Mikesell, Robert Mineo, Lydia Ondrusek, Don Pape, Donita K. Paul, Candace Pope, Melba Pritchard, RD Reider, Bud Rogers, Paul Rose, Jr., Paul Rose, Sr., Cheryl Russell, Jay & Jamie Swartzendruber, Mary Sergent, Keith & Roxanne Shaw, Tony Shore, Kerry Smart, Katherine Gutwein Smith, Kathie Sprout, Kathleen Sprout, John Thompson, Richard Vance, Jay Vineyard, Shirley Watkins, Rosa Lee Well, Judy Wetherbee, and Susan Zartman. You have been more help than you can know.

Thanks also to my fellow novelists in Sta Akra: Brandilyn Collins, Tim Downs, Creston Mapes, Melanie Wells, Kathryn Mackel, Robert Liparulo, T.L. Hines, and Eric Wilson. Your advice and fellowship is incalculable.

And thanks to Noah Strebler and Tanner Strebler. You are two of the finest nephews an uncle could ever hope for.

— ~ —

Men of Galilee, why do you stand looking into the sky? This Jesus, who has been taken up from you into heaven, will come in just the same way as you have watched Him go into heaven.

ACTS 1:11

Of that day and hour no one knows, not even the angels of heaven, nor the Son, but the Father alone.

MATTHEW 24:36

— ~ —

"I MIGHT AS WELL JUST TELL YOU RIGHT NOW, I KILLED REVEREND DANIEL GLORY."

– 1 –

I might as well just tell you right now, I killed Reverend Daniel Glory. Back there at the church, in his study.

But this is my story. Don't let anyone tell you different. My dad always said we all write our own story. Of course, I guess that's why it worked out so well for him.

Why did I kill Reverend Daniel Glory? Sure, it was an accident. More or less. At least, I think it was.

I don't know, we were arguing about the Rapture and it kind of got out of hand and then I just—

Wait. Wait. I'm getting ahead of myself. Let me back up.

This all started about three months ago, when Reverend Daniel Glory told us we needed to do our Tribulation House earlier than—

Oh. Wait.

Okay, I guess this actually started last year when Marvin Dobbs left the church. Our church. The Last Church of God's Imminent Will.

A year ago last summer, Marvin left with some of the other families to start a new church, and he took his Armageddon House multimedia show with him.

You do know about Armageddon House, right? Every Halloween for the past three or four years, Marvin and our team put together a special multimedia presentation explaining the Great Tribulation, which ends with the Battle of Armageddon.

Wait—you don't know about the Great Tribulation? It's that seven-year period between the Rapture and the Triumphant Return of Jesus Christ, as described in the prophecies of Daniel and Ezekiel and the apostles Paul and John. After the Lord Jesus takes His Bride home, there are going to be seven years of horrible judgment inflicted on those who are left b—

What? The murder of Reverend Glory? I'm getting to that.

Well, anyway, when Marvin left to form his little offshoot splinter group, we discovered he had actually trademarked the name "Armageddon House." Imagine that.

When the board at church met to discuss the matter, we considered doing Armageddon House anyway without him. Just reconstruct it from memory and copy or use materials from previous years. Use the same name, business as usual. Just ignore the cease-and-desist letter, let God and His angels work that out.

But we decided we didn't want to be associated with Armageddon House anymore. I mean, if Marvin and his new "fellowship" planned to stage their own Armageddon House, the risk of confusion in the marketplace was enough to rebuild ours as a brand-new event.

Which is how we ended up with Tribulation House. It was an opportunity for a new beginning. We went through a whole list of possible names—I came up with Kingdom Come, but was voted down—before we settled on Tribulation House.

We sat down and worked through the whole grid. Instead of imagining how to simply explain or show a picture of each bowl of wrath and each trumpet of judgment, we created an entire theatrical event.

Yeah, we could have set up the charts and graphs and the overhead projector. But today's audience, this last generation, they're kind of jaded about flannelgraph presentations, know what I mean?

These kids today, with their *SpongeBob SquarePants* and their *American Bandstand* and their *Buffy the Vampire Slayer*, they need the bells and whistles and the like.

They don't need a lot of explanation. They need a *demonstration*.

You see, that was the challenge, wasn't it? It's one thing to say "the moon was blackened" or "the waters turned to blood" or "men were stung by enormous flying scorpions"—but how do you make it happen right *here,* right before their eyes?

In the end, we created Tribulation House: A full-sensory immersive interactive dramatic theatrical evangelistic event that simulates what it will actually be like to live through the events of the Great Tribulation. An entire full-service prophetic experience.

You'd be surprised how much of it we accomplished with sound and light. We developed the various rooms throughout the church basement. Some college kids created soundscapes for each event. We wrote up a full script for the actors; they played everything from people caught up in the events, to the world armies fighting the Most Holy, to the father of lies himself, bound and thrown into the pit for a millennium.

The murder of Reverend Glory? I'm getting to that.

So we were working out the blueprints for creating Tribulation House as a major theatrical evangelistic full-sensory ministry outreach. We had debated the merits of various slogans for the event—the leading contenders were WE'LL SCARE THE HELL OUT OF YOU; GET RIGHT OR GET LEFT; and THE TIME IS CLOSER THAN YOU THINK. While the first slogan was a favorite of several board members for its bracing, truthful stance, in the end we worried that the neighbors would misunderstand. So we went with the second slogan, for its simple, instructional message.

And I remember the meeting where our chief carpenter, Bill Broadstreet, was giving us his estimate for the physical construction to be done on the project. Suddenly, Reverend Daniel Glory burst in with some news.

"Friends!" There was a glow on the Reverend's face unlike we had ever seen before. The man stood there in the doorway to the church basement, leaning against the door frame, wheezing to catch his breath. "Jesus is coming back!"

The room was silent. We all stared. At first, we wondered why he was saying this right then. After all, he preached on this topic every week. But then he dropped the bomb: "And I know when!"

Okay, that was a new one. Collectively, everyone in the room gasped. One of us, I don't even remember who it was, asked, "When, Reverend?"

"October 17."

Five months.

"5:51 AM." Reverend Glory waved the papers clutched in his hand. Later, I would wonder what he was waving at us. His Bible study? His calculations? All I know is he grinned from ear to ear and said, "The Rapture is going to happen at 5:51 AM on October 17."

Everyone around the meeting table reacted differently. Some were stunned into silence, others screamed with joy. One noisy woman loudly sobbed and clapped.

Reverend Glory came into the room, face aglow with thrill and exhaustion, and dragged a chair from the wall over to our table. He sat, waiting until everyone was silent again. "I now have incontrovertible proof that the Rapture takes place this coming October."

I'm sure I grinned bigger than anyone in the room. "What reason do you have to say that?"

Reverend Daniel Glory looked at me and winked. "Why stop with *one* reason, boy? I got one hundred and seven of 'em!"

Of course, you know what this meant. We were going to have to step up the production of Tribulation House.

(I still can't believe it's not Kingdom Come.)

– 2 –

Out in the car, Ross Cleaver was bored. He and associate Bill Lamb had been sitting for maybe forty minutes in the gravel lot across from Zykes Drugstore. They were new to the territory, just wanted to get to know their future "clients." This was the edge of the business on this street. Drugstore, barbershop, church. Then you hit the houses. In front of the church, the sign read GET RIGHT

OR GET LEFT. Underneath, in smaller letters, it read, THE TIME IS CLOSER THAN YOU THINK.

Cleaning his fingernails with his teeth, Cleaver once more thought over his mental to-do list: *towing operation, check; numbers-running, check; insurance cooperative, check.* ("Insurance cooperative" had a much better ring to it than "protection racket.")

Cleaver turned and regarded the other man. Saw Lamb finish off yet another plastic bottle of water and drop it to the floor of the Pontiac with the other empties. Cleaver grunted. "Got a bladder problem?"

"Whut?"

"The water." Cleaver, still trying to clean under his thumbnail with his bottom teeth, nodded toward the empties piled at the other man's feet. "You drink a lot of water. Got a bladder problem?"

Lamb turned and stared with wide, glassy eyes. Twitched. "Why would drinking a lot of water mean I have a bladder problem?"

"Why not?"

"If I had a bladder problem, I would drink *less.*"

Cleaver grimaced, wishing he never brought it up. "I'm just saying, a person with a bladder problem might want to flush something out of his system."

"If I had a bladder problem, I'd have no trouble flushing—"

Cleaver held up a flat hand. "Hold it." He pointed to the windshield at the back exit of the drugstore across the street. The old man was closing up for the night. "There he is."

Cleaver opened the driver side and exited the car, carefully—he really needed to lose that last thirty or fifty pounds (or think about a bigger car). As he rounded the front of the car, Lamb joined him. The man was a head taller and decidedly thinner.

He sometimes wondered how Lamb stayed so trim. After all, the two had about the same eating habits, got about the same amount of exercise. Give or take a shakedown or the odd beating of some welsher.

Maybe it was the nervous twitching. That had to burn off calories.

Cleaver and Lamb crossed the empty street, smelling fresh tar, reached the drugstore exit just about the time the grizzled old man was locking up, fumbling with the key ring.

Cleaver glanced quickly at Lamb, hoping this time his associate kept his mouth shut. He turned eyes back to the old man locking up. "Evening, Padre."

The old man jumped, whirled around. "Oh! You startled me!" He was on the frail side, Cleaver noticed. Should be no problem.

"Don't worry, Padre," Cleaver said. "You're safe. We just—"

"Yeah," Lamb snorted, rotating his shoulder blades. "Safe."

Cleaver shot his associate a glare. "Do you mind?" He turned back to the old man with a forced smile. A little more predatory than he intended, but the only smile he had. "You'll have to excuse him." He started over. "Um…" He had lost his place. *Evening Padre don't worry Padre you're safe we just…* "We just wanted to express our concerns for you in this neighborhood."

The old man stared back. Blankly. Serenely.

Cleaver motioned to the buildings around them—the church, the gas station, the greasy diner, a row of houses. "This ain't the safest area. Know what I mean?"

The old man's eyes narrowed, his gaze sharpening to a point. Trembling, he raised a bony, misshapen finger at Cleaver. "You have no business here," the man said in a trembling voice. The two mobsters stepped back. "Get thee behind me."

What was with this guy? Cleaver forced a grin, held up conciliatory hands. "Hey, old-timer, you got this all wrong. We represent an insurance cooperative."

"Sure," Lamb tossed in, nodding like a jackrabbit with a neck problem. "An insurance racket."

Cleaver shot Lamb angry eyes. "The grown-ups are talking here."

The old man picked up steam. "In the name of our Lord Jesus, I cast you out!" Still pointing that skeleton finger. "I rebuke you!"

Cleaver waved his hands. "Okay, okay." Turned to Lamb. "Let's hit it." To the old man, "We're sorry to have troubled you, sir."

As the two thugs walked, Lamb let out this sort of whine. A

signal he was about to make a comment that would endanger his quality of life right now.

Cleaver held up a hand. "Whatever it is, stifle it."

"But—"

"I don't wanna hear it." Cleaver snorted and spat snot on the tar.

The two men were silent as they reached the car. Key in the ignition, hit the gas, tires spitting gravel as they drove away. Checking the rearview mirror, Cleaver punched the gas again and swerved out into the road. In seconds, they were back at the main drive.

He wasn't sure what had happened back there. All he knew is he would never trouble the old man again.

— 3 —

Detective Charlie Pasch was assigned to clean the toilets.

The toilets. The public restrooms that every public person came and used when they forgot to go before they left home.

Of course, here, today, he was not "Detective Charlie Pasch, Kansas City Police." Here he was just "Charlie," one of the dozens of volunteers helping on the annual cleaning day at Mercy Street World Mission Church.

Back when he'd signed up to help, he had not expected to be cleaning toilets. In fact, that had been his one secret hope: that he not get stuck cleaning toilets.

Sure, there were no glamorous jobs when cleaning a major facility like the WMC. Some volunteers were sweeping the parking lot. Some were weeding the grounds. Some were repainting the gym.

Charlie was cleaning the toilets.

Not that he was alone: He and Grady Webb were the adults

supervising a gaggle of 12-year-olds also wishing they had been stuck with something else.

But Charlie was not going to let it get him down. He was here to *serve*. He would make sure the mirrors were cleaned, the commodes polished white, the tile along the walls mold- and mildew-free.

Occasionally, though, Charlie felt a gripe rising in his throat, and fought it. Down on hands and knees, polishing the base of the toilet, he searched his mind for an appropriate scripture. He couldn't think of anything related to cleaning toilets, so he grabbed hold of 2 Corinthians 10:5: *We are destroying speculations and every lofty thing raised up against the knowledge of God, and we are taking every thought captive to the obedience of Christ.*

Rubber gloves on hands, Charlie scrubbed the inside of the urinals. Fighting the urge to retch. Every time he felt the humiliation or anger rising, he reminded himself to "take every thought captive" and scrubbed harder.

Grady's voice echoed from over by the shower: "Hey, you hear about that Second Coming booklet?"

Charlie was thrilled to have something to take his mind off the job. "Which one is that?"

"107 Reasons Jesus Is Coming Back in 2007."

"I saw something about it in the paper."

"Pastor Mac talked about it Wednesday night."

"I missed church Wednesday," Charlie answered, squeezing his sponge into the bucket, then getting more liquid soap. Not sure whether he was doing this right. "I was on a stakeout."

A younger voice asked from behind, "Where do you want these, Mr. Charlie?"

Charlie, wiping sweat off his forehead with the back of his arm, sat back on his heels and looked at the kid. Justin, he thought the name was. "What do you got?"

Justin held up a wrapped cylinder of paper towel in one hand, another in his other hand. Breathing hard from running back up the stairs.

Charlie nodded toward the front sink. "Set them over there. I guess you have the rest out in the hall?"

"These are all I could carry."

"What do you mean?"

"You know, two hands, two rolls."

"We need a whole case. Didn't you take the cart?"

The kid shrugged. "No."

Charlie sighed, fighting to retain his patience. *Don't lose it, Charlie.* "Take the cart to the elevator, go downstairs, and get a whole case of paper towels. I think there's like a dozen rolls in each box."

The kid nodded and ran for the hall. Charlie knew Justin would get a kick out of using the service elevator; it was normally off limits to the kids.

Charlie turned his attention back to the job. *Blech.* A few minutes passed before he thought of something. Yelled across the room, "What did he say?"

From around the corner came the echo of Grady's voice. "Who?"

"Pastor Mac."

"Oh. He was saying how this guy's whole worldview is focused on the wrong thing. Instead of, you know, 'Do the job, follow Jesus' commands,' this guy is telling people to put everything down and watch the skies. Pastor Mac calls it 'X-Files theology.'"

"Wow." Charlie nodded as he scrubbed. "That's good."

"And since the guy is telling people he knows when Jesus is coming back, that makes him a liar. Although I'm not sure why Pastor said that."

"That's easy." Charlie dropped the sponge in the bucket, dragged the bucket to the sink. "Jesus said that even *He* doesn't know the day or the hour He's coming back." He dumped dirty water down the drain. "Consequently, no mere mortal is going to have that answer."

"Huh."

Charlie glanced toward the showers at the far end of the men's room. From this angle he saw Grady and a couple of the kids sponging mildew off the walls. Charlie wondered how thick it had gotten.

The bucket filled with clean water, Charlie dragged it to the next urinal. He heard Grady continue the story: "So, apparently, this guy was here at church Wednesday."

"What guy?"

"The *107 Reasons* guy."

Charlie dropped the bucket, water sloshing around the edges. "He was *here?*"

"Apparently he's got a local church. But for some reason he was here and he heard Pastor Mac say he was a liar."

"What, did he stand up during the church service or something?"

"No, he came up after service and told Pastor Mac, 'I'm the guy who wrote that book.'"

Charlie grabbed the sponge, started scrubbing again. "He said it like that?"

"Well, I don't know *how* he said it, but the guy told Pastor Mac he wrote the book. And then he says he doesn't appreciate being called a heretic. And Pastor Mac just keeps smiling and says, 'One of us is a liar. And on October 17, everyone will know which of us it is.'"

Charlie stopped scrubbing. "He *said* that?"

"Yep."

"Wow."

The conversation soon turned to other topics—Grady wanted to talk about music and sports, Charlie wanted to talk about comic books. They split the difference and discussed rock songs about superheroes. Grady was surprised to learn there were more than 300 songs that referenced Superman alone.

By the end of the morning, the adults and their young helpers had finished: The trash cans were empty, all the porcelain polished, paper-towel dispensers reloaded, closet stocked with paper goods, and the shower sparkling clean.

Charlie and Grady stood at the front, admiring the group's handiwork. One of the boys gave Charlie a weary look. "Can we go to lunch now?"

Grady looked at Charlie. "What time is it?"

Charlie checked his wrist, remembered he left his watch in the car to keep it clean. "Wait, I'll check." He started to reach into his pocket for his cell phone, then remembered how filthy his hands must be. As he washed his hands—*thoroughly*—he asked, "Have they started setting up lunch downstairs yet?"

Another boy said brightly, "I think so."

Hands clean, Charlie reached an elbow toward the dispenser and pushed for a towel, then blotted his hands dry. He threw the crumpled towel in the trash and pulled out his cell phone. 11:47 AM. The box lunches would be available at noon.

Back aching, he said, "Go ahead." As the boys ran off, rubber soles squealing on tile floor, Charlie called after them. "After lunch, back here so we can clean the ladies' room!"

Which, of course, was something he'd hoped he would never have to yell in his life.

— 4 —

I remembered having a spirited discussion about a week later. I was at the office, Sherman's Realty. I work there as an agent.

The workday had barely started. I was in the kitchenette, getting the coffeemaker going, when I started talking with one of my co-workers, Helena Wheeler. She was a regular churchgoer, so she and I would sometimes discuss religious matters, but I often found her to be kind of loose in her eschatological leanings.

"I saw the story in the weekend paper," she said as she grabbed her coffee mug and poured from the decanter.

"Oh?" I was playing it cool. "Which story is that?"

"About the little nightclub y'all are putting on."

"Tribulation House is certainly not a 'nightclub,' " I bristled. "It is a full-sensory immersive evangelistic event."

"Of course." As she tapped powdered cream into her coffee, I caught a faint smirk. "But I thought y'all usually did that on Halloween."

"I guess you didn't read the story very carefully." My turn to smirk. "We only have until October 17 to warn the people. Noah had 120 years to preach before the flood came. We have less than three months."

"Uh-huh."

"So we're pulling together our most creative members from the church," I continued. "You know, carpenters, sound engineers, electricians, craftspeople—the whole gamut. This is going to be a top-notch event."

"Hope y'all have some decent production values. Christians have a hard enough time in the culture without making ourselves a laughingstock."

I felt the anger rising in me, but tried to laugh her comment off. It came out as a snort. "The world mocks what it cannot understand."

"No," she said, her voice already thick, "Jesus is the stumbling block. We don't need to make it worse."

"How can we make it worse? Jesus is the—"

She cut me off. The nerve! "Christians make it worse by the way we behave," she said. "We make it worse by the way we talk. By the things we do."

I shook my head, voice trembling. "I don't think—"

She raised a hand. "Let me finish."

"Now, Helena—"

"If you represent the Lord, y'all need to put together a 'Tribulation House' that is without reproach. Better construction, better sets, better acting, better makeup, better everything."

"This is not some flannelgraph presentation," I said, voice rising against my best efforts. "This is an immersive theatrical sensory event."

"This needs to be Broadway-quality stuff."

"What does that mean?" I cleared my throat. "Do you mean more worldly?"

Helena made an awkward grin, like grinning was hard for her. "It's the apostle Paul on Mars Hill. He spoke to the pagans in their own cultural idioms."

"Sure. We are competing with the pagan venues"—I had to think about the names for a second, continued—"places like Slaughter Swamp, and Severed Arms, and Horror High. We have looked at the entertainment value they offer their audience and matched it. We get 'em in the door with our Broadway production values and then hit 'em at the exit with the option to turn or burn."

"Now that is just the sort of jingoistic, sloganeering, ambush evangelism—"

"I am sorry if serving the Lord is more important to me than for—"

"Let me finish." Helena put up that annoying hand again. "It took God hundreds of years, dozens of writers, and sixty-six books to tell us the Bible. Why do you think it's an improvement to reduce it to a series of bullet points?"

"Fine." Wishing the conversation were over, I pulled the decanter, poured into a mug. "I think we have the same goal here. We're just looking at this from different angles." I set the mug down, adding powdered creamer. I took my coffee and left the room for my desk. Wishing she would tire of the discussion and go away.

She followed me. "Jesus almost never preached sermons," she yammered as I reached my desk. "He told stories. About farmers and about fishermen. That was his crowd."

I started sorting through the folders in my box, just trying to look busy, keep the anger at bay. "That's it, that's exactly it," I said, slurping from my coffee. I should have let it sit longer. "And then we come in at the end and explain everything—"

"No, no, no." Helena's voice shook. "Jesus did not explain everything—He told the stories and let them hang in the air. He let the audience think about them, let the stories work their own way into the minds and hearts of listeners."

"Of course He explained his stories." I must have made a face, a sort of confused smile, shaking my head. "How else would we have the explanations in the Bible?"

"He explained them privately to His disciples. Just twelve people. He never explained them to the crowd."

"I don't know about that."

"That's what it says in my Bible."

I sat back in the chair and used my fingers to form one of those steeples, trying to look thoughtful. "Helena, I understand your points. I do. But we do need to remember that our time is short. When Jesus told His little stories, He had all the time in the world. We have less than three months."

"What are you talking about?"

I didn't feel like telling her. Instead, I just looked up and smiled. "Isn't it about time we got to work?"

– 5 –

City Councilman Lester Goode, Seventh District, was living the high life. Goode had the money, Goode had the power, Goode had the connections—and the connections were going to bring him more money and more power.

Ted Massey made it work. Goode was connected to Massey. And Massey was connected to organized crime.

This particular afternoon, Councilman Goode was preparing for his rendezvous with his mistress. They met every Monday afternoon. He was in the men's room adjusting his tie. He wanted to look good for his lady. He made bug eyes at the mirror; he thought it made him look sexy. He ran fingers back through thinning hair, grabbed his briefcase, and exited back into the hallway.

In the hall, he ran into Jerry Kirk. "Les, m'man!"

Goode smirked. "Jerry. What's the word?"

"Nuclear!" Kirk bellowed with laughter, like he had just said the greatest punch line in the world.

Goode chuckled, pretending to be amused.

Kirk finished laughing, wiping a tear from his eye. "But seriously, how is the case for the defense going?"

"It's coming along." The other man stared, waiting for him to elaborate. Goode added, "My lawyer says I have nothing to worry about. The prosecutor has no proof of any improprieties—"

"I thought they had a list."

"A list?"

"The list of dead people who supposedly voted for you."

"No. No such list could exist." He glanced at his watch. Zelma was waiting. "Listen, I have to go to an afternoon appointment. I'm going to be out of the office."

A grin spread slowly across Kirk's face, eventually reaching both ears. "Hot date, huh?"

Goode blinked. "I don't know what you're talking about. It's an appointment with a client."

"Sure." Kirk just kept giving him that look.

Goode squelched the urge to punch that face in. "You have the worst imagination of anyone I know."

Walking away, City Councilman Lester Goode, Seventh District, could not help but grin in spite of himself. The "list" mentioned by Kirk did, of course, exist, but Mr. Massey said it was taken care of. Massey took care of everything.

Reaching his car, he plopped his briefcase on the passenger seat, where he could keep an eye on it. The case full of unauthorized photocopies regarding certain zoning issues.

Punching a few buttons on the radio until he found some good country and western, Goode headed for the open road. A little outside of town, he took the usual circuit, checking the rearview mirror often.

During the careful process—as long as he covered his tracks, who would ever know the difference?—he sang along with the radio. Trick Henderson had a new rodeo song, and Goode mumbled along.

I look in her eyes and feel the luck
I just know this bronc ain't gonna buck
I can taste that trophy now
I ain't gonna plow
I ain't gonna bow
I look in her eyes and feel the luck

The song didn't make much sense, of course, but Goode liked the chords. And when the strings kicked in at the end, you just felt it, you know?

After he decided the coast was clear, he zeroed in on the Daylight Motel. It was a rundown operation outside of town, the safest place he knew to meet with Zelma. You weren't likely to run into anyone important there. (And, at a place like this, if you did run into somebody important, they were just as likely hoping you didn't notice them either.)

Goode pulled into the uneven gravel parking lot. Zelma's coded message indicated they had a room in the "J" wing. Of course, it was one continuous building, with the same series of numbers on the door. If you knew the number, any two rooms would help you triangulate where to go.

He pulled around back. The pool sported a big crack across its dry, dirty green basin. No danger of passing swimmers stumbling across the little tryst between Councilman Lester Goode and dancer Zelma Collins.

Not that he was doing a bad thing, mind you. He had long ago decided what he was doing was best for everyone concerned. A man had needs. But it was better to protect his wife and children this way. Keep them in the dark.

When Councilman Goode attended a prayer breakfast a few weeks ago, the preacher had made a few questionable remarks, something about staying with "the wife of your youth." And something or other about your prayers not being answered because of how you treat your wife.

Goode had not heard much. He was thinking about the scrambled eggs. They should have been a little runnier. There should have been more.

Locking up the car, clutching the briefcase close to his chest, Goode headed for J-14. He thought about his life and decided maybe he didn't need any prayers answered. His luck was just fine. He had more money than his wife or the IRS knew, he had power and more of it coming, and his connections meant he was on his way.

And now he was seeing his best gal. At his special knock, Zelma opened the door, all grins and not much else. "Whaddaya know, Goode? Are you governor yet?"

Lester was deflated. "Not yet." Setting the briefcase on the little desk, he loosened his tie. "But I'm working on it."

"Workin' on it," she whined. "Always workin' on it."

"That's right, Buttons." He leaned in to kiss her bare shoulder. "I got connections." He saw her pouty face and matched it with a broad grin. "If I help Ted Massey and his friends with their little zoning problems, Ted's going to help me on the ladder of success."

"That's what you always say."

"With Warren Blake out of the race, Massey has me lined up to be the next mayor." He rubbed his hand across the briefcase. "All I have to do is work out this zoning situation for him." Goode pulled off his tie, started unbuttoning his shirt. "Stick with me. I'm going places."

Later that night, on the way home to his wife, Lester Goode, City Council, Seventh District, had a heart attack, right there in the car. Hit a telephone pole two blocks from home.

It was all over the papers the next morning.

- 6 -

Detective Tom Griggs and his wife, Carla, were at the grave about 10 AM. Floral Hills cemetery. Standing there, holding hands, the Monday morning sunny and cool, but inside Griggs felt grey and cold. The air around them silent but for the sound of birds not yet flying south, the sound of cars passing in the distance.

Griggs took a light step forward, carefully, like he was walking across something brittle. He got down on one knee by the headstone. *KAYLA RAE GRIGGS. OUR PRECIOUS DAUGHTER. September 6, 1991–July 20, 2003.* They had lost their little girl exactly four years ago today.

Fighting back any emotion, he set the flowers down on the ground in front of the stone. Back at the flower shop, he had wanted to buy roses. But Carla said it was better to buy the floral arrangement. Apparently, these were what Kayla had liked. It all looked the same to Griggs, so it was fine with him.

He stood again next to Carla, who wrapped her fingers around his hand. They stood there a while, her staring at the stone, lip trembling, him looking around at the foliage. Taking note of the orange and yellow leaves. Falling and turning brown. Around their daughter's final resting place.

There was a long silence, just the birds and cars and Carla sniffling. Finally, she pulled a wrinkled tissue out of her coat pocket and wiped her nose. "All this time, you would think the pain would go away."

Griggs felt like he should say something. He grunted. "As long as you carry the pain, you can always remember." Not as profound as he had hoped, but it was all he had right now.

This was the first time in months they had visited the grave together. Griggs and Carla had spent years allowing the death of their daughter to drive a wedge between them. Griggs refusing to talk about what happened. Carla always leaving an extra place at the dinner table. Both wallowing in their private pain. Both wallowing in their private guilt. Blaming each other for the events that had stolen their little girl from them.

In the past couple of years, the two had started seeing a marriage counselor, who told them to work through their grief together. Until the counselor assigned it to them—made it an action item, in fact—it had never occurred to Griggs the importance of doing such a thing. You walk down the wrong road long enough, you forget there is a right road.

Carla sniffled again. "It's strange."

"What?"

"Being here." She squeezed his hand. "Together."

He shrugged. "She's our daughter."

"I know." She wiped her nose again. "It's just..." She let the sentence trail off. Finally, she said, "I guess it's just important to work through our grief together."

"Mm-hmm."

"You know, talk about things."

"Mm-hmm."

There was another silence, birds and cars. Then she asked, "What are you thinking?"

Griggs inhaled deeply. Shook his head. Could not find the words. Could not risk expressing what he felt, for fear of crying.

"You know, it's important to talk," she said. "The counselor said."

"I'm not in the mood."

Griggs stared at the headstone a few more seconds. Felt his knees going weak and turned for the bench by the pond. When Kayla Rae was little, they had brought her out here to feed the ducks. Griggs remembered stopping at the convenience store for a loaf of bread. Remembered showing tiny hands how to break the bread into small pieces, small enough for the ducks.

It seemed like yesterday. It seemed like a hundred years ago.

He sat down on the bench with a gruff exhalation. Carla sat next to him. As they stared at the pond, he wished he had some bread now.

Carla whispered, "It's important to stay connected." She tried holding his hand again. "The counselor says it's the key to working our way through this. You can't keep it bottled up."

"I know."

A family showed up on the far side of the pond. Small children fighting over a plastic bag of bread. Griggs watched the man, apparently the father, mediate between the two kids. As he watched, Griggs felt a smile cross his lips. He almost didn't hear what Carla said next.

"You should reconnect with your father."

He could barely believe his ears. "What?"

"It's not healthy to keep all this bottled up. I'm worried about you."

"This is not the place."

"Kayla Rae loved her grampa."

"She didn't know him." Griggs felt the bile in his throat. "He abandoned her when she was little."

Carla's voice was small, a hoarse whisper. "She visited a few times before he disappeared."

"He did not 'disappear.' He *left*."

"Of course he disappeared. You don't even—"

"Get it straight." Griggs jumped off the bench and whirled on Carla. "He abandoned his family. He cleaned out the register and left my mother with the bills. Facing an audit. Facing an illness without health insurance." He felt his fingers working by themselves and stuffed his hands in his coat pocket. Gritted his teeth. "I lost a promotion because of him." Suddenly full of bitter energy, he found himself pacing. "Why are we even talking about this?"

"It's important to—"

Griggs, still pacing, not even listening, cut her off. "I came to the cemetery to see my daughter. To remember my daughter. I did not come here to—" He stopped at the sound of his cell phone. Carla gave him a sour look as he checked the caller ID. It was the station. He turned away from her and answered. "This is Griggs."

"Oh. I thought I would get your voice mail." It was his partner, Detective Charlie Pasch. "I didn't meant to bother you this morning."

"It's okay. What do you have?"

"O'Malley has some dirt on Ted Massey."

If Special Agent O'Malley was passing along a tip, that meant it was something of special interest to the Kansas City Police/FBI Joint Task Force against organized crime.

Griggs suddenly felt a hand on his shoulder. "Tell them you're busy. Tell them you're in the middle of something."

He shrugged her off, took a step forward. "What did he say?"

"Massey has his people working a protection racket."

"You called me for that?"

"This one has an interesting twist. He's using the leverage to buy up real estate."

That was weird. "Why? What is he doing?"

"We're still trying to figure that out," Charlie said. "But you don't have to worry about it right this moment. I'll catch you up about it when you come in tomorrow."

"Sure." Griggs paused a second. Weighing the options. Finally, he said, "I'll be right in. I'll see you in about an hour." He pocketed the phone and turned back to Carla. Ignored the hurt look on her face. "I gotta go."

"I should have known. You didn't have the time for her when she was alive, why should you…"

Griggs didn't hear Carla finish. He was already walking away.

⟞ 7 ⟝

Why did I kill Reverend Daniel Glory? Ask my family. Really, all this trouble is their fault. I would never have killed Reverend Glory if not for them.

I remember when I first sat the family down and told them there were going to have to be some changes. With the Rapture coming in so many weeks, we needed to reprioritize. But were they supportive? Of course not.

Take my no-good son, Clint. He wants to be a writer. A writer! Can you imagine it? Sure, he has excellent grades and has won some awards. He even gets published in the local newspaper. But how do you make an honest living out of that?

Now, selling real estate—that's useful. That's productive. It's a trade that affects everybody. If the economy collapsed tomorrow, whoever owns the land owns the world.

But words? What good are they? Nobody needs words. Just give me a newspaper or a copy of *U.S. News & World Report* or a good detective TV show and I'm fine. You can keep your words.

Before dinner that particular night, the boy asked about money for his SAT tests coming up. It seemed as good a time as any to call a family meeting. Everyone gathered around the dining room table, the daughter with her cell phone unglued from her ear, almost paying attention. I decided to share the good news. "As you have heard, the Lord is coming October 17."

The boy gave me one of his smart looks. "You don't really believe that?"

I started sharing about Reverend Daniel Glory's *107 Reasons Jesus Is Coming Back in 2007.* Before I got far, my son jumped into it, picking it apart. "But you can't pick the time and day!"

"Don't give lip to your elders, boy," I said.

"The Bible says nobody can know the time or the hour. The Bible says *Jesus* doesn't know the time or the hour. How arrogant you must be to think that you're smarter than—"

"That's enough!" I slapped my hand on the table. It hurt. But I wasn't going to let them know. "This is my story. I don't need you stepping in here, Clint." I forced myself to relax, set my elbows on the table. Locked my fingers together. "We have irrefutable proof that we are not going to be here on this world much longer. So some changes are in order."

The wife suddenly looked alarmed. "Changes? What changes?"

"Well, this test, for example. There is no point in throwing our money away on a future that ain't coming."

"Wait." The boy again. "You're saying I can't do the SAT test?"

I sighed. "I don't know what the point would be."

"The point?" His voice rose, shrieking. "I need those SAT scores to go to college!"

"I don't even know what you need college for. You need a real-estate license to go into the family business." Why couldn't he get a real-estate license like a normal person?

He stormed out of the room. Punk kid. Never supportive. Always worried about his grades and about getting published. And my wife had the nerve to glare at me. My daughter just snapped her gum.

Anyway, it was all my wife and kids' fault that I killed Reverend Glory. It was what you call "exterminating circumstances."

The family has never been supportive. When I became deacon in the church, they didn't buy me presents or anything. When I started teaching Sunday school and I would come up with my lesson idea, I would ask my son for help with my research, but he refused to give me the Bible verses I needed. I would say, "I need to find some verses that teach such and such," and he had the nerve to tell me no such verses existed. Look, if I want to preach on the importance of washing your car...

Ahem. Anyway, there you have it. The family was never supportive.

That was why I needed a boat. A yacht, a schooner, whatever—something to take out on the water. Anything to rescue me from the cares of the world.

When our Lord Jesus needed time to be alone, He would take the boat out on the lake. Sometimes He would fish, sometimes He would sit and think.

I needed that. A refuge from this world. A refuge from all my cares, from all my worries. A boat to make me feel like I had it all under control.

When the kids were younger, we'd take long Sunday drives after church, go out to the big lots where they sold boats. Spent hours just looking at those magnificent creations, propped up, sitting on trailers and mounts, in all their glory.

The kids'd get bored, sure. And Marge had to work hard to keep the grin on her face. That's when the boy started his habit of reading in the car; eventually, we never went anywhere he didn't have at least one book on him.

But none of that mattered when we were in the lot. Looking at the boats. Dreaming. Dreaming of my chance to escape. To get out on the water like our Lord and just be away from it all, from all the people asking for loaves and fishes and healing.

A chance to get away.

That's what the boat represented to me.

For years, I would dream and plan and wait. It was okay because there was always a "someday" waiting for me, you know.

But when I heard that Jesus was coming back October 17, I knew that "someday" was about to pass me by. I couldn't enjoy Eternity if I didn't have a boat.

⁓ 8 ⁓

Following yet another semisuccessful attempt to extort money, humiliated thug Ross Cleaver drove the car a few miles down Airline Drive. Fuming over what his associate had blurted this time.

During the brief drive, the dummy tried to make small talk. Like he had no idea what had happened. "What do you think about monkeys that play musical instruments?" As usual, no rhyme, no reason, no connection to anything that had been said before.

Cleaver just gritted his teeth. "Shut up."

They reached the broken-down part of the neighborhood, past the row of gas stations and empty lots. Fuming, he parked the car in front of the now-closed Mister Bee's Grocery. When they reached the empty parking lot, he hit the brakes, the car abruptly stopping and then jerking forward. Lamb let out a surprised shriek. A stack of magazines slid off the seat and onto the floor.

Cleaver unsnapped his belt. He grabbed his occult magazines off the floor and threw them into the back. Without looking at the other man, he jabbed a thumb toward the passenger door and grunted, "Get out."

Lamb giggled nervously. "Whut?"

Cleaver jerked his thumb toward the passenger door more savagely. "Get out, get out, *get out.*" He shoved the driver door open, rocketing out of the car seat. Boot heels clacking on asphalt, he circled the car with quick, purposeful strides, ignoring the smell of fresh tire marks on asphalt.

He reached the other side of the car as Lamb dazedly exited his side. Cleaver clenched his fist and, white-knuckled, reared back and just popped Lamb right in the chops.

The other man yelped and fell backward, scraping palms on the parking lot. The dummy had a shocked look on his face, like he never saw it coming. Like they hadn't just come from his worst display yet. The man struggled with words. "Whut're you—"

Cleaver growled, "Git up."

Lamb just sat there on the ground, staring with wide eyes. Struggled with a shaky voice. "Whut?"

Cleaver stood over the man, breathing in and out, gritting teeth, clenching and unclenching his fists. "I said git up." He stepped forward with three big strides, took aim with the point of his boot, and kicked the man in the side. "Git up, git up, *git up.*" Kick, kick, kick.

Lamb was scrambling backward, trying to get his balance, trying to get up. "Wait!" The wail of a hurt child on the verge of tears.

Cleaver stood his ground. Breathing, gritting, clenching fists. Waiting. Waiting for the man to get a fraction of an ounce of a clue.

Lamb, one hand on his jaw where the bruise was forming, staggered to his feet. Inching backward, inching away. "Whut's the cheese?"

Cleaver sputtered, "Why can't you talk like a normal person? Huh?"

"Whut're you—"

"I mean, 'What's the cheese?' Who talks like that?"

"I got my own style."

Cleaver angled forward in a menacing pose. "You best drop your 'style' and get with the program. Somehow you convinced the boss you're connected, so he trusts you're connected."

Lamb, nursing the bruise, stepped back again. "I do got connections."

Cleaver stepped up, stepped in, close. "I ain't seen it." Hot, angry breath in Lamb's face. "All I seen is you spitting off a lot of dumb stuff, you stumbling over yourself, you tripping me up. You are the biggest dum-dum I ever seen." He pointed his index finger up. "You screw up once more, I ain't taking it." He angled the finger forward, jabbed Lamb in the chest. "I ain't taking any fall for you." Jab, jab, jab.

Lamb, trembling, stepped back, back, and tripped on the edge of the parking lot. He landed in grass and mud. He worked his mouth, but nothing came out.

"We stop here again, it won't be for another pep talk. You read me?"

There was no answer, so Cleaver stepped forward and growled. "*You read me?*"

Lamb, still sitting in mud, nodded vehemently. "Y-yes."

Cleaver's rage dropped from his face. He'd had his say. Glancing around the empty lot, he turned and looked at Lamb with cold eyes. Then whirled and headed for the car. He yelled without turning back: "You ain't tracking that mud in my car."

Cleaver got in the driver side. Snapped his belt without glancing into the rearview mirror. Punched the gas without looking out the window. Squealed away into the night.

As he swerved and joined traffic on Airline Drive, he imagined Bill Lamb alone in the Mister Bee's parking lot. With his thoughts and his mud. And a long walk home.

Wondered what Lamb had told the boss to get this gig. Who'd vouched for this dummy?

And if things got touchy and Cleaver had to deal with the kid, who would gripe? Who cared whether the kid lived or died?

But maybe Lamb was the brother of somebody important. Maybe he was somebody's nephew. Somebody's illegitimate son. Whoever the secret benefactor was, Cleaver needed to make sure he did not make a false step. Did not do something to make the problem worse.

But this dummy, he was just an atom bomb waiting to go off.

And take everybody with him. Whoever he was, he needed to be dealt with. And soon.

Cleaver thought back to the old man at the drugstore. Weird. With his bony finger and his unseen power. Like the man had some psychic connection or something.

He would have to figure that out too. Cleaver made a mental note to check his horoscope again when he got back to the apartment.

- 9 -

Detective Charlie Pasch was sitting in Pastor Mac Raymond's office. Wondering how much cash was in his wallet. "I didn't realize this was a lunch appointment."

Pastor Mac grabbed his suit jacket from the chair. "Well, I'm starved. Do you mind?"

Charlie, unsure of his monetary status, was surprised when he heard himself say, "Sure."

And that's how Charlie and Pastor Mac ended up at New Famous Chinese Super Buffet. Between egg rolls and General Zao's Chicken, Pastor Mac wiped sauce off his mouth with the paper napkin. "So, Charlie, how are you doing?"

Charlie stopped fiddling with the chopsticks and looked up. This was his opening. The whole point, in fact, for the appointment. But he looked back down at his cashew chicken. "Doing good, Pastor, doing good." Gave up on the chopsticks and unrolled the silverware from the napkin. "Still fighting crime."

"Is that right?" The pastor smiled, amused with the phrase. "So you're still investigating homicides?"

"No, I've been in organized crime." Charlie shoveled in a mouthful of lo mein before he realized what he'd said. Chewed quickly, swallowed, then corrected, "Excuse me," wiping mouth with napkin, "*investigating* organized crime."

"Well, I should hope so!" Pastor Mac, twinkle in his eye, started munching on a plateful of Crab Rangoon. Charlie had no idea how the man kept from getting it all over his face. Amazing.

Charlie tried it for himself, quickly felt failure smeared across his cheek. He was trying to artfully remove it when he heard Pastor Mac say, "I have always liked mystery stories."

"Mm-hmm." Charlie nodded, pretending he wasn't a mess. *Cool, play it cool.*

The pastor slurped a noodle. "You know, good versus evil, right versus wrong, the bad guys are caught and put away, and God is in His heaven."

Charlie dipped his egg roll in red sauce. "Sure."

"I have always felt like a mystery story is a great nonconfrontational way to share your worldview." The pastor spooling lo mein on his fork. "I don't know what Agatha Christie's personal beliefs were, but there were certainly some fascinating faith discussions in her Hercule Poirot novels. Especially the early ones."

"Really?" Charlie had Agatha Christie on his "to read" list, but had never gotten around to it. "I didn't know that."

"Not obtrusively, but simply as part of the fabric of the characterizations. Just little bits and pieces there."

Charlie nodded again. Wanted to nibble some more on the Crab Rangoon, but didn't dare.

The pastor continued. "And of course, Dorothy Sayers and G.K. Chesterton were both strong Christian writers and also pillars of classic mystery fiction."

Charlie started peeling apart his egg roll. "A real-life detective is probably the worst audience for a made-up crime story."

"You already see so much of it in real life?"

Charlie munched a fragment of crust. "Because we see all the mistakes. It's why a doctor can't watch doctor shows."

The conversation petered out. The two ate a bit in silence. Then Pastor Mac pushed aside his plate. "So, Charlie—we aren't here to talk about Agatha Christie, are we?"

Charlie blushed. "I guess not." He took a sip from his water and set the glass down. Pushed back the plate, set elbows on the table. "I wanted to ask you about...girls."

"Girls?" The pastor blinked and gave Charlie a sideways smile.

"I keep getting attached to girls and they keep going away." He grabbed one of the chopsticks and started making invisible patterns on the tablecloth.

Pastor Mac kind of pursed his lips. "Hmm. Do you mean that you always go out and then have a bad breakup?"

"No. I mean, I grow attached to them and then they leave town before anything can come of it. They suddenly get engaged to someone else and move away, or they go back home to reunite with their family, or whatever. Is there something I'm doing wrong?"

The pastor gave a fatherly smile. "You know, the concept of dating is a modern invention. It gives the unrealistic impression that relationships are meant to be casual, a matter of convenience."

Charlie nodded. "Okay." Where was this going?

"You're a young man," the older man continued. "Your whole life is ahead of you—focus your energy on God and career. In the Lord's perfect timing, when He knows you're ready, He will open the right doors for you. And if there is a woman out there for you, He will bring the two of you together. When the time is right."

"So...what do I do in the meantime?"

"Dig in and serve." The pastor regarded Charlie for a second. "It might not be a bad idea to serve in children's church."

Charlie raised an eyebrow. "What?"

"It really gives you the right perspective when you start working with the next generation."

Charlie thought about cleaning day. "I've never been much of a leader."

"You'll do fine. And, I daresay, you'll learn as much from them as they will learn from you. Too many in the church today are so blinded by this 'Second Coming' hysteria that they take their hands off the plow and start watching the skies. But if we are to be faithful to our calling, we need to keep building for the future. It's for the

Lord to decide when to come back. And those of us who are faithful will be found doing the work."

Charlie nodded, thinking.

The pastor sipped from his glass of water. He set it down on the table, nodding thoughtfully. "What about a mystery series where the pastor preaches the gospel and solves crimes on the side?"

Charlie frowned. "Don't you think it's kind of predictable?"

～ 10 ～

Hank Barton had a lot on his mind. After the home Bible study, the group broke up for after-meeting snacks. The ladies and gentlemen headed for the island in the Surtees kitchen, a smorgasbord of nacho chips and brownies and various soft drinks in two-liter plastic bottles.

Hank and his best friend, Sven Surtees, found themselves with their plastic cups of punch in the den by the big television, discussing whether the lady machine in *Terminator 3* was or was not a step backward from the killer model in the previous movie.

"But in *T2*," Sven was saying, "you have this killer machine made out of superhard liquid that can make itself into anything."

"Right," Hank replied.

"And then you have this woman robot who's just like the first model, but with this added liquid thing. It just seems—"

"She was the best of both models," Hank said.

The two went on like that for a while, neither man budging from his position. Soon they were joined by some of the other guys in the group, and eventually the talk turned to politics.

"If I were president, I would fight to make the world safe for everyone." Hank was full of red punch. Sugar and food coloring always got him worked up. "You know, protect free speech, protect our rights as Americans to worship who we please, believe what we please."

"Yeah," one of the other guys said. "We are guaranteed freedom *of* religion. Not freedom *from* religion."

Sven grinned at Hank. "So that's only if you're president, huh?"

Hank nodded, his lips pursed. "When the church turned its back on the culture, it reaped the results. It's the simple law of seedtime and harvest, where—"

One of the others—the guy with the Royals cap—frowned. "The what?"

"You know, the promise God gave to Noah: Whatever you plant will grow."

"Did God say that?"

"Well, something very much like that." Hank, nervous about his sloshing cup of punch, set it on a coaster on top of the entertainment center. He continued his speech, ticking points off on his fingers. "When the ark came to rest on the top of Ararat, God promised Noah several things—"

The other guy, in a *JESUS* shirt where the middle "S" was the Superman shield, broke in. "God said there wouldn't be another flood."

Hank looked at the man with a knowing smile. "God promised Noah several things: One, no more worldwide floods. Two, the sun and the moon—the passage of time. Three, summer and winter—the seasons. Four, seedtime and harvest—whatever you plant becomes something." He looked around the circle. He had their attention. "Now, we have no control over the first three items, but the law of seedtime and harvest—that is something that is up to us. We have to be active. We have to do something for that law to work."

Royals Cap scowled. "But grace is free."

Hank shook his head. "I didn't say anything about grace. I'm talking about farming here. Grace does not make the corn come by itself. You have to do the work. Grace does not make the cows milk themselves. You have to—"

Sven cut in. "I don't think you plant cows."

"Whatever, man, I'm making a point here. God told Noah to build the ark, but Noah had to hammer the nails himself."

Royals Cap nodded, his eyes lighting up. "Or he would have drowned with everyone else."

"Right!" Hank nodded. *"Or he would have drowned with everyone else."*

"So you're saying we should all be…farmers?"

"We already are, my friend. We already are." He put an arm around Sven. "Look, everything you do or say is a seed that you plant. How you treat your wife. Whether you give at church. How you act around your co-workers. Everything."

"Everything?"

"Everything. If you plant a lot of anger and distrust and unfairness, well, that's your crop. That's what you're going to get back."

Jesus Shirt frowned. "Sounds a lot like karma to me."

"You're right, it does." Hank grabbed his cup of punch and took a sip. The corner of his mouth twitched up as he wiped it. "Where do you think they got the idea?"

Royals Cap: "So this is in the Bible?"

"Look it up."

Sven smiled broadly. "And how does this make you president of the United States?"

Hank's eyes looked into the distance. "I just feel like we need to do more. We need to invest in our future. Do you know that the percentage of Bible-believing Christians in America drops with each generation?"

Jesus Shirt: "I don't know what a few percentage points—"

"Between the World War 2 generation and now, it's dropped from something like sixty percent to only four percent."

Royals Cap almost spit out his punch. "What?"

"Only four percent of teenagers today believe in the Bible. We have planted laziness and doubt in our kids, and now we're looking at a post-Christian America in just a few years. Like five years. Or less."

Sven asked in a whisper, "Five years?"

"In five years, this generation coming up will be in their

twenties—they'll be in the workforce. And statistically unreachable with the gospel." Hank looked around the circle, all the men now waiting for him to go on. Stunned into silence. "So what do we do? We need to pray for grace—that God will save us from the crop we've planted. As for me, I've had on my heart for sometime that maybe I should enter public office."

Sven looked at Hank soberly. "So you're serious about being president?"

Hank grinned. "Well, maybe I should start a little smaller and work my way up." He sipped from his punch. Nodded slowly. "But yeah, I want to be a part of the solution. Too many Christians are pulling back, watching from the sidelines. Waiting for Jesus to return and rescue them. I think we should be more proactive. When Jesus comes back, I want Him to catch me doing the work."

Royals Cap was impressed. "But running for office, man. That's so…grown up."

Jesus Shirt agreed. "Yeah, where in the world would you start?"

Hank was mulling over the question when his eye caught the newsbreak on the TV. He hit the volume button to turn it up: "Seventh District City Councilman Lester Goode died of an apparent cardiac arrest…"

— 11 —

At our next Saturday planning session at church, I was still fuming over the family's unsupportive reaction. Tribulation House was a big deal to me, and as the head of the household, that should have made it a big deal to them.

I was able to put it out of my mind, however, as I got to the meeting. Soon I was engrossed in the practical facets of the event.

Before the meeting, I was given a tour of the control room,

which had recently been upgraded to "state of the art." Normally, the church budget would not allow for that, but given the coming Rapture, we no longer had to worry about what would happen when the bill came. (If you know what I mean.)

My tour guide was cute little Sandra Robertson, who I have known since she was a little girl. She showed me to the room, back behind the sanctuary. As I gazed at the enormous soundboard, with all those switches and dials and the bank of video screens, I could not contain my excitement. "This is incredible! Like something on a spaceship!" Not that I believe in spaceships, mind you, I was making a point.

Sandra grinned and sat down in the center chair. "We have cameras set up all throughout the church." She flipped some switches, pointing to a series of screens along the console. "We'll have these operational for Tribulation House, but the Reverend also wants us to set them up for security."

I leaned on the console, my eyes flicking from one monitor to the next. "This is amazing." On one screen, Fred Garber was in the sanctuary, setting out hymnbooks for the next service; he was picking his nose. On another screen, a couple of kids were in the gym, playing handball with the old brown basketball. Yet another screen showed Reverend Daniel Glory in his study, preparing a sermon. "So, someone sitting in that chair can watch everything as it happens all throughout the facility?"

She tapped a black box to her left. "More than that, we're recording everything." She grinned, showing her braces. Bless her heart. "When we do Tribulation House, we'll have all sorts of footage." Her grin fell as she looked again at the screens. "If only we would be here long enough to make some kind of documentary." She grinned nervously, chuckling. "You know, if not for the Rapture."

I smiled at her, didn't know what to say. Maybe we weren't going to have time to make any documentaries, but I also knew it meant we did not have to worry about paying off this new high-tech control room, either.

I patted her on the back. "So we can run the whole Tribulation House event from here?"

"Right, sound, special effects—everything is fixed to come through here."

I made a mental note to call former deacon and former friend Marvin Dobbs and rub it in. There was no way his Armageddon House would have this sort of setup.

When we got to our planning meeting, we broke down how the various events of the Great Tribulation would be demonstrated throughout the full-sensory immersive evangelistic event.

Now, the Great Tribulation is broken up into three categories of judgments: seven seals, seven trumpets, seven bowls. The trick for Tribulation House was to show the sinful state of life on Earth—video games, R-rated movies, Christian rock—and then demonstrate in spectacular and dramatic fashion each judgment: each seal, each trumpet, each bowl.

The first four seals are the Horsemen of the Apocalypse. Since we could not have four real horses indoors—our zoning did not exactly permit that—we needed to demonstrate what each horseman wreaks upon the earth. You know, dramatize how it will be like to live through these events.

The first Horseman brings persecution. We thought the best way to stage this would be a mock witch trial—except, instead of witches, they are burning true Christians at the stake.

The second Horseman brings war. We wanted to create a mock battle scene, each army fighting to prove they love the Antichrist more. We thought the best way to show that was to have them yelling. You know, "I love the Antichrist more!" and "No, *I* love the Antichrist more!" Stuff like that.

The third Horseman brings famine. We set up these store shelves with a lot of really awful canned stuff, and then all these desperate people rioting over what's left. You know, canned possum and pigs' feet and thin mints.

The fourth Horseman is pestilence. We had all these actors in makeup, you know, to look like they're dying of all these plagues, flesh rotting, really scary stuff—and as we walk the customers through, these plague people are, you know, reaching out, begging for help, begging for medicine, grabbing at the customers.

Now, the fifth seal—

Pay attention. I'm giving you context. We went to a lot of trouble to put this thing together.

—the fifth seal is martyrdom. We had a room where these Christians were being killed for their faith. A little like the other room with the witch trial, except these are the executions. There's a guy getting his head chopped off on a guillotine; we actually figured out how to make it look like a man's head is really chopped off. Pretty scary stuff. We have people hanging from nooses…

Most of these martyrs are dummies, but one or more are real people, who can scare the attendees. You know, as the kids are walking through, some of the supposedly "dead" people start shouting, "How long, Sovereign Lord, holy and true, until you judge the inhabitants of the earth and avenge our blood?"

It's in the Bible. Don't you think you should write this down? It's important. *"How long…Sovereign Lord…holy and true…until you judge…the inhabitants of the earth…and avenge our blood?"*

The sixth seal is the earth moving and stuff falling out of the sky. This is good—to simulate an earthquake, we have the floor raised up and it tilts back and forth while the kids walk across.

And the lights are all flashing, like the sun blackening and the moon turning red and stars falling from the sky. And we have these actors dressed like kings hiding in caves. The caves are off to the side. We could never get the lights just right so you could see them, so we have them shouting stuff too. I don't remember what they were shouting, it was something we had to make up. I'm sure it was scripted.

Now, when the seventh seal is opened, it reveals the seven trumpets and seven bowls. So, the first trumpet—

Look, I'm just trying to give you context. A lot of people worked really hard to stage all this. We had souls to save.

— 12 —

Detective Charlie Pasch. Sunday morning. At church. Working the parking lot. Badly.

Somewhere between first and second service, all the outgoing traffic got locked up with all the incoming traffic. Charlie too flustered to understand the directions being barked through his walkie-talkie.

About ten minutes into service, folks abandoned their cars along the front lawn and hoofed it for the sanctuary. Charlie wanted to crawl under a rock.

— 13 —

Ross Cleaver was waiting in the car. Cleaning his nails with his teeth, reading his book about the ghost girl of Watseka, Illinois, trying to focus. Occasionally glancing out the window to see if their appointment had arrived.

Bill Lamb, already through with his last bottle of water, fiddling with the radio. Punching the buttons, jumping from one option to the next. Hair metal. Schmaltz pop. Honky-tonk.

Cleaver set his book on his lap. "Do you mind?"

The other man flinched, pulling his hand away from the radio. "What? I'm trying to find something to listen to."

"I'm trying to read here."

"Okay."

Cleaver went back to his book. He was only a few paragraphs in before he heard the radio jumping around again. Classical. Oldies. Rap. Without looking over at the other man, Cleaver reached up and turned the keys. No more power to the radio.

A few paragraphs later, he heard the other man ask, "What are you reading?"

Cleaver sighed and set the book on his lap. Glanced out the window. Nobody yet. Without looking at the other man, he answered, "It's about the ghost girl of Watseka."

"Who?"

"The 'Watseka Wonder.' Back home in this little town of Watseka, Illinois—"

"Where is that?"

"Close to Chicago. Anyway, in the 1870s, there was this thirteen-year-old girl who could speak with spirits. Doctors said she was retarded or something and should be sent to an insane asylum. Then this other guy in town says his daughter had also actually spoken to spirits, and was also sent to the asylum, where she died."

"Huh."

"So the second girl started—" Cleaver saw the car arriving and held up a hand. "Hold it. Here's the boss."

As the luxury car pulled up, Cleaver and Lamb got out of the sedan and walked across the gravel. The back window lowered and cigar smoke curled out and left on the wind. The sun in his eyes, the boss, Ted Massey, squinted at them. "What you boys got for me?"

Cleaver and Lamb looked at each other nervously. Lamb coughed, "Um, boss? We didn't know we was supposed to bring you a present."

"News! I'm asking what news you got."

Cleaver elbowed Lamb. Turned and gave the boss his most serious face. "Everything is on schedule, boss."

Lamb blurted, "We tried to press the drugstore guy, but he scared us off."

The boss puffed a few moments on his cigar. He squinted from one man to the other, then straight at Cleaver. "Is this true?"

"In a...way, Mr. Massey."

The boss smiled. "Was he a big fella? Real bruiser?"

"Sure, he—"

Lamb added, "Little old man. Kinda shaky."

The boss glared at Cleaver. "Shaky old man, huh?"

Cleaver pretended to ignore his associate, trying to think of the best way to kill the dummy. "You see, it's like—"

Massey smiled helpfully again. "He was packing, right? Shotgun or something? The guy got the drop on you?"

"Of course, boss—"

"Naw," Lamb blurted. "Just this old man shaking his finger."

Massey gritted his teeth, quivering. "Some harmless old man scared you off? All by himself?"

Cleaver had nothing to say.

Lamb did. "He wasn't by himself. He had the armies of God hanging over him."

Massey almost spit out his cigar. "You gotta be kiddin' me." He squinted at Cleaver. "You been feedin' his head with that ghost stuff?"

"No, sir!" Cleaver shook his head vigorously. "Honest!"

"Better not." The boss turned away, thinking, shaking his head. He looked back at Cleaver and Lamb. "Tell me about the church."

Cleaver nodded. "Working on it. But these guys seem like some kinda flakes."

Massey looked at Cleaver and then Lamb and then again at Cleaver. "They got armies of God over them too?"

Cleaver grinned nervously. "Nothing like that. We just have a hard time figuring out who's in charge, you know? We're ready to apply the pressure. We just need to know which joints, you know?"

Lamb blurted, "Their board is going to discuss it."

The boss squinted. "Their what?"

Cleaver had to keep himself from slapping his forehead. "When we spoke to the preacher at the church there, he said he was not allowed to make 'contracts' until he spoke with his people."

Lamb repeated, "Board."

"Boar?"

Cleaver shook his head. "No, like 'board of directors.'"

"Why din't you say that?" Massey looked toward his driver, then back. "So this board is gonna vote on whether we can do a protection racket?"

"He doesn't know what he's talking about, Mr. Massey." Cleaver gave a light shrug in Lamb's direction.

The boss raged. "What do you mean he doesn't know what he's talking about?" Eyes still on Cleaver, he pointed his cigar toward Lamb. "I vouched for him. Are you saying I don't know what *I'm* talking about?"

Cleaver, dismayed, waved his hands. "No, sir, that's cr...that's wr..." He sighed. "No, boss, I ain't sayin' that."

Massey puffed on his cigar. Leaned and tapped ashes into the tray. "Look, we gotta put the screws to this church. Our friend in Congress is no longer able to help our cause."

The dummy asked, "You whack him?"

Cleaver once again squelched the urge to punch him.

The boss, almost amused, shook his head. "No, I did not 'whack' him. Our friend had a heretofore undisclosed ailment. He had a heart attack."

"Oh," Lamb said. "The guy on the news."

Massey sighed. "Yes. The guy on the news." Waved his cigar. "Anyway, now he is unable to get that property rezoned for our purposes. As long as that church is sitting there, it will be problematic."

Cleaver blurted, hoping to end the conversation before the dummy got them in any further, "You want we should burn it down?"

"No. That could bring the Feds down on us. We need these people to move of their own free will."

"So..."—Cleaver looked at Lamb and at the driver and then the boss—"...we need to convince the entire church to pack up and move away."

The boss puffed on his cigar and grinned. "Oh, I don't think it will take all that."

"No?"

"No." The boss leaned forward and tapped the driver on the shoulder. Looked back at Cleaver with a wicked grin. "You just gotta convince the board of directors."

The back window rose and the car drove off. Leaving Cleaver and Lamb standing in the parking lot.

⌐ 14 ⌐

Hank Barton's best friend, Sven Surtees—now, apparently, Hank's campaign manager—leaned across the coffee-shop table toward Hank. "A man who *can* make a difference, *must* make a difference."

Hank sat back in his chair. Stared at the logo on the coffee cup, just trying to let the idea sink in. He mumbled, to himself more than Sven, "Make a difference."

It had been a few days since that evening at Sven's house. When, during fellowship time after the Bible study, Hank had started spouting off about the importance of participating in the culture. Storm the gates of hell, as it were. While they were standing there, the announcement had come over the TV that a member of the city council had died, and now there would be a special election to fill that open seat.

The men at the Bible study had decided it was not a coincidence. They said it was a sign.

Hank was not as sure. But he certainly couldn't rule it out.

From that night on, Hank found himself debating whether to run for that open seat. It was on his mind constantly—days at the repair shop, evenings at home.

As the local news followed the story, all manner of citizens had thrown their hats into the ring. Hank wondered how he could compete with all those people. Some of them seemed to be pretty sharp. Some were rich, some were famous, some were proven leaders.

"I just own a small repair shop," Hank pointed out. "Lawn mowers in the spring and summer, small appliances to fill out the rest of the year."

"You own your own business, Hank," Sven replied. "It shows you are responsible. You can be trusted."

"I don't know…"

"You know how to fill out paperwork."

"Yeah, but—"

"You have to keep track of licenses and things, right?"

"Sure, but—"

"Then you are qualified."

Hank rubbed the side of the empty cup with his thumb. "You think so?"

"I know so." Sven leaned across the table again and tapped Hank on the forearm. "You are one of the best people I know. Hard working, honest, loyal…I think you should do it. Besides, the hallmark of a good leader is that he surrounds himself with great people." He winked. "And you got your friends right behind you."

"Uh-huh. Looking for free parking spaces or something?"

"We'll work out the perks later. The important thing is that you have a vision, Hank. You shared it with us the other night."

"I was just talking."

"No, you were passionate. You had us convinced. We were ready to vote for you right then and there. And you weren't even running for office yet." Sven sipped from his coffee and set it back down. "These other people, what have they done?"

"Some of them seem pretty smart. Some of them are pretty rich…"

"Look, I've been watching the news reports."

"We all watch the news."

"No, I have been studying this. These people are out of touch."

Sven raised an eyebrow. "The people need someone who knows them. Who understands them. Who will represent them."

"You do know this is just for city council, right?"

"Sure."

"Not mayor."

"I hardly see what—"

"Not governor."

"Look, if the people vote for you—*when* the people vote for you—they are sending a message to the rest of that council. About what they believe in. About what they want our community to be like."

Hank was still rubbing the empty coffee cup with his thumb. He also found himself nodding. "Yeah." He looked up at Sven. "Okay, you're right. I need to do this. If I fail, I fail. But I have to do what I can to make a difference."

"That's the spirit, mister."

"What was that thing you said before?"

"What thing?"

"About the 'difference' and the 'making a difference'?"

"Oh—'A man who *can* make a difference *must* make a difference.'"

"Right." Hank reached over and gripped Sven's hand firmly. "Let's make a difference."

— 15 —

Detective Charlie Pasch. Wednesday night. At church. Working as a greeter. Badly.

At some point before the evening service, a whole case of bulletins ended up in the baptistery. Charlie too flustered to get them out of the drain before there was a "problem."

About ten minutes into service, the choir was forced to abandon its place up front as water poured from behind the curtain.

— 16 —

Mob soldiers Ross Cleaver and Bill Lamb were in the car, Cleaver driving. Lamb looked out the window, wrinkled his nose. "So, where we going?"

Cleaver didn't bother taking his eyes off the road. "Whaddaya mean? We're going to the church house to speed up matters. Like the boss said."

"This doesn't look like the way to the church."

Cleaver rubbed his thumb against his nose. "We're swinging by my ex-wife's on the way."

"So this isn't the way to the church."

"We're swinging by my ex-wife's on the way."

"So this isn't the way to the church."

Cleaver growled, "Do you want me to stop this car?"

"I'm just sayin'—"

"You want me to stop the car?"

"I'm just—"

Cleaver directed his palm at the passenger. "You do *not* want me to stop the car."

For the next few minutes, Lamb sulked, staring out the window. Finally, he squeaked. "Why are we stopping at your ex-wife's?"

"I don't think that is any of your business." Cleaver drove a few blocks, then grunted. "I'm meetin' a guy."

"What kinda guy?"

"I swear, I will stop this car."

Reaching the neighborhood, Cleaver pulled the car up to the curb in front of a little yellow box house. Some guy with a clipboard stood on the slanted porch, waiting.

Cleaver turned off the ignition, pulled the keys, and held them in his hands for a second, jangling them. Without looking, he asked, "You staying in the car or are you coming in?"

Lamb didn't say anything. Just yanked the handle, shoved the door open, and jumped out of the car. He scampered toward the porch while Cleaver sauntered, taking his time.

When Cleaver finally got there, the stranger, a tall, broad-shouldered man, stuck out his hand and grinned. "Bull Winkler."

Cleaver ignored the outstretched hand. "You with the company?" At the sound of Lamb chuckling, he sighed and glanced toward his partner. "What?"

Lamb mock whispered, " 'Bull Winkler.' "

Cleaver rolled his eyes. Shook his head, pulled open the storm door, and unlocked the yellow wooden front door.

As he pushed through, the dummy squeaked, "Why don't we knock?"

Stepping inside, Cleaver didn't bother to answer. He walked into the middle of the living room, where sunlight streamed through the crack in the curtains. He turned and regarded Winkler, who stood a good two feet taller than him, linebacker shoulders almost bursting out of the polo shirt.

The company man glanced around. "So, where do we start?"

Cleaver motioned toward the fireplace, across the room. "This trim is all messed up here." In front of the mantel, which sported an assortment of framed photos, he waved a hand at the shoddy craftsmanship around the edges. "Your boys shoulda finished the job."

Winkler pulled a pen from his ear, clicked it, and scribbled notes on the clipboard. "Uh-huh."

Cleaver turned and stormed toward the kitchen. "And then back here." He got to the room and flipped on the switch. Pointed toward the sink. "This counter is all wrong."

"What do you mean?" Winkler, pen poised over clipboard.

Cleaver waved his hands like a game-show host. "It's crooked. It don't fit the wall."

"You mean it isn't flush?"

Cleaver gritted his teeth. "It is crooked. It does not fit the wall."

From the next room, Lamb yelled. "Hey, is this your wife?"

Cleaver furrowed his brow. Yelled toward the hall. "What?"

"These pictures here. This your wife?"

"I guess."

Lamb appeared at the kitchen opening. "She looks like a young Jessica Lange."

Cleaver paused. Set his palms on the counter, trying to get back on track. "This is cut all wrong. It leaks around the edges of the—"

The dummy squeaked, "Like in *King Kong*."

Cleaver pressed on. "Around the edges of the, uh, the edges of the counter here. The sink." He turned to see Winkler scribbling and nodding again. "It leaks around the edges of the sink."

The dummy added, "I mean, the '70s *Kong*."

Cleaver waved him to shut up. Glared at Winkler, who was still scribbling some notes. "Now, you gonna finish the job right?"

Winkler dropped the clipboard against his side. Puffed his cheeks and exhaled. "I'll be honest with you. It's going to be tough." He pointed the pen toward the counter. "You can't really fix something like that. The counter needs to be recut. But it's a time-intensive and cost-intensive procedure to just do that over again." He headed for the living room. "Plus, we have a full schedule in the near future. Now in here…"

Clenching and unclenching his fists, Cleaver followed into the other room. The big man kept yammering, pointing that pen of his.

But Cleaver wasn't listening. The room was turning a shade of red. He calmly, quietly headed for the staircase, nodding. He heard the guy still yammering.

Cleaver kicked at the banister, and the man stopped talking. He kicked again and one of the posts came loose. He grabbed it and walked over to the big man. "You gonna finish the job right?" The big man just standing there, Cleaver swung the post hard, hitting the man across the side of the head.

The man shrieked, "What are you doing? You can't—"

Cleaver swung again, the wood hitting the man in the back with a meaty *thunk*. "You gonna finish the job right?"

Winkler, on hands and knees, spit blood. Nodded. Cleaver grabbed the man by the arm, helped him up. "Good." He wiped his hands on the man's polo shirt. Then he turned and motioned toward the broken banister. "You're gonna hafta fix that too."

Later, in the car, headed to the church, Cleaver had his eyes on the road. The dummy squeaked, "I think it was the best one."

Cleaver turned and furrowed his brow. "What are you talking about?"

"The '70s *King Kong* was the best one. They used a big robot."

"Do you want me to stop the car? I swear, I will stop this car."

They made the rest of the trip in silence.

— 17 —

I first met the mobsters when they came by the church to introduce themselves. There was a taller guy who twitched a lot. The shorter guy seemed to do all the talking.

I had heard about a previous visit, when they apparently told Reverend Daniel Glory they would torch the church if we didn't pay them money.

Did they say it that bluntly? I don't know the actual conversation, I just know what I heard. He said he just laughed them off. After all, we weren't long for this earth—there was no point worrying about the future.

The trick was to put the men off just long enough that one day they come back and knock on the door and nobody's home but the janitor, you know?

Why don't I think Jesus is going to rescue our janitor? Well, he's not a member of our church. I don't know his eternal plans.

Anyway, sometime after Reverend Glory related this story about the mobsters, they came around again after one of our Tribulation House planning sessions. I remember we were still working out some of the logistics before each team leader broke off with smaller groups. You know, so the script department could work on their script, and so the sound engineers could—

Wait, I explained this.

Okay, so we come to the end of the meeting, and there are two guys hanging around the foyer up front. The tall guy who was twitchy and the shorter guy. I asked if I could help them—I figured they were lost—and the shorter guy said, "Who's in charge around here?"

I said, "Tonight, I guess I am. Unless you're asking about Reverend Daniel Glory."

The shorter man shook his head. He had this weird sort of grin, and leaned in like he was trying to pull me into his confidence. "If you don't mind, we already talked to that Glory guy. I'm not sure that he has all his oars in the water, you know?"

I wasn't sure how to answer that, so I nodded. Puffed my lip out thoughtfully.

The guy said, "We just wanted to express our concerns for you in this neighborhood."

I didn't know how to answer that either, so I just nodded thoughtfully again.

The man motioned around the foyer with his hands, bobbing his head toward the neighborhood outside. "This ain't the safest area. You have such a lovely church here, I would hate to have something happen to this place. Know what I mean?"

I smiled. "The Lord protects his own." Of course, the end times being upon us and all, I was not sure how true that was these days. "Besides, what do you suggest?"

He glanced to the taller man, who kept rotating his shoulders and picking his ear, and said, "My partner and I represent an *insurance cooperative* that will guarantee this establishment will be free from disaster and harassment."

I asked him what sort of harassment he was talking about.

"It's a real crazy world out there," he said. "Why, I just heard tell of a ring of tow-truck operators who circle the town just looking for unsuspecting vehicles to tow, and then hold them until the owner coughs up the charges."

"You mean when people park in handicapped spots, stuff like that?"

"That's the thing—these vehicles are actually parked *legally*. But once a car's been towed away, who can prove it?"

I was aghast. Just another sign of the end times. "Who would do something like that?"

"I know. It's rough." The man leaned in and put an arm around my shoulder, leading me toward the glass door exit. "Just think, some of your members might be enjoying your little church meeting, and they come out ready for their Sunday chicken dinner and find their car towed away."

I imagined that happening to one of the older congregants. "That's terrible!"

The man squeezed my shoulder. "We can prevent that sort of thing happening. As long as we're on the job, everything is under our protection."

I hate to admit it, but it took me until about this point to realize what he was actually talking about. That these two men were the gangsters who had threatened Reverend Daniel Glory. And here they were, right in front of me, these men of violence, one with his arm around me.

Suddenly, his grin seemed more wicked. His eyes more threatening. I wondered whether they were hopped up on juice or weed or whatever it is that worldly people do these days.

Not quite sure how to broach the subject, I cleared my throat and sent up an unspoken prayer request for some extra guardian angels. All I could think to say was, "Your offer sounds…important." It was hard thinking of the right words that would be inoffensive without lying to the man. Tougher than you might think. "But here's the problem," I continued, hoping my voice was not quivering as much as my stomach, "I am not authorized to make decisions regarding the church's funds. We actually have a board of directors who handle that. If you would like to come make your presentation to the board—"

"We already got that song from your preacher man." The man's eyes flashed something dangerous, and his grin morphed into this face where he was just gritting his teeth. "Sounds to me like a stall."

"No, sir. No, um, 'stall.'" Based on his expression, it did not seem to satisfy the man. I added, "I could take your proposal to the board myself."

The man sidled up alongside me and squeezed my neck from behind. His grip made it hard to breathe. I could see spots. He said in this sort of low voice, "You do that."

It was hard to talk with that grip on the back of my neck. "I will take it to them at first opportunity."

He lightened up, his eyes glowing again. I wondered what spirit was on him. "Glad to hear it." He took his hand off the back of my neck and patted me on the back. "Stress to them the—*importance*— of this offer."

The taller man rotated his shoulders again. I noticed a shiner on one of his eyes. Who would have the nerve to inflict violence on men such as this?

The shorter man made for the exit, motioned for his partner to follow. As they were shoving the door open and going out into the night, the shorter man said, "I would hate for something to happen to your fine church. Or to one of its members."

Then he made this *click-click* noise with his lips—it's one of those noises my dad used to make, but I can't really do it myself. Then they were gone.

And Jesus forgive me for saying this, but it was scary. It was like looking into the face of Satan. Is this how Jesus felt after His temptation in the wilderness?

— 18 —

"I would have to say that Rich Johnston is the best source of comics news anywhere." The speaker, Lucas Hendrickson, fiddled with the cards in his hand. "He's outstanding."

Across the table, Daniel Dawson looked up from his own cards. "What, the Internet guy?"

"Right, he has an online column."

The game: poker, aces high. Around the table: Alice Malone, Detective Charlie Pasch (although tonight he was just "Charlie"), Jimmy Chase, Daniel, and Lucas. The stakes: story pitches for comic books, winner gets his or her pick of any ideas on the table.

Charlie kept his eyes on his cards. "I read his column every week." Tried to remember the order of the hands.

Alice, the dealer, pointed to Lucas. "So what are you putting in?"

Lucas grinned, popping a handful of Skittles. "Superman and *Jurassic Park*."

"What is that supposed to be?"

"It's my idea."

Alice frowned, shaking her head. "That's not an idea, that's two names. Try again."

Lucas's grin faded. "Huh." Then his eyes lit up again. "Okay, check it out—there's this outstanding island where they have cloned dinosaurs." He blinked. "And, um, this scientist and these two kids are lost on the island—"

Charlie piped up. "Okay, that's just the plot to *Jurassic Park*."

Lucas sighed loudly. "Okay. I'm out." Slapped his cards on the table.

The dealer looked at Charlie. "All right, you're up. What do you got?"

Charlie grinned, leaning forward. "Think *Robinson Crusoe* meets *War of the Worlds* on Skull Island. This guy is shipwrecked on the island, like 1800s, maybe, and he finds it's populated with dinosaurs."

"Go on."

"Wait!" Lucas sat up. "He can't have dinosaurs on his island!"

Alice held up a hand. Looked at Charlie. "Are your dinosaurs clones?"

Charlie shook his head. "No."

"Go on."

"So Shipwreck Guy finds this previous wreckage and finds this guy's diary and his Bible—"

Daniel sighed loudly. "Wait, this isn't one of your Christian stories again, is it?"

"It's a free country." Charlie frowned. "Still."

"Yeah, but if one of us ends up with your story, what are we supposed to do with it?"

"This is an homage to the original *Robinson Crusoe*. And that was a Christian novel."

"Fine." Daniel folded his arms. "What does Shipwreck Guy do next?"

"He sort of figures out the island. How to work it, how to survive the dinosaurs. He finally gets to a sort of routine for how to live on the island, real *Gilligan's Island* stuff. And then comes the strange part—"

Lucas threw up his hands. "Oh, *this* is the strange part."

Charlie smiled, blushing. "This cluster of alien spaceships lands on the island. It's an invasion force, and they put their base of operations on this island."

Everyone sat forward. Charlie had their attention. "So this one lone 1800s guy has to figure out how to sabotage this alien army. And he uses his knowledge of the island to defeat them. You know, set jungle traps, start dinosaur stampedes, stuff like that."

Alice nodded thoughtfully. "I can see it. Accepted." She turned to the next player, Daniel. "What have you got?"

"I think DC Comics should license a line of novelty soft drinks called Soder Cola."

"How is that a comic-book pitch?"

"Ah, but I am pitching a product to a comic-book *company*."

Alice frowned. "Uh."

Lucas popped another handful of Skittles. "Why Soder Cola?"

Charlie leaned in. "Soder is the brand name of the fictional cola in the DC Comics stories."

Daniel's eyes twinkled. "Right. And they would make these novelty flavored soft drinks. And the Superman Soder would be bright blue, and the Batman Soder might be purple—"

Alice shook her head. "Clever as your idea is, I don't think we can use it. It is not a comic-book pitch."

Daniel's face fell. He looked at his cards, then dropped them on the table. "I'm out."

"Hey," Charlie said, "did you see that *CSI* comic where Rich Johnston was the murder victim?"

"What, you mean the character was named after him?"

"No, I mean they did a miniseries where the murder victim was…Rich Johnston."

"Really?"

"Yeah. The mystery took place at a comic-book convention. And all the suspects were real-life comic book pros."

"Wow." Daniel smirked at Charlie. "I bet you figured out the murderer long before the end of the series."

Lucas perked up. "Why, who was the killer?"

Charlie frowned. "I'm not going to tell you that."

Adjusting his glasses, Daniel asked Charlie, "So, did you work it out right away?"

"Actually, no."

"But isn't that your job?"

Charlie wasn't sure how to answer that.

~ **19** ~

Hank Barton threw water on his face and looked at himself in the men's-room mirror. As a new candidate for City Council, Seventh District, he finally had his chance to make a difference. To change the world. To storm the gates of hell.

But right now, he just needed to get past this morning press conference. He pushed back the doubts. Grabbed onto what Sven Surtees—now his campaign adviser—said: "A man who *can* make a difference *must* make a difference."

Hank had thought long and hard about this new chapter in his life. Had prayed long and hard. Had discussed it with his friends, his co-workers, members of his family. Dissected the idea of running for the open seat on the city council, poked and prodded at the idea from every angle. Weighed the pros. Weighed the cons.

In the end, he knew Sven was right. *A man who can make a difference must make a difference.*

Hank knew that he might make the run, might even get the seat on the council, and find that one lone voice could not make a difference. But to make the run and fail was far better than to not run and never know.

With a sigh and a prayer, he put on the suit coat, stretched his arms to make the sleeves fall in place, and headed for the exit. It was time for his press conference.

~ ~ ~

HENRY BARTON IS CANDIDATE FOR CITY COUNCIL, SEVENTH DISTRICT
September 20, 2007

Today, I am proud to announce my hope to earn the support of my fellow citizens of the Seventh District of Kansas City as their representative on the City Council. With the untimely demise of Councilman Lester Goode, the special election to fill the vacancy for the rest of his term forms an opportunity for the people to make their voices heard.

This is an incredible city. But our local government is broken; and for far too long we, the God-fearing local taxpayers, have been paying the price. Our freedoms are threatened by activists on the left and organized crime on the right. For far too long, we have been too polite, too lax, too willing to go with the flow. But the sleeping giant needs to awaken and deal with these problems.

I will do an honest job of representing our interests in Kansas City. I will be beholden to no one but the people who elect me. I would be thrilled and honored to represent the people of the great Kansas City neighborhoods of August Heights, Dusthoover, Dutch Park, Garrick, Joelton, King Hill, Mt. Lincoln, South Vincenzo, and St. Clair Square.

We have an opportunity to start over in Kansas City. Attention to safe neighborhoods and parks, adequate numbers of police, well-maintained streets, clean sidewalks with buildings unspoiled by graffiti, and a welcoming climate for new businesses that provide good-paying secure jobs will make us that kind of city. We can now all wake up to the new morning of Kansas City and get ready for a great day. All of Kansas City must stand together, or we will fall together.

I hope to be elected to the seat that was vacated by Council Member Lester Goode. The special election to fill the remaining two years of Mr. Goode's term will most likely be held in October. No exact date has been set.

We have our work cut out for us—so let's get started!

— 20 —

So I was still thinking about the whole thing the next day at work. That would be, what, Thursday? Yeah, I guess it was Thursday. The worst day of the week: So close to the weekend you can see it, but still too far away to taste it.

If I were running the show, we'd have Thursdays off. Or Wednesdays. I guess Wednesday is the halfway point, and if we had Wednesday off, maybe that would make Thursdays better.

Of course, that would make Thursday the new Monday, and nobody likes Mondays. I wonder if the coming Kingdom has Mondays? I mean, when Jesus comes and sets up his Millennial Kingdom, that would be, what, 1000 years? That sounds like a lot of Mondays. I never really thought of it that way before.

Sorry. Context. It's all context. I just want you to understand I am not some religious nut.

So anyway, I'm at my job. I work in a real-estate office at the corner of Foster and Moon. Sherman's Realty. I can give you a card—

Oh. I don't seem to have any on me right now. I'll have to get some for you.

Anyway, I was sitting in the office there and it was sort of a slow morning. I was supposed to go out and take some pictures of some new listings. That would be property that has recently gone on sale through my agency. But I was sort of preoccupied with thoughts of the men from the night before.

You know, I don't remember either of them dropping a name. But that short one, the look in his eyes was like the devil in the wilderness, you know? How he must have looked at Jesus during the Temptation.

I hadn't mentioned the meeting to Marge. I didn't want to worry her.

I probably should have mentioned it to someone at the church— especially Reverend Daniel Glory. But something about the man's look…a spirit of oppression reached down my throat and grabbed my heart.

Plus, his comment about Reverend Glory made me stop and think. What did he mean about the Reverend not having a full deck? When the enemy bad-mouths your leader, it doesn't really instill confidence, you know? I suppose I should have considered the source.

At the time, it really stopped and made me wonder. I struggled with my faith then and there, that morning at work, I don't mind telling you.

To keep my mind off things, I spent the morning online reading about the end times. Who the Antichrist might turn out to be. What role the UN would play in the Tribulation. Where the Koreans having the bomb fit into Daniel chapter 10.

Soon, I was searching to see what I could find out about gangsters. I tried some different keywords—"gangster," "mobster," "organized crime."

By lunchtime, I was checking boat prices. The clock was ticking. And I wanted a boat.

I work hard, you know? I deserve something for me. Why couldn't my wife and kids be more supportive? Why did they make it feel like I was *dragging* them out to boat lots and the docks all the time? Why couldn't they understand a man needs to be free? To feel the salt in his hair…

Um, I got lost there. What was I talking about?

Oh. Reverend Daniel Glory? I'm getting to that. But this is my story. Just let me tell it.

Anyway, I deserved a boat. Some fathers go golfing, I needed a boat. I made the kids move everything from the garage out into the backyard, their bikes, everything. We needed room for the boat. I didn't own one yet—and believe me, I got grief from the kids over emptying the garage in faith—but I was believing for a boat.

I told my son, Clint, "Other dads go golfing, I'm going boating."

The boy had to give some lip. "I'd wax your golf clubs, no problem," he says. "At least then I could still do my homework."

As if taking him out to the docks a few nights a week to stare at boats was a crime. Sure, we were out late, so he was a little red-eyed when he got up at three-thirty for his paper route—but he just needed more faith, you know?

So that Thursday morning, still sort of recovering from the meeting with those gangsters, I decided that in the interest of mental health, I needed to take a break.

So, come lunchtime, after a couple hours of gazing at virtual showrooms, looking at runabouts, cuddys, deck boats, cruisers—I still hadn't made up my mind—I told the receptionist I had an afternoon meeting and headed out to the boat lot.

First, I stopped at the newsstand and grabbed some magazines—*Passage Maker, Cruising World, Go Boating*. I bypassed the classified ads in the paper—I didn't think Jesus wanted me to have a used boat. When our Lord got in the boat to preach to the crowds from the lake, do you think He went second-class? No sir, He went first-class all the way.

Which is how I ended up at Midwest Auto & Marine on 48th. Just to take a look.

But you see—and this is what I'm getting at—I was still terrified of these men. I knew it was a test of my faith. It was a test of my spiritual fortitude.

Did Jesus run from the devil? No. He stared him down. After the church leaders beat them and threw them in prison, did the apostles run? No. They stood their ground.

I knew this was my test. I stewed over it a few days. But I needed to go back and face the enemy. I needed to find those men and prove to them and to God that I was not scared.

Standing there at Midwest Auto & Marine on 48th, looking at that boat...I did not know it at the time, but that was when I first started to consider the form my contest of faith would take.

I wondered what former deacon and former friend Marvin Dobbs would think of *that*.

～ 21 ～

Detective Charlie Pasch. Sunday morning. At church. Working as an usher. Badly.

Somewhere between the first and second service, the metal trays of communion grape juice were knocked over, staining the carpet in the back hall. About ten minutes into the second service, Charlie was fighting traffic to the grocery store for more juice.

— 22 —

It was a Monday morning when Hank Barton, candidate for City Council, Seventh District, decided to go after the church vote. The morning turned out to be hit-and-miss, mostly miss. Of the five churches he visited before lunch, only two pastors agreed to offer him an opportunity to connect with the congregants. Of the rest: One pastor was unavailable for a meeting this week (how about next week?); one pastor wished him well, would probably even vote for him, but categorically refused to mix politics with the pulpit; one pastor got mad and threw Hank out before they even had a chance to discuss the state of the community.

When Hank broke for lunch, he stopped for a burger, watching people as he chomped. He wiped his mouth often, reminding himself the importance of public image.

But how to get the votes of these people? Hank went over in his mind the awkwardness of just jumping up, reaching out, and pumping a stranger's hand. Of explaining himself and asking them to vote Barton. These days, it was impertinent enough to ask a person to vote at all.

He just decided to remain seated. Finish his burger and side salad, and get back to his church campaign. Build his power base, gain the support of important influencers in the community. Then he would feel more comfortable about going to the average folks for their vote.

The first stop after lunch was The Last Church of God's Imminent Will. Out front were a series of huge signs touting its upcoming Tribulation House event.

Hank was a bit nervous about meeting with Reverend Daniel Glory. The man was a major player in the local community, regularly on the news for one reason or another. He was one of those bigger-than-life preacher types. He also had a popular book right now about the Rapture, which was all the buzz on the local talk radio.

The meeting went very poorly. In retrospect, Hank realized he should not have expected any different. After all, the Reverend's book should have been the clue. "Why bother running for office at all," Daniel Glory asked him point blank, "when you know we won't even be here long enough for you to be sworn in?"

Hank attempted to stammer a reply. But Reverend Glory kept at him with those TV-closeup-ready pearly whites. Hank almost had to shield his eyes. "But I don't think we're supposed to drop out on our duties to the culture. Responsible stewardship—"

"That's all fine, young man"—Reverend Glory kept his cool, unflappable tone—"but there's no point digging the vineyard after the season is already over."

"What?" Hank had not followed any of that.

Reverend Glory leaned forward and grabbed a booklet off the top of his desk. Held it up. *107 Reasons Jesus Is Coming Back in 2007*. "As you can see, young man, the time of the end is near. The Lord Jesus will be here on October 17 of this year. He will take His church out of harm's way, and there will follow a judgment such as this world has never seen."

Hank stared at the man stupidly, struggling valiantly to think of a way to answer. But came up short. Within a matter of minutes, he found himself politely escorted out to the parking lot.

He dusted himself off and considered his next move.

~ 23 ~

The FBI/Kansas City Police Joint Task Force was meeting in the office of Detective Tom Griggs. The group, still a token unit as far as the higher-ups were concerned, was now back up to a robust four: representing the KCPD, Griggs and Detective Charlie Pasch; representing the Kansas City division of the FBI, Special Agent Martin O'Malley and Special Agent Kathie Harper.

As the others dragged in chairs from the outer office, Griggs flipped open the folder he had been reading since the day he was at the cemetery. He put aside the guilt he felt for coming in early to grab it—there had been no call for that, no reason. Nothing in this file that couldn't have waited. If only Carla had not pushed his buttons. If only Carla had not been so pushy.

Charlie brought in four Styrofoam cups of coffee: black for Griggs; cream, two sugars for O'Malley; black for Harper. His own coffee was heavily flavored with Swiss Miss and Froot Loops. The others had long ago gotten used to it.

Once the meeting came to order, the four compared notes, shared what each side was doing in the war against organized crime.

"One item of new business," O'Malley said. "An ex-judge is turning state's evidence."

Charlie perked up. "Judge Reynolds?"

O'Malley nodded, chomping his gum loudly. "*Ex*-Judge Reynolds. He made a deal to get out of prison early. We have to babysit him until we get him to court to testify."

Griggs grunted. "Need any help?"

"When we get ready to move him, we'll let you know."

The team also discussed various cases being pursued by other divisions of both the KCPD and the FBI that had suggestions of a connection to organized crime. A homicide investigation. A cold case that had suddenly turned up new evidence. A missing-persons case. A fraud investigation.

O'Malley was particularly interested in the fraud investigation, a business called Frozen Futures.

"What," Griggs asked, "fraudulent ice cream?"

Charlie piped up, as he was wont to do. "Frozen Futures claims to put its customers in a state of suspended animation. It claims to keep them in this state until such time as they can be, er, defrosted and cured of whatever illness they would have died from. Er, from which they would have died."

Griggs looked at O'Malley and Harper. Did they understand what the kid was saying? Griggs tried not to feel like the dumbest man in the room. "So they just grab people off the street and, um, freeze them? Put them on ice, as it were?"

"Naw," O'Malley said, chomping gum like a cowboy. "This is for rich geezers."

"So they're bilking old people out of their money? For what? I still don't quite understand—"

"It is like this, Detective Griggs," Charlie said, slipping into his lecture tone. "The clients at Frozen Futures are the sort who are terminally ill. Modern medicine cannot help them. A place like Frozen Futures promises to put them in suspended animation, keeping them alive—or so the claim goes—until such time that the medical community can cure whatever illness they have."

O'Malley snorted. "It sounds like the kid believes it." He turned to Harper and murmured. "He's a Trekkie."

"My TV-viewing habits aside," Charlie said, "I don't know whether I believe in suspended animation."

Griggs waved the conversation off. "So what?" He tapped the folder in his hands. "We're short-handed enough as it is. Why do we even care about—"

O'Malley pointed a finger. Griggs saw a Band-Aid wrapped around it. "You missed something on the sheet there."

Griggs furrowed his brow. Looked down at the memo provided by O'Malley and Harper. He skimmed the report, skimmed the description of the business, got to the names of the proprietors.

Ah. There. "Winthrop Parker," Griggs read aloud. "Businessman. Entrepreneur. Well-known for laundering money through assorted business enterprises."

"Fronts for the mob," Charlie said. "If we could ever prove it."

"Parker usually keeps such a low profile," Harper said. "We would never have even noticed his connection if not for Mr. Mike."

Griggs frowned. "Mr. Who?"

"Mikolaczyk."

"Oh." Griggs nodded. "Mik."

"Right." O'Malley raised an eyebrow. "That's a guy who could never keep a low profile." He sat back in the chair and sighed loudly. "So we got a van parked across the street from this Frozen Futures."

Charlie grinned. "The usual stake-and-bake?"

Harper frowned. "What?"

O'Malley stopped chewing his gum and rolled his eyes. "Nobody calls it that, Charlie-boy."

"I do."

O'Malley looked back at Griggs. "Anyway, there is a stakeout across the street. They're working the fraud angle, but as soon as they spotted Mikolaczyk, they knew our task force would be interested. They promise to keep us posted if anything of interest should happen."

"In the meantime," Griggs said, flipping open the file on Massey, "what do we know about Ted Massey?"

"You don't know?" O'Malley stopped chomping his gum momentarily, flashing a toothy grin. "You had the file all weekend."

Griggs did not want to admit he had been in no condition to focus. Just shrugged and claimed, "I read it thoroughly. It just seems flimsy, is all."

Charlie sat up in his chair. "Massey has kept a low profile until the past few weeks. Suddenly, he started sending goons out to work protection rackets."

"I heard, I heard." Griggs put the folder down. Grabbed the autographed baseball off the plastic stand on his desk. "But I heard there was something involving real estate or something. What's that about?"

Harper spoke up, "Massey is by trade a developer." She almost sounded like Charlie. "You know, real estate, construction. He bought out the Catalano operation a couple of years ago when it suddenly became...available."

"Right." Griggs started rolling the baseball from one hand to the next. Not really paying attention to it, just to keep his hands occupied. "So, why the big question mark? Is he working a protection racket or not?"

"That's the weird thing," O'Malley said. "He is actually trying to push people out of their businesses. And homes. It seems like his employees are the ones working the protection racket."

Charlie was finally confused. "What do you mean?"

"Actually, a guy named Cleaver is the one who got our attention," Harper said. She consulted a notebook. "He started pressing a couple of store owners for protection money. That's what got our attention."

O'Malley took over. "But when we started to listen real closely, we discovered he was not actually ordered to collect protection—he was ordered to push certain parties to pull up tent stakes and move."

"So Cleaver is actually doing some extra work for himself. Working a protection racket to line his own pockets."

"That's what it looks like. The whole thing might have gone unnoticed if Cleaver had not added the extracurricular activity."

"Greedy bum." Griggs leaned forward and replaced the baseball in the stand. "How does a guy like Massey hire a guy like Cleaver?"

Charlie snorted. "Have you seen the market out there? Organized crime ain't what it used to be. Thanks to people like us."

"Pin on your medal a little later," Griggs said wryly. "Right now, we got a question. What does Massey want with all that property?"

~ 24 ~

Saturday morning, I got stuck driving the boy to his SAT test. It was against my better judgment, of course, but it was the only way to shut the wife up. Know what I mean?

There wasn't much conversation as we drove. Me watching the road, humming some country music song to myself, Clint reading through his book. Books, always books.

About fifteen minutes into the drive, we were maybe a couple of miles from the school when I had a thought. I took a left onto a different route.

The boy got his nose out of the book. Looked around. "Where are we going?"

"Just need to make a stop somewhere on the way." No big deal, right?

"These are the SATs. I have to be on time."

"We'll make it," I said. Not sure if it was true, but I was the one driving, that's all that mattered. "If it weren't for your mother, we wouldn't be going at all."

He huffed, "This is important."

"What, so you can be a 'writer'?"

"Writers are important."

"You can keep your writing." I flicked on the radio, punching buttons to find me some good country-and-western music. "Just give me a newspaper or a copy of *U.S. News & World Report* or a good detective TV show and I'm fine. You can keep your writing."

The boy slapped his textbook shut. Slumped back in the passenger seat. "Where do you think those things come from?"

"What do you mean?"

"Somebody had to *write* them."

I wasn't sure what he was getting at, but I saw the sign coming up ahead. I tapped the brake and hit the blinker. "Let's just make a quick stop."

"Wait, what are we doing here?"

"Just making a quick stop. To look at some boats."

I may have felt a twinge of sympathy for my son. I may have even felt a twinge of memory...of my dad dragging me out to look at tractors.

But I put those feelings aside. This was important.

— 25 —

Detective Charlie Pasch. Wednesday night. At church. Working the soundboard. Badly.

Somewhere before the evening service, a thermos of iced tea was spilled. Charlie too flustered to figure out how to get the spill contained before there was a "problem."

About ten minutes into the service, there was a loud pop and the lights went out.

— 26 —

Outside the Last Church of God's Imminent Will, sitting in a car parked across the street. Ross Cleaver, cleaning his nails with his teeth, reading his book about the ghost girl of Watseka, Illinois. Bill Lamb, having lost his radio privileges, hummed some private song to himself.

The parking lot across the street was packed, the church a full house on a Wednesday night.

Lamb finally got tired of his made-up song. Kicked at the last of his empty water bottles collecting on the floorboard. "Still reading a book, huh?"

Cleaver glanced up from his book. Scowled. "What?"

"I see you're still reading that book."

"No, you said, 'still reading *a* book,' like this one book represents all the books in my life."

"I was just—"

"Like this was the only book I was ever gonna read."

"I didn't mean nothin'."

Cleaver went back to his book, Lamb tried to reconstruct his private song. Started rapping his knuckles against the passenger window to keep time.

Cleaver snapped, "Would you stop it?"

"What?"

"The noise. Stop smacking the window there."

"*Sorr*-ee."

Cleaver kept his thumb in the paperback, set it down, and looked square at his partner. "Look, we gotta do a thing here."

Lamb nodded nervously, eyes wide. "Uh-huh."

Cleaver picked up his book again, looking for his place. "So you just let me know when the truck gets here."

"Uh-huh."

A few minutes passed before Lamb interrupted again. "So what's so great about the book there?"

"This is what you call 'research.'"

"Why?"

"This book is about something that happened around my hometown."

"If you're from there, why are you researching it?"

"Because I'm going to write the book."

"But there's already a book."

Cleaver exhaled savagely and set the book down. Glanced out the window, wishing the truck would get here. "It got some of the details wrong, so I'm going to write a book of my own. Get the details right."

"What sort of details?"

"Names, places—it's like this author never even visited the place for himself."

"How do you know if—"

Cleaver lunged and clutched the other man's arm. "Shut up!" Relaxed his grip, tried to unclench his teeth. Couldn't do it. "Just. Watch. For. The. Truck."

Cleaver looked across the street. Church was in session, or whatever you called it. The big sign announced something called

Tribulation House, with the tagline, *GET RIGHT OR GET LEFT.*
An additional line read, THE TIME IS CLOSER THAN YOU THINK.

You better believe the time is close, Cleaver thought to himself.

"You're going to write a book?"

"What have we been talking about? Do you listen to *anything?*"

"I know, but that seems so…huge."

"How hard could it be?" Cleaver saw some familiar lights. "Hey,
I think this is us."

"What—here?"

"No, dum-dum, I think that's the truck." Thrilled at the prospect
of getting out of the car with the dummy, Cleaver flipped open the
door and jumped into the night air. Glanced around to see if anyone
was around who didn't need to be.

The tow truck pulled up. The driver leaned out his window,
elbow hanging out. "Hey, man. What's the sitch?"

Cleaver skipped the explanation—the driver already knew the
"sitch," if he understood the word correctly. "This way." Cleaver
crossed the street to the gravel parking lot, the tow truck pulling
in behind him. Went right for the car parked by the front door,
behind the sign marked *PASTOR REVEREND DANIEL GLORY.*
"Right here."

The driver parked it. "Okay."

"No. Wait." Cleaver thought better of going right for the pastor's
car. If you get the top man's car, it went right to confrontation. They
needed to grab a car belonging to one of the man's sheep.

Cleaver turned, pointed to a beat-up station wagon parked in
the second row. "This one."

The driver paused. "Okay." Climbed back into the truck. Pulled
it forward a couple of yards, then backed up toward the station
wagon.

Cleaver watched the man set up the chains on the car. He smiled
to himself. This was gonna get results.

— 27 —

On Friday, we had a big media showcase for Tribulation House. In fact, I was on the way to church for our big media showcase when I stopped in at the sporting-goods store. I wanted to see my options. When a man has a boat, he needs to know his options. Snorkeling gear. Life vests. Wetsuits. Underwater cameras.

I was comparing scuba masks when I saw former deacon and former friend Marvin Dobbs. He was looking at golf stuff. I don't play golf. Some fathers golf, I go boating.

I thought about whether I should say something to him. But checking my watch, I saw it was time to head to church for the media showcase.

Eyes down, headed for the door, I heard the familiar gravel voice. "Hey! What's the news?"

I stopped, looked over. Tried to play it cool. "Hey, Marvin." Preempting any awkward pause, I gestured with my watch. "Actually, I gotta head out. Meeting."

Dobbs gave me a face. Kind of scrunched-up. "Not your Armageddon House, is it?"

I shook my head. "No. Of course not."

"You'll be getting a letter soon." He flicked his eyes away. Breathed in through his nose, then snorted and cleared his throat. "Armageddon House ain't yours."

"We don't need your secondhand flannelgraph show, Dobbs." I felt the anger in the back of my throat. "We're just fine—"

"You think I haven't heard what you're doing?" Dobbs straightened his neck, tried to look taller. "You don't know—"

"I know plenty!" I felt my fists clench, ready to—

"You're probably going with the Horsemen as bikers cr—"

"That's it!" I threw myself at the man, going for the throat. His eyes went wide and I shoved him into a mannequin, it and the two of us crashing into a display of golf balls. Little white spheres careened in every direction.

~ ~ ~

I extricated myself with an apology and a check made out to the store for damages. I barely made it to church before our dress rehearsal for the media. We had sent out invitations far and wide—everybody from the network news to the big talk shows—but in the end, it was just the local media. And some guy from Comedy Central. (I'm not even sure who sent the invitation to them.)

Some of the board members had worried about showing their hand too soon to the secular media, concerned about throwing pearls to swine. But, I argued, we needed to get our warning out there to a perishing world. After all, even old Noah preached to the unwashed masses during the building of the ark.

So the journalists came through with their cameras and equipment and we demonstrated various stages of the event. The kids dressed up and performed some of the skits. The tech guys did up the special effects. The reporter for the *Kansas City Blade* asked a lot of questions, but the rest of the bunch conducted themselves in a respectful manner.

The guy from the *Blade* had the temerity to question the intent of our full-sensory-experience evangelism event. He carried his doubts around like a badge of honor all through the demonstration. Like, we were standing in the middle of the Third Scroll and the lights went out—part of the show, you know—and the sound system is rumbling and this guy starts mumbling to himself.

And then we get all the way to the end, and the guy from the *Blade* opens his trap again. He asks whether Tribulation House is an example of "ambush evangelism"! The idea! He implied that the entire event was just a giant arcade to advertise Reverend Daniel Glory's book, *107 Reasons that Jesus Is Coming Back in 2007*. And he had the gall to ask how the expense of staging this event compared to the funds we spend on reaching out to the community.

"*This* is an outreach to the community," I told him.

"No—I mean, how does the expense of this operation compare

to your spending on say, aid for disaster victims, social programs—stuff like that?"

"This *is* a disaster situation we're facing," I told him, putting on my sternest face. "We are putting all our efforts into rescuing lost souls before the trumpet sounds."

The other reporters were scribbling this in their notebooks or getting it on tape. But this guy, he says, "What if the trumpet doesn't sound this year? You have persuaded your converts to disengage themselves from the community—to disengage themselves from politics and the culture as a 'lost cause.' But if your timing is off, do you think the 'conversions' made under these conditions will stick?"

Can you believe it? Pfft. The unbelief of some of these people.

— 28 —

The church campaign going so-so, Hank Barton, candidate for City Council, Seventh District, knew it was time to switch gears. He started his door-to-door campaign. At first, he had the wide-eyed innocence to believe he would try to reach every single house in the district.

Again, hit-and-miss, but slightly better than it might have been. A lot of unanswered doors (including those where you could see movement through the drapes, where you could hear the TV being shut off). Several bored faces attempting to listen politely. Many more impatient faces pretending to listen before shoving the door closed in his face.

Most frustrating of all, however, was the surprising number of people who apparently owned Reverend Daniel Glory's book. And believed it. They were certain the Rapture was coming in a matter of weeks.

And looked Hank in the eye and said, "Why bother voting?"

～ 29 ～

Ross Cleaver and Bill Lamb were on errands for the boss. Sometime after lunch, Cleaver drove down a familiar street. Parked in front of the ex-wife's house. He slipped the book about the ghost girl onto the dash.

Lamb struggled to escape his seat belt. "What are we doing here?"

Cleaver grinned. "Gonna check on the repairs."

The two men walked up the driveway—Cleaver checking his key ring, yelling at Lamb to get off the grass.

Inside, Cleaver walked through the house randomly, checking objects sitting here, sitting there. Looking at postmarks on mail, looking at framed photos to see if he knew anybody in them.

Somewhere around the kitchen, Lamb asked, "So, was this your house?"

"What?"

"You know, when the two of you were married."

"No."

Somewhere around the den: "But you started fixing it before you split? So this is unfinished business for you?"

"No."

Somewhere around the guest room: "So this is all part of your settlement, right? You gotta take care of the house?"

"No. She got this place a couple of years ago."

Back in the living room: "If she is your ex-wife, why are you doing this?"

"A man has to keep his options open." Cleaver chuckled. "Know what I mean?"

Lamb let a few seconds pass. "Why is she never around?"

Cleaver shrugged. "She's got a job. Woman's gotta work." Nodded. "Well, modern women."

"So why don't we ever stop in when she's at home?"

Cleaver eyed Lamb dangerously. "You wanna get a look?" He

shoved the other man. "Huh? You trying to put the moves on my wife?"

Lamb put up his hands. "No, man." Shaking his head. "I'm just trying to understand this. You keep saying you and your ex-wife are on friendly terms, but you're never in the same place at the same time. Just seems weird. She does know you come in here, right?"

Cleaver grabbed his partner by the arm and dragged him toward the front door. Opening the door, he shoved him out onto the porch. The man lost his balance, tripped, fell on hot concrete on his rear and palms. Ignoring the dum-dum's baby pouting, Cleaver jabbed a finger. "You got a big mouth." He glared down at the man a second, then reached inside his jacket and gripped the gun. "Are you gonna shut up or am I gonna hafta shut you up?"

On the concrete, Lamb rubbed his mouth with a skinned hand. Verge of tears. Shook his head. Whimpered, "No."

Cleaver stepped forward. Menacing. "You ain't gonna shut up?"

"Yes!" Lamb nodding wobbily. "I mean, no! I'm not saying anything." Huffing. Puffing. Holding back the blubbering. "Not saying anything." He stopped talking, just breathing heavily through his open mouth.

Cleaver stood there, holding the pose. Finally, relaxed. Let go of the gun, smoothed his jacket out. Turned toward the door. "Let's see if they made those repairs."

— 30 —

At the office, I just hadn't been able to get my head in the game. Who wants to sell real estate when you're about to rocket out of here?

Eventually, my work dropped off. And the boss, Elias Sherman, noticed. "Where is your head?" On a good day, the man was a teddy bear. This was not a good day. "Your sales are in the crapper!"

"Come on, Mr. Sherman, they're not that—"

"We're going to be watching your numbers for the next few weeks."

Huh. Next few weeks. "Okay, Mr. Sherman."

"You've gotta do better."

I gave the man a smile. It was genuine. "Yes, sir."

Back at my desk, I did get one big call in the office that morning. Big sales opportunity. But I figured, why bother?

I spent the morning thinking. Dreaming.

That afternoon, I was at the boat dealer. And I had finally decided on what I wanted: a 2008 Bayliner 192. In a fine craft like that, I could boat around all day and then spend the night in the great outdoors. Nineteen feet, dependable 3.0-liter engine for extended cruising. Comfortable enclosed cabin and portable head. Cushioned V-berth with storage below. AM/FM Stereo CD with input for MP3. Jump seats and sleeper seats that convert to loungers. Self-bailing fiberglass cockpit liner. In-floor storage. Padded side panel storage with shelves and cord locks...

A sweet deal at only $22,428.

"Can I help you?" The young salesman was all grins and bursting with helpfulness. His nametag said *FRED*.

"Yep." I must have had the twinkle of Christmas morning in my eyes. "I think I may need this Bayliner."

"Oh, that's a nice one. Comfortable enclosed cabin and portable head..."

"I know."

"...cushioned V-berth with storage below..."

"Right."

"...AM/FM Stereo CD with MP3, jump seats and sleeper seats that convert..."

"I know," I said, grinning. "I read up on it online." I reached out and touched the smooth surface. "It's a great boat."

I told the guy to draw up the papers.

Sure, $22,428 sounds like a lot of money for a guy like me to drop down all at once. So I went into the office there and tried to work it out on credit.

No big deal, right? After all, I wasn't going to be around to have to pay for it! It's not like you think—I would not stiff my brothers in Christ. But I figured that after the Rapture, anyone who is my brother in Christ would not be around to worry about whether I paid off my boat.

As for whoever was left—who cares? Even if the condemned come after me, I'll be long gone.

I sat down with Fred, the salesman, and we went through the paperwork. I had a twinge of doubt about whether I would have the credit, but sent up a silent prayer that it would all work out okay. After all, it had worked out the other day when I got the truck.

Wait, I think I forgot to mention that before, didn't I? I'd purchased an Avalanche earlier in the week.

Yeah. Chevy Avalanche 2500 LT. Red with the black molding. I needed something to pull the boat. The wife was not happy when I drove home with that. But I needed to step out in faith, so I cut into the family account for the down payment.

I signed for the boat on the dotted line, and Fred took the papers to another office. Left me sitting there, analyzing the items decorating his desk and tacked to the wood-panel walls. There was a bobblehead on the desk. I didn't know who Ozzy Osbourne was, but I patted it just the same, watching the plastic head jitter on the spring.

I was squinting at the certificate on the wall when Fred came back into the room, his smile a little forced. "I'm sorry, sir," he said. "Your credit has been declined."

— 31 —

Wednesday afternoon at Randy's Comics Empire. New-comics day. Detective Charlie Pasch digging through long boxes of old comics on sale for 50 cents apiece. A treasure trove of back issues of *Mighty Thor* and *Batman Family* and *Transformers* and *Green Lantern/Green Arrow.*

Charlie thrilled with his stack of *The Brave & The Bold* drawn by Jim Aparo (R.I.P.), starring Batman and a series of classic DC Comics B-characters, from Metal Men to Adam Strange to Plastic Man. No Irv Novick/Cary Bates issues of *Flash,* but this was still a good find.

He paid Jeevan at the register and wandered to the back room, where a couple of buddies were hanging out at the back tables. Charlie plopped his white plastic *THANK YOU* bag of comics purchases on the table. Daniel and Lucas were sharing a bag of Skittles and chatting about obscure comic-book continuity. Daniel was busily drawing on his sketchpad.

"It breaks my heart to see what he's doing," Daniel was saying. "Judd Winick is a competent writer—he can do the pacing, he can do the dialogue—but he is so focused on this one single incident that happened in his life, every single comic he writes becomes about the same tragedy. He did it in *Green Arrow,* he did it in *Batman,* he did it over in—"

"Judd Winick is like John Grisham," Lucas broke in. "He writes the same story over and over and over."

Charlie didn't know what they were talking about, but felt comfortable debating the last point: "You shut up about John Grisham!"

Lucas laughed. "Hi, Charlie." He pushed over the open bag of candy. "You can have the green Skittles."

Charlie shook his head. "Thanks, but I don't eat green candy."

Daniel looked up from his sketchpad. "Because it has a mango-ey flavor?"

"No, I just don't eat any green candy."

"Really?"

"At all."

Daniel leaned in, raising an eyebrow. "Is it because of all the rumors...?"

Charlie squinted. "What rumors?"

"You haven't heard the rumors?"

"There aren't any rumors about green candy."

Lucas laughed and grabbed the last of the green Skittles by the handful and popped them in his mouth. Charlie dug into his white plastic *THANK YOU* bag to admire his treasure. "So what are we doing today?"

"The tournament was postponed." Daniel scribbling a figure on his drawing pad. "We're working on our comic."

"Did I tell you about my idea for Quicksilver?"

Lucas took his chair again, and he and Daniel looked at each other, rolled eyes in unison. Daniel sighed. "Yes, you did." The figure on the pad had wings now. "We're coming up with something *original*."

Charlie nodded. "Uh-huh." Trying not to be offended, fiddling with the white plastic *THANK YOU* bag. "So, what have you come up with?"

"Check it out." Lucas leaned forward, elbows on table, all aglow. "We've created this outstanding superhero universe."

Charlie blinked. "Do tell."

"Check it out—this group of teens endowed with special abilities are recruited by a government agency."

Charlie nodded. "So...*X-Force*."

Lucas shook his head. "No, dude, this is outstanding—check it out, these kids were captured by aliens and imbued with these special abilities—"

"Oh." Charlie nodded. "*Teen Titans*. Circa Dan Jurgens."

"No, man, these kids are brought together by this secret organization to fight the very same aliens that imbued them." Lucas leaned back in the plastic chair triumphantly. "Huh? Huh? Isn't that outstanding?"

Charlie nodded. "So...who's in this group of yours?"

Daniel started to say something, but Lucas jumped in. "It's outstanding! Check it out, check it out—Even Steven, Anne-X, Bruce Force, Colin Cold One, Maggie Magna, Edgar Headgear—"

"Yeah," Daniel cut in, "and the name of the group is M-Pact."

Charlie raised an eyebrow. "Impact?"

"No—*M-Pact*," Lucas overenunciated.

"Uh-huh." Charlie blinked. "So, the 'M' is because they're... mutants?"

"No, dude," Daniel said, looking up from his scribbled figure. "Misfits." He grabbed a big square eraser and rubbed off a section of his pencils.

Lucas touched Charlie's arm and grinned. "Check it out, the name of the mentor is Auntie-M."

Charlie nodded. "Cute." Smiled awkwardly. "Let me guess—is she in a wheelchair?"

Lucas dropped the grin. "Maybe." Frowned. "Why?"

Charlie sighed, slipping into his lecture tone. "You have somehow created an amalgam of *X-Men* and *Doom Patrol*."

Daniel looked up from his sketchpad. The figure now had bat wings. "You gotta shoot everything down?"

A voice from the doorway said, "Why even do superheroes?" The men turned to see Jeevan Kapoor, the employee at the front counter. "If you're doing indie comics, you can do anything you want."

Charlie furrowed his brow. "Did I tell you about my idea for Quicksilver?"

Jeevan rolled his eyes. "Yes, you did." He sighed. "Man, you need to give up on pitching to somebody like Marvel."

Charlie wrinkled his nose. "What do you suggest?"

Jeevan pursed his lips, thinking. "You should write a novel." He started nodding. "I think it would be funny."

— 32 —

Hank Barton, candidate for City Council, Seventh District, was still unpacking boxes in his new headquarters when he was paid a visit. A couple of tough-looking guys who did not bother to introduce themselves. Simply claimed to represent a Mr. Massey, simply demanded that Hank promise to uphold the previous councilman's agreements to help with certain zoning issues.

"I can't make a promise like that." Hank hoped his voice sounded stronger than he felt. "If elected, I have a responsibility to the people."

The shorter man, stubble darkening his face, offered him a grim smile. "I am not sure you understand the nature of your responsibilities." He shared a glance with the taller man, one who seemed a little confused by the whole conversation. The shorter man looked back with a grimace. "I also think you may have an unrealistic view of your opponent's chances."

"In a fair, democratic election—"

"If one of your opponents say 'yes' and you say 'no,' Mr. Massey may have to throw his considerable weight against your campaign." He leaned in. Eyes blazing. "And when he throws his weight, you'll feel it."

Hank blinked rapidly. "A-are you threatening me?"

"You got me all wrong, councilor," the shorter man said. Wicked smile. "We're just worried about you, that's all." He put a hand on Hank's shoulder and squeezed. "We'd hate for anything to happen to you."

– 33 –

Driving home from the boat place, I was sort of steamed. But the drive gave me some time to put it in perspective.

After all, even after taking out the down payment for the Avalanche, the wife and I still had the money put away for a rainy day. And since we were not going to be around for that rainy day, what were we saving it for? We could just dip into that. Not be enough for a cash sale, but it would make for a much bigger down payment. And soon I would have my Bayliner.

I was feeling pretty good, in fact, by the time I got home. When I pulled into the garage with the Avalanche—I know, I made everyone put everything out in the yard, but when you have a brand new Chevy Avalanche 2500 LT, you don't leave a beauty like that out in the weather—I was on cloud ten.

That did not last long. Making my way inside the front door, I found the wife standing in a living room full of dresses, and shoes, and jewelry, and coats, and I don't know what all. I said, "Marge! What did you do?"

She looks at me and says, "What?" All innocent. Like she didn't know. "I just got a few things."

"A few things? It looks like you bought the whole store."

"No, I left a couple of things for other people." She makes this smile, trying to laugh it off. "I'm kidding. It was not—"

I tried to keep my voice at a reasonable level. Tried to sound merely disappointed. "You bought all this without consulting me?"

"Without...?" She scrunched her nose angrily. "You mean the way we discussed that truck of yours parked out in the driveway?"

It wasn't parked in the driveway, but that wasn't important then. "That's different," I said, struggling valiantly to keep my voice level. "I am the man of the house."

"Check your Scriptures, mister. 'Man of the house' does not give you the license to take money out of the kids' college fund and buy a truck without discussing it with your family."

"I need the truck to pull the boat."

"Boat?" Her voice was close to the pitch only dogs can hear. "You bought a boat?"

"Don't act surprised. This is not new information."

She stormed over to the window and violently pushed open the blinds. "Where is it?"

"I haven't bought it yet. But I'm going to."

She gave me the look. "Without a family discussion."

I had an answer, but bit my tongue. Decided it was time to try and reason with her. "Honey, there was no time for a family discussion. Look, Jesus is coming back in a month. Before that happens, I have to get my boat so I can feel the ocean breeze through my hair."

She laughed and made a gesture toward my thinning hair. "Breeze? Through that?"

She had no call to make this personal. But I kept my cool. "Look," I said, using my end-of-discussion voice, "we're not discussing this." I motioned at her haul scattered around the room. "How much does all this come to?"

The wife's eyes blazed a second, like she was thinking of a reply. Then she calmed down a bit and looked around at all her purchases. "I don't know," she said in a timid, reflective voice, "Two…three…" She looked up and shrugged. "Six thousand, give or take."

Wow. I tried to put a positive spin on it. "So there should still be about fifteen thousand in our savings. We gather up all this stuff and take it back, we could—"

"You're going to spend the rest of the kids' college fund?"

I shrugged and tried to be calm. "In a month, it's all moot. So we have the fifteen—"

"You already took ten out for that truck."

"Oh. Down payment. Right. Okay, that leaves maybe five—"

"I gave each of the kids some money. As a last fling."

"You did what?"

"It was their college fund."

"Fine. How much?"

"A thousand."

"A thousand."

"Each."

"Each." I mentally calculated, "Okay, that leaves—"

"And then I wrote out a check for charity." She had this look on her face, so I knew it was bad.

"You what?"

"I gave three thousand to charity."

"Three thou…are you insane?"

"I thought we should do some good with what we had left."

I felt the air go out of me. I had to sit down. "Marge, you just threw that money away."

"But I—"

"All the good people will be raptured up in a month," I told her. "And anyone left after that doesn't deserve our money. It's too late for them."

"I didn't...I don't..." She was out of words.

"It's like you took that money and threw it down the hole."

She tried to explain it away, weakly. "I don't think..."

I just had to shake my head, hands hanging over my knees. Staring at my shoes. "I can't believe you did that."

I looked up at her. Saw her lip trembling, but I was too defeated to care about that. "I can't believe it, Marge. All I ever wanted was a boat."

— 34 —

Parked outside the Imminent Will church, Ross Cleaver tried to figure out what had just happened. What was with these people?

He and his associate, Bill Lamb, had paid a visit, following up on their little tow-truck stunt. The first problem was, it hadn't seemed to make any impact.

"A shame what happened the other night," Cleaver had said to the man in the church lobby. He'd looked down at the hat in his hands, shaking his head sadly. "You fine folk having your little church meetin'...and somebody's car has gotta disappear like that."

The man in the church lobby had frowned. "I don't understand what you mean."

Cleaver looked up at the man. "You know, your little church meeting. The other night."

The other man had nodded. "Yes." Blank stare.

"Here...at your church."

Nod. "Uh-huh." Blank.

"The...other night."

"Right." Stare.

Cleaver, accustomed to talking in circles, found his usual mode of operations was not working. "It has come to our attention that a certain person's car may have been towed away by operators unknown."

"Really?"

"Right out of your own parking lot there." Cleaver smiled, all friendly. *We're all friends here.* "I don't see why you folks don't keep track of the comings and goings of cars in your own parking lot." If the incident hadn't spread through the church, it was a wasted act.

"Well, it is a big church." The man shrugged, apologetic. "We can't keep track of every little thing that happens to every single member."

Cleaver had nodded doubtfully. "Surely there was a complaint."

"Not that I've heard."

"Well, it happened." He clucked his tongue. "Now, I only wish that my partner and I had been in a position to halt this atrocity before it took place."

The other man's eyes had widened. "Oh."

Contact. Cleaver had smiled. "I see you appreciate our situation." He'd shrugged amiably. "We only wish to serve." Paused. Added, "We would hate for these sorts of incidents to escalate."

The man had nodded. Shrugged again. "Well, I'm sorry, but I still have not had a chance to bring this matter before the board."

"The board."

"Yes. Our board of directors."

— — —

Back in the car, Lamb scrunched up his eyes. "If they're supposed to move the church somewheres else, why haven't we told them to move?" Twisted the top off another water bottle.

Cleaver, gripping the steering wheel at 10 and 2, kept his eyes on the road. "What are you talking about?"

"Mr. Massey wants that property, right?" Took a swig of his water. "So why are we worried about insurance if they're actually supposed to be folding up the tent and moving on?"

Cleaver was silent a second. Eyes fixed on the road. "I got my ways." Cleaver didn't trust the kid anymore, bit his lip before any elucidation came out. No reason to tell the kid he was looking for some cash on the side. If they kept pushing on the church, it would get tired of the neighborhood and move.

He just needed to figure out how to maximize his efforts. Apparently, towing one random car hadn't done it. It still didn't make sense to him.

Maybe he shoulda towed the Reverend's car after all. That woulda put the stink in it. Surely the gang woulda heard about *that.*

Cleaver made a mental note to knock on a few cars at a time. The risk of getting caught in the act would go up, but the attack needed to hurt. It needed to be *noticed.*

But he would figure the church out, figure these weirdos out, figure out what put the fear of man in them. And he would yank the chain until they finally gave up. Finally moved somewhere else. Out of the neighborhood. Out of his hair. Out of his life.

But if he could get the church to shell out a few bills before then, no harm in that, right? A man could always use some pocket money. The boss din't have to know the difference.

He could even get Enid a nice present. Show her he was not exactly worth tossing aside. Show her he had a handle on things. Show her he knew what he was doing.

Cleaver thought again of the ex-linebacker at her place of work. Mikolaczyk.

Cleaver frowned. Cleaver planned.

~ 35 ~

Detective Charlie Pasch. Sunday morning. At church. Working in the kitchen.

The fire department was very prompt.

~ 36 ~

At our final meeting before opening the doors for Tribulation House, my heart was barely in it. All I could think about was that 2008 Bayliner 192.

Still, we made it through the final checklist. The local press had done their stories, so we were expecting a big turnout. The actors were in makeup, the special-effects crew was making their last adjustments to the lights and sound and fog machine and such. Our carpenter was doing a walk-through to make sure every nail and every board was in place.

We had our merchandise all set up by the exit. Black T-shirts proudly displayed the slogan *GOT LEFT?* An assortment of stickers and key chains echoed the theme.

We also had our counselors standing by to grab prospects as they came through the line. The end of the tour was set up so you got your biggest shock at the end—the black room would burst into a bank of floodlights, exhibiting the blinding glory of the Lord. Every person who came through that final room would be dazed, would need help to get through to the exit.

The merch table doubly guaranteed that traffic would slow down by the exit. Thus, the counselors had ample time to swoop and grab their prospects. They were armed with their copies of *107 Reasons Jesus Is Coming in 2007* and various cartoon tracts.

I looked around myself. We were almost ready for Jesus. I checked the blueprints again, comparing it to the charts and graphs. This was our map of Tribulation House, the demo model, if you will, of the "hell on earth" that would afflict mankind during the seven years of Tribulation after the faithful had been taken, "rocketed through that escape hatch known as the Rapture," as Reverend Daniel Glory liked to say.

And it was good.

Every bowl of wrath, every scroll of judgment was represented: There was the Scorpion Room, the Boils Room, the Blood Room—it was all coming together.

The directors of the project had also taken the liberty to modernize the project, help patrons understand the evils of drinking and TV and Christian rock. None of these were specifically mentioned in Scripture, of course, but that was just how Old Scratch worked, and we needed to make that clear even if the Bible didn't. The pleasures of the flesh were the undoing of sinners.

Not that every pleasure was wrong. I was still praying for a boat. I could imagine myself out on the water, conquering the waves. Could imagine following the path of a modern Jesus, using the boat to minister to the masses. Just float up to the dock, and preach to the huddled masses too poor to afford a boat of their own.

And the more impressive the boat, the more impressive the ministry.

It was a beautiful thing.

"Sir?"

I turned and jumped a bit. A frightening skull mask was glaring down at me. Tissue-paper flames erupted around it, crackling in the breeze of the office fan. "Yes, um…"

"It's Tod McGinnis, sir."

"Of course, of course. It's just so hard to recognize you inside that makeup. You did a great job."

"I'm Ghost Rider."

"What?"

"Ghost Rider. It's a guy in Marvel Comics."

"Oh. Of course." I remembered when the concept had first been floated during planning: a burning skull face. The directors of the project shrugged their collective shoulders. *Sure, why not?* There probably would be some burning skulls during the devil's reign on earth.

How could there not be?

I turned and regarded Ghost Rider. "So, which horse does he ride?"

"Horse?"

"Yes, son," I said, trying not to roll my eyes. "Which horse: Famine, Plague, what? He's a 'rider,' he must be a Horseman of the Apocalypse, right?"

"No, he rides a motorcycle."

I nodded doubtfully. I did not really appreciate these Marvel Comics people putting a rider of the Apocalypse on a modern convenience. But of course, they would get theirs. If they did not come to Tribulation House and see the error of their ways, they would be trapped in that hell on earth with all the other sinners, waiting for Jesus to return in judgment.

~ ~ ~

The evening went better than expected. We were packed. Most of the special effects went great. Our man in the video room—the control center, so to speak—kept track of everything, recorded everything, was able to spot trouble before it got out of hand. He saw the fire that started in the room of the fifth bowl—a loose wire touched a curtain—and dispatched someone with a fire extinguisher before anyone found out. He saw the power problems with the third trumpet room and sent another power strip, which seemed to fix the problem.

As the night went on, I went outside for air. Thinking about my 2008 Bayliner 192.

The parking lot was packed, cars packed bumper-to-bumper all the way up and down the street. One car was being towed away.

I don't know whether they were in a no parking zone or something.

Then I heard a smacking sound and a gruff voice coming from over by the corner of the building. "How many times I gotta tell ya to shut up?"

I saw a flicker of light by the dumpster. My eyes adjusted to the moonlight, and I saw the taller man and the shorter man from before. The shorter man pocketed his lighter, took a long drag off his cigarette, spoke up. "How ya doin'?"

I didn't want to be unfriendly—Tribulation House was, after all, a community outreach. "Hello." Then a thought hit me and I walked over to them. "How are you boys tonight?"

The shorter man said, "Keepin' warm." I noticed the chill in the air. "How about you?"

"All the excitement is inside," I said. "You should come and join us."

"No, thanks, man. We're waiting." Another long drag on his cigarette. "We're meeting someone."

The taller man apparently had nothing to say.

I looked again at the tow truck, now driving off with someone's car. It made me think of my Avalanche and my 2008 Bayliner 192. I looked back at the two men. Pretty sure what sort of men they were. "If I needed to borrow a large sum of money..." I let the sentence trail off. I felt something harden in my chest. Someone trying to steal my faith.

"Yes?"

I started over. "If I needed to borrow some money, do you have any...suggestions?"

The taller man didn't look at me. Seemed off in his own little world.

The shorter man threw his cigarette down and stamped it out with his boot. He looked right into my eyes. "How much do you have in mind?"

~ 37 ~

The two men sat in the Dodge watching the apartment building across the street. Behind the wheel, Detective Tom Griggs, Kansas City PD. In the passenger seat, Detective Charlie Pasch. Their FBI pal, Special Agent O'Malley, was inside the building with former judge Hapsburg Reynolds, who was about to turn state's evidence in exchange for a reduced sentence. If O'Malley and his associates could get Reynolds to court alive, it would be a major coup for the district attorney.

When they'd gotten to the car, there had been a flyer on the windshield, stuck under the wiper blade. Announcing some church event named *TRIBULATION HOUSE,* with the added warning, THE TIME IS CLOSER THAN YOU THINK.

Griggs shook his head, pointing to the printed flyer in Charlie's hands. "I don't know how you can stand that stuff."

"What do you mean?"

"All that end of the world malarkey. It's so depressing."

"It doesn't have to be." Charlie looked up, grinning that Charlie grin. "Come to church with me and see for yourself."

Griggs turned his attention back to the sidewalk. "Uh-huh." The guys on the sidewalk were milling around the entrance to the apartment building. Maybe a coincidence. Maybe not.

Griggs checked his watch. Give it another five minutes. If the guys were still milling around, he and Charlie might need to go have a talk with them.

Charlie pointed out the passenger window. "Lookie there."

Coming toward them, a car was creeping slowly up the road. Griggs squinted, couldn't quite make out the model. "What?"

"It looks like a Taurus." Charlie checked his clipboard. "It has to be some of Patterson's brood."

"How can you tell from here?" Griggs squinted harder. "I can barely see the car."

"The headlights remind me of Batman's cowl." The blush in Charlie's voice unmistakable.

Griggs gave Charlie a sideways smile. Turned his eyes back to the entrance of the apartment building. The three men still there. Griggs leaned toward Charlie and whispered. "At this point we just know it's *like* Patterson's car...?"

Charlie found his place on the third sheet on the clipboard, pressed his index finger on some figure. "As soon as we see the license plate, we'll know for sure."

Griggs grabbed the night binoculars. The faces in the car seemed vaguely familiar. He aimed the glasses for the license plate, but the car kept moving toward him. Eventually, he read the letters and numbers off to Charlie.

Charlie looked up from the clipboard, smiling. "Yahtzee."

Griggs put the glasses down, shaking his head. Not sure whether he was more annoyed that Charlie kept calling out the name of the wrong game, or that the kid was happy there was going to be trouble. "Call it in."

Charlie nodded and grabbed the mic. Called for backup.

Griggs was already on his cell phone, hitting speed dial for Special Agent Martin O'Malley. The phone on the other end rang twice. A voice clipped, "What?"

"Wake-up call."

O'Malley cursed. "How bad?"

"Three guys milling around by the front door, and a carload of Patterson's boys coming up the street." Griggs looked out the window. "Wait—the car turned for the side street. They might be headed for the back way."

"There is no back way."

"You always know how to pick 'em." Griggs looked up the street. "We called for backup. I didn't know what arrangements you might also want to make."

"Like call for a priest?"

Griggs chuckled. "How close are you to moving the subject?"

"We're circling the wagons now."

"All right, cowboy. We'll try to get you an opening out front. Wait for my call—or until you hear sirens." Griggs snapped the cell phone shut and pocketed it. Began checking his weapon.

Charlie unholstered his gun and followed the elder cop's example. "What'd he say?"

"He didn't expect anyone to find them tonight."

"Pfft. Feds." A playful jab—O'Malley was one of the good ones. As part of the KCPD/FBI Joint Task Force against organized crime, Griggs and Charlie had gotten to know O'Malley pretty well. And right now, he was sitting upstairs with a federal witness who was ready to testify against Boss Pratt tomorrow morning. More like a sitting duck.

Griggs checked the street with his night glasses one more time before exiting the Dodge. The three guys who had been milling around the front door were now walking to the alley. "Hey, Charlie, I think we might—"

The sounds of automatic gunfire erupted from the alley across the street. Griggs dropped the glasses and popped his door. "Now!" The two detectives hit the pavement as two gangsters climbed into the big Taurus backing out of the alley.

Charlie raised his weapon. "Police!"

Gangster #1 turned and replied with automatic gunfire. Griggs fired through the windshield. The driver slumped over. As the car rolled to a stop, Charlie and Griggs ran forward, guns ready.

Gangster #2 pushed the driver from behind the wheel and hit the gas. Charlie unloaded his weapon at the fleeing car, then turned for the Dodge.

Griggs charged up the alley, fired a couple of shots at the Taurus barreling toward him. It kept coming. The car narrowly missing Griggs as he rolled onto a parked car.

Charlie pulled the Dodge into the street, blocking the Taurus. The other car smashed the big blue postal drop as it hit the sidewalk, to go around. Charlie backed his car to make a U-turn, waited for Griggs to hop in the passenger seat.

Griggs heard the sirens in the distance. "Step on it."

Charlie hit the gas and the Dodge was off. Griggs slapped the flashing light on top of the car and hit their own siren. He grabbed the radio. "This is Detective Griggs in blue sector, in pursuit of a silver Ford Taurus." He read off the Kansas plates and then looked up at the compass ball hanging from the rearview mirror. "Heading north on Woodmont at high speed. Subjects armed and dangerous. We need roadblock units."

Charlie behind the wheel, intent. Aglow. As they closed in, gangster #1 unloaded more gunfire. A bullet punctured the windshield, Griggs heard it whiz by and hit the backseat.

The Taurus hit a hard left, darting through cross traffic. Charlie followed suit with the Dodge, which got clipped in the rear. Charlie gripped the wheel and stomped on the brakes as the Dodge spun 360. He and Griggs exchanged a look. Charlie turned front with his determined face, let out a hot breath, and punched the gas. Tires squealing, the Dodge rocketed back in hot pursuit.

Within a few seconds, they had the Taurus in sight again. They had to run a red light, Charlie touching the brakes, making a deft right and left to avoid frantic pedestrians. He grinned darkly. "All we need is the guys with the big pane of glass crossing the street."

Griggs smiled, said nothing. Braced himself against the door as the Dodge kept rocking. The old car not as good with high-speed chases as he remembered. Maybe it was time to trade it in. What would Carla say? Another hail of gunfire got Griggs's attention—they were closer to the bad guys than he realized.

Charlie swerved left and floored it, coming up around the Taurus. Griggs had his handgun ready, thought better of it and unlocked the shotgun. Griggs rolled down his window and, as gangster #2 aimed toward him, unloaded the shotgun at the back window. The gangster ducked for cover, glass exploding into the bad guys' car.

The guy behind the wheel eyed the Dodge nervously now. Before the gangster in the back could reappear, Griggs pumped the shotgun and leaned out his window, aiming for the front tire.

Suddenly, the Dodge hit a bump—Griggs lost his bearings, fired wildly. He cursed into the wind, pumping the shotgun again, when the gangster in the back of the Taurus reappeared, aiming his automatic dead at Griggs.

For years, Griggs would remember the instant with slo-mo clarity. Slivers of memory bobbing to the surface, regrets, unresolved issues. His wife. The estranged father he still had not forgiven. The daughter he and Carla had buried.

The world stopped.

Then Charlie hit the brakes and cut a hard right, avoiding the angle of the spray of bullets, smashing hard into the side of the Taurus. The gangster behind the wheel lost control and bounced up on the sidewalk, smashing hard into brick. The driver went through the windshield and splashed all over the pavement. The gangster in back still coiled up in the wreckage.

Charlie shifted into reverse and pulled the Dodge out to the curb. Taking air in loud gulps. "A-are you okay?"

Griggs gave the kid a weary grin. Fought the urge to tousle his hair. "You done good, Charlie."

— 38 —

"You can't do this, Hank. It's too risky." Sven Surtees set down the coffee mug labeled *BETTER WITH BARTON,* echoing the slogan on the banner draped behind him. "At the very least, you need to hire bodyguards or something."

Sitting at the new headquarters for Hank Barton, candidate for City Council, Seventh District, surrounded by unopened boxes and unfurled posters, Sven at the table with his longtime friend Hank, and the two men's wives, Wendy Surtees and Lisa Barton. The room was dark, moonlight coming through the storefront window. The volunteers all gone for the night.

Three sets of eyes boring into him, waiting for his decision, Hank shook his head. "No." Stuck out his chin, striking a pose of strength. "No. I will not bow."

Lisa gently put her hand on his. Her voice trembled a little. "But to be threatened by the Mafia—"

Hank pulled his hand from hers. He pushed back from the table and stood. "We don't know that it's organized crime." He held out his hands, calling for calm reason. "Look, we don't even know it's a threat." He turned from the table and walked tentatively over to the moonlit window. He looked out to the street, gazing at the passing traffic. Checked his gut, held in his own fear. Kept his voice calm. "It could be nothing."

Sven walked over to the window and stood next to his friend. "You don't know that it's nothing." He looked back at the women at the table, then back at Hank. He put a hand on his friend's shoulder and sighed loudly. "Right after they talked to you, you sure thought it was a threat."

"That was before I had time to think about it." Hank shrugged. Shook his head. "I must have misunderstood them." He turned and looked Sven in the eye. "That's all." He smiled weakly. "Besides, even if it is trouble—if God be with me, who can be against me?"

Lisa's voice still shook. "God didn't ask you to take on the mob."

Hank turned and chuckled. "In the Bible, the men of faith took on mobs all the time."

"That's not what I mean!"

"I know, honey." Hank nodded, furrowed his brow. "But it's the same thing. Daniel survived the lion's den. David survived Goliath. Shadrach, Mesha, and…and…" He shrugged. "Those three guys survived the fiery furnace."

Sven frowned. "Shadrach, Meshach, and Abednego?"

Hank nodded. Smiled. "Right. Those guys."

At the table, Lisa bit her lip in tearful silence. Wendy leaned over and took Lisa's hand. "That was in Bible times, Hank." She turned and looked at him with stern eyes. "Don't be a fool."

"I don't know if I agree with that." Hank fairly puffed out his chest. Anger rising. "Is He God or not God?"

Sven reached out and touched Hank's shoulder. "Easy...we're not saying that—"

"No, seriously." Hank's eyes held flecks of rage. "Is Jesus Lord or is He not Lord?"

Sven rolled his eyes. "Jesus is Lord, Hank." Looked dead at his friend. "But you're not Jesus."

"If He is the same yesterday, today, and forever, then what He did yesterday, He can do today." Hank felt the faith rising up in him. He privately hoped it was not false bravado. "I have a mission. I have a purpose. I have a plan. And I cannot lose heart at the first sign of trouble." His voice dropped low, controlled. "I cannot be swayed by the first sign of opposition." He started pacing in front of the window, forming a sharp silhouette in the moonlight. "Anything worth doing is hard. If it weren't, more people would do the right thing. But the church has spent the past thirty or forty years disengaging from the culture—removing its influence from entertainment and art and science and the ordinary lives of ordinary people. Not being light. Not being salt. Hiding its light under a bushel."

The others watched him pace, saying nothing. He was on a roll. No stopping him now. "In 1962, they banned prayer from schools. Without that influence, the country was soon broken forever."

"How can you say—"

"Starting in 1963, there was the murder of JFK, the murder of Martin Luther King Jr., Vietnam..." Hank wheeled toward Sven, pointing a finger. "Did you know that until the 1960s, the church actually had a say in the ratings of movies?"

Sven shrugged. "Hollywood stopped listening."

"No." Hank shook his head, eyes lighting up. "The church walked away. The church chose to stop speaking into the film industry. And if you look at your film history, you can see the decline in values from that point."

At the table, Wendy sat up straighter. "Are you serious?"

"I am very serious. In centuries past, all of the real advances in the arts and sciences and humanities were the result of the church. Or, at least, church influence."

"You mean, they were all invented by Christians?"

"Not necessarily. But they were created in a biblical culture. In the environment of decency and wonder provided by a healthy presence of the church."

"Don't tell that to Galileo." Sven grinned in spite of himself. "He might pick an argument on that point."

Hank eyebrows went up. "That was not Galileo versus the culture of the church, that was Galileo versus the specific leadership of the church at that time. He still made his discoveries inside a Christian culture."

"I don't know." Sven shook his head. "If the church leadership—"

"I never said the *people* were infallible." Hank stopped in front of the window again. He looked out, found himself imagining all the lost souls who passed by on the sidewalk from day to day. "We can make a difference." He turned back to the room. "We can do this. We *need* to do this."

The other three let their arguments drop. Hank could still see flecks of doubt in their eyes, but felt like Sven, Wendy, and still-sniffling Lisa all saw that he was full of his convictions. He watched them slowly, finally nod despite their reservations.

He looked back out the window. Still thinking about the mob.

~ 39 ~

Detective Tom Griggs got home pretty late. Carla had left the kitchen light on for him. As he emptied his pockets on the kitchen table, he saw the note on the microwave. *DINNER.*

He opened the little door and found a plastic container with some sort of meat dish inside. "Aw, Carla," he whispered. "I already ate." He smiled to himself and put the container in the refrigerator.

Upstairs, his wife was already in bed. He sat down on his side and undressed as silently as he could.

She stirred. "Tom?"

"Yeah, baby. Go back to sleep."

She turned and rubbed shut eyes. "Are you okay?"

"Yeah. We got the guy moved to a safe place."

"No trouble?"

"No trouble." He pushed his pants off onto the floor. "Much."

She sat up and turned on the lamp on her nightstand. "Okay, Tom. What happened?"

"Nothing, baby."

"Just tell me."

"There were some bad guys and there was some shooting."

"Uh-huh."

"And there may have been a car chase."

"Did anyone get hurt?"

"Some of the bad guys. Me and Charlie came out okay."

"Who was driving?"

"Charlie."

She squinted at him. "Whose car?"

Tom pushed off one sock. Then the other. Then he said, quickly, cleanly, "Yours."

"Great."

"It's not bad."

"Of course it's bad."

"Why would you think it's bad?"

"Because you don't want to tell me about it. If it weren't bad, you would've just told me about it."

He leaned and kissed her on the forehead. "You're dreaming. Go to sleep."

"How can I sleep now?"

"It's no problem, baby. Just close your eyes and continue sleeping. We'll take care of this in the morning."

"I put some goulash for you in the microwave."

"I grabbed something on the way home."

She nodded sleepily, turned off her lamp, and put her head back on the pillow. "I'm glad you're home."

"Me, too, baby."

— 40 —

Saturday, October 6. I had a lovely day on Blue Springs Lake, out in Fleming Park. With my new boat. My 2008 Bayliner 192. Cool breeze in my hair, the sun dancing on the surface of the water. It was heavenly.

Before I brought it out here, I made a point to show off to the neighbors. Parked it out on the street there, where everyone could see. I made a point to knock on a few doors, tell a few neighbors to watch my house for any suspicious activity—I was going to be out on the lake with my new boat. My 2008 Bayliner 192. Have you seen my new boat? So if you could watch my house while I'm out on the lake, I would surely appreciate it, neighbor.

Sure, they tried to play cool. Like it was no big thing. I knew they were wrestling with jealousy right then and there, with the fact I had a boat they could never afford. (Okay, a boat *I* could never afford, either—if it weren't for my special arrangement with Jesus.)

Doug Waters nodded and said he would keep an eye out. "That's a nice one there," he said politely, hiding the fact that he was surely seething.

Felix Mendel shrugged. "Sorry, I'm headed out this afternoon." He didn't even bother to look at my boat, but I'm sure it was because he knew he wouldn't be able to hide his coveting.

Mrs. Henson just gave me a disapproving look. But I think her face is frozen that way.

My 2008 Bayliner 192 hitched to the back of my Chevy Avalanche 2500 LT, I waved to whoever watched as I pulled away from the curb. Driving to Blue Springs, I made one slight detour. But Marvin Dobbs wasn't home. I couldn't apologize to him for the unpleasantness the other day. Worse yet, he couldn't see my new boat.

Getting the boat out on the lake, I was soon sitting back on the lounge chair, sipping from my lemonade and munching on Oreos. I really got a sense of what it must have been like for our Lord on the Sea of Galilee, ministering to the crowds on the shore.

Did I preach to the crowds at the dock? Oh, Lord, no. I didn't think much of that crowd. I had already stapled some flyers about Tribulation House on the telephone pole and stuck one on the bulletin board. If those people wanted to get saved, they could come to church like everybody else.

Of course, no Eden is without its snake: Even though I was out there on the lake like Jesus, the enemy tried to squelch my good time, with flickers of memories about those gangsters. And, I must confess, I wrestled with the shadow of doubt. Had I been right to speak with them? Had I been right to share my dilemma with them? Had I been right to take their money?

Something about the situation made me think of what happened when I was sixteen. That time I was babysitting my little brother. But this was a completely different situation.

Allowing the breeze to wash over me, the smell of the lake, the sweetness of the Oreo, I closed my eyes and listened to the sounds on the water. The waves gently lapping against the side of the 2008 Bayliner 192. The birds announcing themselves as they passed overhead. The others on the lake, boating and skiing and laughing and envying me on this day that the Lord hath made.

I pushed the doubts out of my mind. I held fast to the promise that we faithful should benefit from the money of the unfaithful. (I am not exactly sure where it is in the Bible, but Reverend Daniel Glory preached about it one time.)

But, man! Being alone on the lake. No nagging from the wife. No nagging from the kids. No contact with another human soul. This was the way God meant for it to be.

It was paradise being away from everybody. I wondered what

Marge was doing right now. Probably trying on her shoes. How could someone expect to wear so many different shoes before the end of the world? I looked down at my sneakers. They were new—you did not wear old sneakers on a brand-new 2008 Bayliner 192—but they would be the last pair of shoes I ever owned. (Will we wear shoes in the kingdom? Jesus wore shoes, I guess—sandals, right?—so we must.)

It was glory here without the daughter. Right now, she was probably brushing her hair or trying out different nose rings in front of the mirror and gabbing with her friends on her cell phone. Wondered whether I should cancel her cell account—didn't want her unsaved friends to come across the phone wherever the daughter dropped it in the Rapture and start running up minutes. Then I chuckled, remembering that it didn't matter what the phone bill came to—we wouldn't be here to pay it.

Jubilee.

I was out of lemonade. It was an effort to peel myself out of the lounge chair to get some more—the rocking of the boat had made me drowsier than I realized. Another glass of lemonade and then a nap on the lake would be exquisite.

Settling back in the chair with my refill and another handful of Oreos—the wife never understood how I could take the sweet and the sour together—my thoughts turned to the boy. Him and his stories. Always writing. When would he learn that fiction is no way to serve God?

My mama read her novels, and it never did her any good. When I was a kid, her library always fascinated me—perhaps because her paperbacks were always off limits. One night, when the folks left me and my brother alone for the night, I snuck a Jackie Collins out of her room. I was reading it when—

"Are you going to copy *everything* I do?"

I knew that voice. Dobbs. I set down the lemonade and peeled myself out of the chair again.

Went to the side of the boat—wait, what do they call that? Bow? Stern? I probably should have remembered that from the test. But I was sleepy from dozing in the sun, so it could be forgiven. I squinted at the boat cruising slowly alongside mine. "What are you talking about now, Dobbs?"

"First you steal Armageddon House—and now you got a boat!"

"Lots of people have boats! How can I be expected to remember you have a boat too?"

"We came out here just last summer. You and all the deacons. On my boat. For our summit."

"I forgot about that."

"How could you forget that? You spent all winter talking about how we need to do it again."

"No, I think I talked all winter about how Jesus went out on the boat. I just want to be more like Jesus."

"No, you want to be more like me," Dobbs said. "Pathetic."

I don't know how it happened, but my cooler was thrown at his boat. And maybe the lounge chair.

Apparently, Fleming Park has a policy against that. I was going to have to find another place to be like Jesus.

— 41 —

"I have a bad feeling about this." Detective Charlie Pasch, Sunday morning, now working Kidz Kingdom in the church gym. He checked his watch—the kids would be coming up from the sanctuary soon.

The children's-church team was doing the final setup for children's church. Charlie and another member of the team, Kara, were waiting by the entrance. "What do you mean?" she asked.

Charlie sighed. Let his shoulders sag. "The last few weeks, I seem to be plagued by disasters every time I try to serve."

"Don't say that!"

"No, seriously, like I was working behind the soundboard the other night and—"

"Don't speak negatively. You invite bad things to happen that way."

After the kids showed up, everything went fine. More or less. Sure, Charlie got nervous in front of the kids—eighty pairs of eyes on him at once was unnerving—and knocked over the cartons of eggs Pastor Wallace was planning to use for an object lesson. Charlie spent the better part of the service wiping yolk off the gym floor before it had a chance to set. Then, during small group time, Charlie was freaked out by the nine-year-old girl with all the questions about the Song of Solomon.

Other than that, service seemed to go okay.

After the service, parents were pooling by the doors, waiting to take their kids home. Most of the parents calmly followed procedure: wait in line by the exit, show the attendant your ticket matching the sticker on your child's clothing, have a nice week.

But Charlie heard one of the men grumbling about the new system. He went up to the man and struck up a friendly conversation. Tried to explain the importance of keeping each child safe. Tried to explain that, as a police detective, Charlie knew what he was talking about.

Before the conversation was over, the man was screaming. He shoved and Charlie reacted instinctively: clutched the man's shoulder with one hand, the man's elbow with the other hand, flipped the man into the sign-in table.

Charlie, horrified, barely noticed the thick silence around him. Young and old alike, eyes wide, jaws dropped.

I knew I had a bad feeling about this, was the phrase that kept going through his mind.

⎯ 42 ⎯

In the middle of Mr. Massey's Monday errands, Ross Cleaver and Bill Lamb stopped in at a place called Frozen Futures. Cleaver turned to the other man, eyes blazing, finger pointing. "Now, we are just here for a minute. No reason Mr. Massey has to hear about it."

Lamb looked hurt. "What are you telling me for?"

Cleaver looked away, checking his temper. "You have a habit of telling things."

"A guy has a right to talk. It's a free—" He stopped dead at Cleaver's glare. Smiled, held up his hands. "I'm cool. I ain't saying nothin'."

As they went up the sidewalk, Lamb looked at the sign hanging over the front door, saw the frosted cartoon effect on the logo. "Are we getting ice cream?" Sounded hopeful.

"Just shut up." Cleaver shot Lamb a look, Lamb shut his mouth. Cleaver pushed through the double doors into the front lobby.

Behind the desk, a woman was chomping her gum and working the crossword puzzle in ink. As the two men approached the desk, she cursed and scribbled out one of the answers. Then she looked up, still smacking her gum. Loud. "Oh. Well, look what been drug in."

"*Cat*, Enid," Cleaver sighed. "The phrase is 'Look what the *cat* drug in.'"

She blinked at him. "I don't got a cat."

Lamb blurted, "So you guys make Popsicles here or what?"

Enid's grin was big and toothy. "Naw." Chomping the gum. "Or maybe I should say, not like you think!" She snorted.

Cleaver turned to Lamb and said in a low voice, "Not that it is any of your concern, but they happen to freeze guys here."

Lamb frowned. "Guys?"

Cleaver shrugged. "People."

Enid stood and handed Lamb a colorful trifold flyer. Under the same frosted logo *FROZEN FUTURES* was the legend, WHEN MODERN MEDICINE ISN'T ENOUG. Lamb read it. *"Enoug?"*

She grinned, smacking gum again. "We got a break on the printing."

Cleaver grimaced. "Y'see, they freeze people who got what you call 'terminus' illnesses. Docs today can't do nothin' for these guys, so they freeze 'em until such time in the future as medical science can save 'em."

Lamb nodded. "Huh." Looked at Enid. "This stuff works?"

Enid turned to Cleaver with a worried look. "This guy for real?"

"He's new." Cleaver shook his head lightly, ready to change the subject. "We got things worked out at the house, baby."

Her amiable demeanor dropped cold. "What do you mean?"

Cleaver spoke in a low, familiar tone. "We had a conversation with the gentleman responsible for fixing up—"

"Who told you to get involved?"

Cleaver stepped back. "W-we just—"

"There is no *we*, mister, there is *you* and there is *me*. The court says there ain't no *we* anymore."

"B-but I just—"

"You made your choice. I told you, 'It's me or it's Massey,' and you chose that, that..." She nodded toward the picture window, sputtering to a stop. "...*crook*."

"I told you, baby, Mr. Massey is a businessman."

"I know what *business* he's in. And I want no part of it!"

"I'm just looking after your best interests."

"Did you do something to them?"

"What do you mean?"

"To the fix-it men." She frowned. Overenunciated for effect. "*Did you. Do something. To them.*"

"Aw." Cleaver lowered his eyes. Shook his head. "We may have had a slight misunder—"

"Oh! Great!" Enid raised her hands to go with the shrieking. "That explains everything!" She stepped around the desk, marched right up to Cleaver, jabbed a finger in his chest. "I don't need your kinda help. I don't need you breaking someone's kneecaps because you're not happy with the dry cleaning or because the pizza is a couple minutes late!" She paced a few steps in front of him. "It was bad enough you pulled this kinda crud when we were married. But now!" Threw her hands up again. "Agh!"

A side door opened, and a beefy guy in a suit came into the lobby. Cleaver recognized him as Herman Mikolaczyk, former all-pro linebacker. Mob thug. Almost fit the suit. "Problem out here, Enid?"

"Naw, Mr. Mike." She sighed loudly. Rolling the gum on her tongue. "Just my idiot ex-husband here forgetting to stay out of my business."

Mikolaczyk stepped up to Cleaver. Stood a foot taller.

Cleaver stood his ground. "Mik."

The other man nodded once. "Ross." Still towering over Cleaver, he turned back to Enid. "Need any help?"

"No." She began smacking gum again. "I think we're done."

Cleaver considered his options against the taller man. Relaxed his demeanor, turned to Lamb. "Let's get out of here."

Lamb pointed to the door from which Mik had come. "What you got back there?"

"You can't go back there." The gorilla cleared his throat. "It's sterile."

Lamb's eyed widened. "Celebrities on ice, I guess?"

Enid rolled her eyes. "We are not at liberty to discuss our clients." She smacked her gum with authority. "It's confidential."

Cleaver growled at his associate. "Let's go." Did his best to saunter casually for the exit. Aware of the eyes burning into his back. It didn't bother him. Wouldn't bother him. Shouldn't bother—

"Ross, wait." The silky voice stopped him. He turned and Enid walked up, smiling sweetly. This might turn out okay. She held out an empty hand. "Keys."

Oh. "I don't know what you're talking about."

"Keys. *My* house. Gimme."

"I don't got—"

"Ross...?"

Cleaver hesitated. Taking note of the ex-linebacker across the room, his shoulders sagged. "Whatever." He pulled out his key ring, picked through the keys, pulled her house key off the metal ring. Handed it over.

On the sidewalk outside, Lamb was smiling to himself. Cleaver let it go. He was thinking about Mikolaczyk.

— 43 —

Back at the KCPD, Detective Tom Griggs and Detective Charlie Pasch were filling out paperwork. Griggs glanced at Charlie as he opened the file folder and checked the papers. "So he told you to write a novel, huh?"

Charlie did not look up from his laptop, which was teetering on the corner of Griggs's desk. "Uh-huh."

"Sounds like a lot of work."

"Maybe. But it's easier than doing comics."

"How you figure that?"

"Well, unlike a comic book, you aren't at the mercy of whether or not you can find an artist. Plus, for the aspiring comic-book writer, there are like three companies that will even look at your stuff. For the novelist, there are hundreds of places to send a book."

"Are you going to do it?"

"Yeah. I think so. I just hafta come up with an idea."

Griggs found the papers he was looking for and sighed. "This is the life. None of that running around fighting crime." He signed a form and placed it in the stack. "It's all about forms and printouts and schedules." Closing the folder, he pushed it aside. He grabbed the baseball off his desk, adjusted his fingering for an imaginary pitch.

"Now, now." Charlie looked up from the laptop. "We had a car chase the other night, didn't we? The witness made it to court, the bad guys are on the run, the good guys win the day." He went back to typing, that crazy two-fingered lightning typing that he did. "Now it's all over but the paperwork."

"*We* didn't have a car chase." Griggs, feet on the desk now, started rolling the baseball casually from one hand to the other. "*You had a car chase.* I was the one who had to go home and explain to his wife that you wrecked her car."

"You don't worry about rubbing the autograph off that?"

Griggs looked at the baseball in his hand and sat up suddenly. "Maybe." He set it back on the plastic stand. "It's one of the only presents my father ever gave me."

Charlie stopped typing. "Uh-huh."

"The signature is probably fake anyway."

"Who is it?"

"Bob Forsch. Pitched for the St. Louis Cardinals 1974 through 1987."

"Do you want to get it authenticated?"

Griggs put elbows on desk, rested his head on his arms. "No."

"It shouldn't be hard. I could probably—"

"No."

"Is it—"

Griggs sighed loudly and sat back up. "It's better to wonder than to know." He leaned back in the chair, swiveling left and right. "Know what I mean?"

Charlie snapped the laptop closed and pushed it toward the middle of Griggs's desk. He sat back in the plastic chair. "I thought you resolved all that."

"I tried, man. I tried." There was a long silence, Griggs staring out the window at the lights of Kansas City. Then he turned back and stared at the desk blotter. "Do you know I have this whole box of unopened letters from him?"

"Sure."

"When he left my mom, he told her a lot of lies."

"There might be two sides. You know, it's always—"

"Not a difference of opinion, Charlie—*lies.* He told her there was not another woman. And then went straight to the woman's house. He said it was spur of the moment, that he had not planned on it. But his bags were already packed."

Charlie did not know what to say. This had been a sore subject with Griggs for as long as Charlie had known him. The only other cop who knew the story would be Griggs's former partner, Jurgens— now sitting in prison, in no mood to share.

Griggs shook his head. "I lost a promotion because of him."

"What, Jurgens?"

Griggs frowned at Charlie, eyes blazing. "What?" He shook his head violently and looked back down at the blotter. "No—my *dad*. I was up for a promotion when we got the report. My dad had embezzled all the money from that used car dealer and run off with the wh—" He struggled with the word choice. Finally sputtered, "—with the *woman*."

"Uh-huh."

"Given the circumstances—I couldn't stop my own father from being a crook and a liar—the higher-ups said maybe I wasn't ready to make lieutenant yet."

"But you are a lieutenant."

Griggs grabbed the baseball again. "I am now. But if my dad hadn't..." He leaned back in the chair. "It might have been different."

"You can't be held responsible for what your dad does."

"It was all politics, Charlie." Rolling the baseball back and forth. "You know how that goes."

Charlie slumped back in his chair. "Doesn't seem fair, somehow." He watched Griggs rolling the baseball a while, trying to think what to say. Finally, he thought of, "Did you ever write back?"

"I've been too ashamed."

"What do you have to be ashamed about?"

"Ashamed of him."

"Oh."

"I still get a letter once or twice a year. It just goes in the box." Griggs turned the ball over in his hands, rubbing a finger along the red stitching. "The first few times, I turned his address over to the authorities. The postmark said he was somewhere in Mexico."

"What happened?"

"Nobody's been able to catch him." Griggs slammed the baseball on the desk. "Nobody."

"But he keeps writing?"

"Yeah."

Charlie leaned back in the chair. "So you have no idea what he says in these letters?"

Griggs shrugged. "I tried again a few months ago. Pulled out the box. The first letter I opened was the same old story—him still trying to play the victim. Defending what he did. Like I was an idiot. Like I wasn't smart enough to see through his lies." He sat back in the chair again, trying different finger arrangements around the baseball. "It was more than I could take. I shoved the whole mess back in the closet."

"After you sent the law, you'd think he'd have laid low." Charlie shrugged. "You know, stopped writing."

"You'd think."

Charlie let the air hang silent a few minutes. Griggs in his private pain. Then Charlie had an idea, spent a few minutes struggling with it. Finally, stammered, "You should come to church."

Griggs dropped the baseball. "What?" It rolled under the desk.

"Seriously. Church. You and Carla could come with me."

Griggs made wide eyes, shook his head. "I don't think so." Then leaned over to try and grab the baseball off the floor. "Besides, Carla goes to church." Griggs came back up with the baseball, set it in the plastic stand. "Sometimes she asks me to go with her."

"Do you?"

Griggs shook his head. "Nope." He let out a big breath. "You know, my dad was a minister."

"You said he sold used cars."

"He was what they call a 'lay minister.' They put him through some seminar and then started sending him out to these little country churches to preach about how God wants you to wash your car."

Charlie felt his cheeks flush. "Look, don't blame God because some little church was stupid enough—"

"How can I trust God if God trusts someone like my dad?"

Charlie sighed. *Lord, help me with the words.* He put a hand gently on the desk, made eye contact with Griggs. "Detective Griggs—Tom—you can't blame God because someone did something stupid in His name."

Griggs said nothing. Looked like he was going to spit.

Charlie looked down. "What about Jurgens, for instance?"

Griggs shot a look. "What about him?"

"He was an officer—he was your *partner*. He betrayed you. He betrayed us all." Charlie dropped his voice to a whisper. "Does his betrayal mean everyone in the force is a criminal?"

Griggs fixed hurt eyes on the desk blotter. "I don't know..."

Charlie leaned forward. "You don't blame the law. You blame the man who broke the law." He sat back again in the plastic chair. "It's the same way with—"

Griggs jumped up. "What about my daughter? Huh? Where was God when my little girl died?" He stormed out of the room.

Leaving Charlie alone with the paperwork.

— 44 —

"So, God told you to run for office?" *Kansas City Blade* reporter Ben Carlson scribbled furiously in his notepad.

Across from him at the small round table, the aroma of coffee floating about them: Hank Barton, candidate for City Council, Seventh District. "I don't know that I would state it that baldly," he answered. "But I do have a mission to make a difference in this district." He added, "My wife and I both feel quite strongly about it."

"So, you're on a mission from God?" Carlson smirked, not even looking up from his notepad. "You know, dark glasses and full tank of gas and all that?"

Hank turned his head sideways, trying to see what all the scribbling was about. Pursed his lips. Tried to figure out where this reporter was coming from. Tried to redirect the conversation. "I am on a mission from the people." He felt himself floundering, went back to his safety net: "I am proud to announce my hope to earn the support of my fellow citizens of the seventh district of Kansas City as one of their representatives on the city council."

"Uh-huh."

"With the untimely demise of Councilman Goode"—Hank crooked his neck to try and see the other man's notepad—"the special election to fill the vacancy forms an opportunity for the people to make their voices heard."

"Uh-huh."

Hank gave up on trying to read the man's notes. He sipped from his coffee. "Look, Mr. Carlson, I was born and raised here. I have traveled all over, and there is nowhere I would rather call home." Practically reciting this info by rote, making a conscious effort to sound casual. "This is an incredible city. But our local government is broken; and for far too long we, the God-fearing local taxpayers, have been paying the price. Our freedoms are threatened by activists on the left and organized crime on the right. For far too long, we have been too polite, too lax, too willing to go with the flow. But the sleeping giant needs to awaken and deal with these problems."

Carlson nodded. "Uh-huh." Scribbling, scribbling, always scribbling.

"When you—that is, when the *people* elect me to city council"—pause, allowing the man's scribbling to catch up—"they are sending a message to the council about what matters to the people of this district."

Hank noticed movement out of the corner of his eye. He turned and saw a woman and a small child looking at him. He grinned big, and the woman brought the child over to the table. "Excuse me, but aren't you Hank Barton?"

He stood. "Yes, ma'am. I am." The reporter did not even look up from his notepad. Shouldn't he have brought a tape recorder?

The woman said, "We look forward to voting for you."

"I appreciate that." He looked at the little girl. "And who have we here?"

The girl blushed and hid behind the woman's leg. The woman said, "This is Suzy." She leaned down to the little girl. "Can you say 'hello,' Suzy?"

The girl, apparently, could not. The woman said it was nice meeting him, and she and the child left. Hank sat down, feeling pretty good.

The reporter picked up as if nothing had happened. "And what do you think matters to the people of this district?"

"I'm sorry?" The reporter did not even give him a chance to get back into the rhythm of the interview. "Where were we?"

"If the people of this district elect you to city council, you claim they are sending a message to the council about what matters to them."

"Oh. Of course."

"And what do you think matters to the people of this district?"

"Well, for one, religious liberties." Pause. "Two, education." Pause. "And three, crime prevention." Hank paused again, sipping from his coffee. Pacing himself. It was all about pacing. "These are the great pillars on which a great society is built. We need the freedom to observe our religion. Our children need to be given the proper education to grow up into the citizens and leaders of tomorrow. And we need to be free from the fear that the criminal element is going to drag our society into the shadows and destroy us." He took another sip from his coffee. Wondering whether he was laying it on too thick.

The reporter just mumbled another "Uh-huh."

Hank continued. "Once these three things are in place, our economy and our community will be free to develop and thrive. I am dedicated to preserving and enhancing District Seven neighborhoods, ensuring the safety of residents, and creating an attractive and healthy environment that will encourage people to live, work, and shop in the—"

"How do you intend to do that?"

Fair question. Hank nodded thoughtfully, smiled. "My plan is to give attention to safe neighborhoods and parks…adequate numbers of police…well-maintained streets…clean sidewalks with buildings unspoiled by graffiti…and a welcome climate for new businesses that provide good-paying secure jobs." Added, "My wife, *Lisa,* and I both feel strongly about this."

"Uh-huh." The reporter scribbled some more in that chicken-scratch shorthand, then looked up from his notebook. "You are aware that this is just a position on the city council?"

"Of course."

"Not, you know, mayor."

"I'm not sure I see what you—"

"So, do you really think you can do all this?"

Hank tried to sound statesmanlike. "This is not about me." Tried not to sound annoyed. "This is not about what I can do. This is about what the council is empowered to do by the people."

"Uh-huh."

"And when the people elect me, they are sending a—"

"A message, got it." Scribbling.

Hank stopped to find his train of thought. Sipped his coffee to stall for time. Wished he had bought another flavor. Finally, "I'm not saying we don't have our work cut out for us," he said. Exuding confidence. "But we can now all wake up to the new morning of Kansas City and get ready for a great day. All of Kansas City must stand together, or we will fall together."

The reporter scribbled furiously. Hank stretched his neck again, tried unsuccessfully to figure out what the man was writing. He thought over his statement, how it would play in the press. It suddenly occurred to Hank that VOTE BARTON FOR A GREAT DAY or VOTE BARTON FOR A NEW MORNING would have been much stronger than BETTER WITH BARTON. He would have to discuss that with Sven when he got back to the campaign headquarters.

"So…" *Kansas City Blade* reporter Ben Carlson stopped scribbling and looked up. "…when God speaks to you, is it like a big booming voice from the heavens, or more like a quiet voice in your head?"

⌐ 45 ⌐

"I'm sorry, Charlie, but you need to stick this out." Pastor Mac, sitting across from Charlie at New Famous Chinese Super Buffet. Between egg rolls and General Zao's chicken, Pastor Mac wiped sauce off his mouth. "You can't just keep bouncing from job to job. I know you had a rough time up there Sunday morning, but—"

"Pastor Mac…" Charlie sighed, gave up on the chopsticks and unrolled the silverware from the napkin, "…you don't know everything I've done."

The pastor smiled, twinkle in his eye. "I think I do." He pushed aside a bowl of egg drop soup, pulled a plate of noodles closer. "By the way, the engineer says the electrical system will be shipshape by the end of the week."

Charlie nodded, peeling apart his egg roll. Struggling not to blush.

"It happens." Pastor Mac spooled lo mein onto his fork. "Look, I understand you're embarrassed."

"You told me to plug in. I'm just trying to find my place."

The pastor blinked and gave Charlie a sideways smile. "You can't just keep bouncing from place to place, Charlie. Lessee, you tried being an usher, I think you tried working in the bookstore—"

Charlie ticked it off on his fingers. "Um, traffic, greeter, usher, sound tech, kitchen—"

Pastor Mac chuckled, shaking his head. "Sometimes you gotta dig in and do the job."

"But God places each of us where we belong. Right?"

"That's right. But you don't move on because things go badly."

Charlie picked at his disassembled egg roll, munched on a fragment of crust. "I flooded the choir loft."

Pastor Mac reached across and gripped Charlie's arm firmly. "Dig in, Charlie. Gotta dig in."

Charlie said nothing. He grabbed one of the chopsticks and started making invisible patterns on the tablecloth. "Yes, sir."

"Pastor Wallace says you're a good fit for Kidz Kingdom."

Charlie dropped the chopstick. "You can't be serious."

The pastor nodded. "He says you have a good heart for it. And I think it is a great place to serve. These are our future leaders, you know. If Jesus waits to come, these children will grow up to be tomorrow's doctors and lawyers and senators." He squeezed Charlie's arm. "And tomorrow's law enforcement."

"But I flipped one of the parents, Pastor Mac."

Pastor Mac shrugged. "Self-defense."

"I flipped a man into a table. They said he's suing."

"He is." Pastor Mac pursed his lips. "I'm not saying it wasn't an unfortunate incident." He gave that beaming, fatherly smile. "But it happened. You don't stop serving."

Charlie chewed on his lip. Looked down at his silverware. "I guess."

"And I think you need to stick it out in children's church. Give it a chance."

Charlie let his shoulders sag. "A little girl asked me about the Song of Solomon."

Pastor Mac gripped Charlie's arm. Grinned. "Dig in, Charlie. Gotta dig in."

– 46 –

Friday. Still trying to figure out the best place to take my boat. My 2008 Bayliner 192.

I also, apparently, needed to get some kind of license. (Who knew you needed a license for a boat?) And of course, I did not have much time: Jesus was calling up His faithful in less than five days. Hardly enough time to go through the trouble of getting any sort of license or permit.

As I searched online for lakes in Missouri and Kansas, trying to find something within driving distance, a scratchy voice jabbed me from behind. "What are y'all searching for?"

I looked up from the computer screen to see wrinkled old Helena Wheeler. I thought about telling her she should shut her stupid face. I thought about telling her to mind her own business. Instead, I said, "I am checking Google for the nearest lakes."

She nodded, sipping from her coffee mug. "Lakefront property?"

Sure, why not? "Yeah, I have a client looking for a nice house on the lake." A little lie, but she would never know the difference. In a couple of days, I'd be gone. And I was pretty sure she would still be here. I was glad she did not ask why I wasn't using our normal search engines, and I was not about to volunteer. To keep her from thinking about it, I asked, "Got any suggestions?"

She slurped again from her coffee. "Naw."

I clicked on another link. So far, nothing I could find seemed to be in driving distance. I had already had to drive far enough to get my 2008 Bayliner 192 to Blue Springs Lake. How much further would I have to go now?

Wheeler said something else. I have no idea what it was. I was already imagining making a road trip of it. Take my boat up to Michigan. Do folks go boating on the Great Lakes? I mean, if they are called the "Great Lakes," they must be pretty good, right? Somewhere in the back of my mind, I mulled over all the natural wonders I wouldn't be able to see before Jesus.

Wheeler made some other point, now pointing somewhere. I nodded and smiled.

I wondered whether Jesus would take up the world's natural wonders with Him. You know, when He's calling up His faithful and we're all flying with the wings of eagles, He waves His hand and then Mount Rushmore and Old Faithful and that waterfall, you know, the one in Africa named after that queen (who was that, Queen Victoria?) all are raptured too.

No, that would be silly. Maybe.

Apparently, Wheeler was still standing over me, droning on. She said, "The best time to buy lake property is in the off season. When the weather turns cold."

"Sure." Move the mouse, click, wish she would just go away. Before she figured out the truth. Before she said anything to Sherman.

Of course, we were not long for this world. What did I care if I got fired at this point?

My cell phone chirped. The caller ID said it came from the church. I cut off Wheeler with a smile as I answered. "Y'ello!"

"Sorry to bother you, sir, but we have a problem." A kid from the youth group.

"Really?" I stood and gave an exaggerated nod for Wheeler's sake. Indicating this call was far too important to stop for her sake. "What seems to be the trouble, sir?" She finally walked off in the direction of her office.

The kid replied, "Well, we have a huge crowd here but we're short-handed. Several of the key people are absent."

This last week, we were running Tribulation House day and night. If we could staff it. "What are you doing about it?" I sat back at my computer, pushed the mouse around, and clicked another link.

"I went through the list and called everyone," the kid said, his voice going up in pitch. "A bunch of them weren't home. I reached a couple of people, and they just said they couldn't come in."

I clicked around some more. "Well, I'm all tied up here at the office, so I don't know what I can do for you."

"Are you going to be able to come in after work?"

"I'm not sure. I'll have to call you back."

⁓ **47** ⁓

Sunday morning. Children's church. Detective Charlie Pasch spent most of the service to one side of the gym. Afraid to wreck any more cartons of object lessons. Afraid to damage any more nine-year-olds' emotional well-being. Afraid to flip any more parents into the sign-in table.

Afterward, he found himself apologizing to the parents waiting in line at the exit to check out their kids. A lot of "I'm sorry" and "It was an accident" with the occasional "I didn't mean it" and "It was a reflex thing."

Charlie humiliated.

Dig in, Charlie, he could hear Pastor Mac saying. *Gotta dig in.*

⁓ **48** ⁓

Ross Cleaver and Bill Lamb had a meeting with the boss. As Cleaver pulled the car in front of the restaurant, The Palm, he wasn't sure what to expect. When the request had come for their presence, he'd been too nervous to ask.

All the way from the front door to the private dining room in the back, Cleaver kept a running tab of everyone he passed. Every person who had to be packing a gun. A knife. Something sharp, blunt, or otherwise murderous.

Cleaver was ushered into the presence of Mr. Massey in the back dining room, where he was having lunch with a couple of other guys. Who were his guests? Bosses from other territories? Was this a sit-down? Muscle on loan from somewhere else? Were they getting their marching orders?

When they reached the table, Massey offered a plastic smile. Nodding for the others to leave the table, he motioned Cleaver and Lamb to sit in the vacated chairs. "Gentlemen. Glad you were able to make it."

Cleaver felt the velvet fabric beneath him. Fancy.

"So, Ross," Mr. Massey said in an even voice, "tell me how things are going in your district."

"Going very well, boss." Cleaver gulped. "Going great."

"Could you be a little more specific?"

Cleaver nodded. "Going very well. We are making…friends. Like you asked."

"I hear you've been taking time to do personal business."

Cleaver tried not to shoot an accusing stare at his partner. "I been faithful, sir. Faithful."

Massey nodded lightly. Maybe in agreement, maybe just to acknowledge that the other man had stopped talking. "We have a busy schedule. A lot of changes are coming."

Cleaver nodded. "I know, sir. We are doing what you told us to do."

"Are you?" Massey flashed a wicked smile.

Cleaver felt the earth might open up beneath him any second. "We're doing everything you said. We're making it uncomfortable for the church there."

Massey sighed. "There are two parts to getting that property. We need to remove the current holders, and we need the city council to rezone it for our…needs."

"Yes, Mr. Massey. We been workin' the church."

"Have you visited the candidates for city council?"

"We have been visiting them. Like you said."

Massey looked away, rubbing his eyes. "How many?"

"Um…a few."

Massey pounded on the table. "There are thirteen different candidates running for that open seat! You go out, and you get all thirteen of them in our pocket."

Cleaver frowned. "No disrespect, sir, but we can't promise support to all of them. I mean…they are running against each other, right?"

"You go to each one of them and you get them in our pocket. And when somebody wins, I don't care what happens to the others."

Cleaver nodded. Surprised Lamb had been silent this long. Of course, he was in trouble enough right now, he didn't need the extra help digging his grave. "Yes, sir." Not quite sure how to implement these new orders, but afraid to ask. "We'll get right on it."

"See that you do."

— **49** —

Hank Barton, candidate for City Council, Seventh District, barely spoke to The Last Church of God's Imminent Will church secretary before bursting into the office of Reverend Daniel Glory. "You've got a fat lot of nerve!" Barely taking note of the man and woman sitting across from the man at his desk.

Reverend Daniel Glory, silver hair and shining teeth, looked up from his desk in surprise. "I-I'm sorry, Mr....?"

"You know who I am." Hank threw the newspaper on the desk.

Reverend Glory tentatively uncrumpled the paper. His guests exchanged awkward glances. He gave them an apologetic smile and scanned the front page. Shook his head. "I don't understand what you are—"

Hank lunged and grabbed the paper, thumbing the newsprint. "Here, on page three." He laid the spread on the desk, slamming his hand on it to flatten the crumpled paper. He jabbed a finger at a headline. "There!"

CANDIDATE LISTENS TO VOICE OF GOD,
THE PEOPLE

Reverend Glory looked up with a quizzical smile. "I think it's admirable if you truly are listening to the voice of the Lord. But you think it somehow makes you sound crazy?"

"The general tone of the piece is bad enough." Hank gritted his teeth, shaking his head. "But you had no right to get involved." He jabbed the finger more specifically at a quote in the story, second column, paragraph three:

> Another local man of God, Reverend Daniel Glory of The Last Church of God's Imminent Will, has his doubts that he and Candidate Barton are listening to the same voices. "I know for a fact that the Lord Jesus is coming back on October 17. Obviously, He would not be wasting good Christians' time with any mandates to participate in worldly elections."
>
> Reverend Glory added that Christians should "let the things of Caesar be the things of Caesar and let the things of God be the things of God."
>
> Reverend Glory outlines his theories about the Second Coming of Jesus Christ, as predicted in the Bible, in his best-selling book *107 Reasons Jesus Is Coming Back in 2007.*

Reverend Daniel Glory looked up from the paper, smugly smiling his pleasure. "Surely you cannot blame me for speaking the truth in love."

"The truth? The *truth?*" Hank was verily shrieking now. "You need to mind your own business. This was a story about my candidacy, my vision, and you jumped in with your opinion. And a dangerous one at that."

"Last I heard, Mr. Barton, we still had free speech in this country."

"And how long is that going to last, if Christian leaders tell their people to withdraw from the culture? To stop serving as salt and light?"

Reverend Daniel Glory stood carefully, straightening his suit jacket. "It's like I told the reporter—let the things of Caesar belong to Caesar, and let the things of God belong to God. We are supposed to be separate from the world. Are we not?"

"But you're quoting that out of context! When Jesus told the disciples the thing about Caesar, he was saying we should pay our taxes! He was saying we should participate in the government—on a local level, on a state level, on a national level. How long will the rights of Christians exist if we—"

"Mr. Barton." Reverend Glory was stern now. "You have interrupted a private session." He waved to indicate the man and woman sitting across from his desk, attempting to shrink into their chairs, to pretend nonchalance. "Now, I have exercised my constitutional right to express my opinion."

"But—"

He held up his hands. "You have said nothing to convince me I was wrong to do that." The Reverend motioned for the office door, where the secretary stood nervously. "I'm going to have to ask you to leave."

Hank lost his temper. Took a swing at the man.

Reverend Daniel Glory must have once been a boxer or something.

⸺ 50 ⸺

That Monday night—I guess that would have been October 15—I was up late making my to-do list. It occurred to me it was the same principle as the "if you were going to die" list, but that was such a morbid thought that I put it out of my mind.

Besides, I had a boat trip to make in the morning.

After a while I found the list was pretty chock-full, so I started another draft. I ended up making several drafts. The wastepaper basket filled with crumpled paper as I reformatted and reprioritized my list. When you're faced with your last day, it is quite daunting to figure out what all to include. A lot of sporting events came to mind, but there was no time—not to mention that some were out of season. Even if I went out and bought DVDs, though, there was no time to watch another Super Bowl, no time for another World Series. For that matter, there was no time for *Little House on the Prairie* either.

Not if I was going to do my list and get on the road to Chicago with my boat.

～ 51 ～

Detective Charlie Pasch pulled into the church parking lot. He checked his watch—he was a few minutes early. The lot was still pretty empty.

As he walked up the stairs to the gym, he pulled the invitation from his jacket pocket and read it again. *BUILDING THE VISION.* The details were scant. Charlie didn't know what the hubbub was about, but he had to RSVP and everything. The pastors must have been planning some major announcement.

In the gym, he found a group of folks congregating around a table of refreshments. There were several familiar faces, but nobody Charlie really knew on a first-name basis. He still had not connected with them personally. He was not a good connecter.

Across the front stage, a big canvas banner showed an artist's sketch of a church building. Hanging from the ceiling in either corner of the gym were screens on which slides were being projected. As the slides rotated, they showed a series of shots of a building project, the groundbreaking, the digging, the construction. Off to the side, a little jazz combo played arrangements of praise songs.

Charlie got a plateful of little quiches and a glass of sweet tea— he wished they had offered Diet Mountain Dew—and looked for friends among the crowd. He was heading for the other end of the gym, when he heard a voice behind him.

"Hello there!" Thick South African accent. Charlie turned to see a tall man with sandy hair. One of the newer members of the pastoral team, though Charlie couldn't place the name right then. Balancing the plastic plate of quiches and cup of tea in one hand, he shook hands with the man, who identified himself as Pastor Switt. The man pointed to the slides on the screen up front. "That picture up there was taken about eighteen hours before the city council shut us down."

"Really?" Charlie squinted at the screen. A picture showed Pastor Mac and other members of his team standing in the middle of a construction site, grinning at the camera. Surrounded by signs of excavation and a wall of cement blocks. Something about the image made Charlie think about the library at August Heights. "I didn't realize any of this construction was going on."

"It's been in the works for a while." Pastor Switt nodded. "The city council tried to block us, but about twelve hours before the deadline, we were able to get the walls up to code."

Charlie nodded. Smiled. "I see." The slide moved on to a shot of the landscaping. He couldn't think of anything else to say, but that was okay—Pastor Switt had already moved on to the next person.

Continuing his trek to the other end of the gym, Charlie found his friend Grady sitting in a red folding chair. "Hey, man." Grady, mouth full, nodded a greeting.

Charlie got situated without making a mess—plate half-full of miniature quiches balanced here, glass half-full of tea balanced there. He looked up at the current slide on the screen: big machines digging.

He felt something in his pocket. Switching the plate to the other knee, he pulled out what turned out to be the flyer emblazoned *TRIBULATION HOUSE.* The controversial end-times theatrical event. *Why do I still have this?* he wondered. Hoping it was not some sort of omen.

"What's that?" Grady talking through a mouthful of corn chips.

"It's a flyer about that end-times deal." Charlie tried to shrug without losing control of his refreshments. "Tribulation House."

"Oh. Right." Grady wiped his hands on his pant legs. He motioned toward the flyer. "Can I see it?" Charlie handed it over. As he watched Grady read the print, the slide show continued overhead.

Charlie saw the rift right there: the flyer in Grady's hand representing a theology of victimization, a church doing nothing but waiting to be rescued; the slide show overhead representing a church following the great commission, storming the gates of hell.

Charlie murmured, "Maybe it's easier to want to sit and be rescued than to be the rescuers."

Grady looked up. "What was that?"

Charlie shook his head. "I was just thinking."

The slide show continued.

─ 52 ─

I know for sure that I had set my alarm for bright and early October 16—5:51 AM, in fact, to give me a full twenty-four hours—but something must have gone wrong. Maybe I hit the snooze alarm. Or accidentally shut it off altogether.

All I know is it was October 16 and it was suddenly almost 11 AM. Blinking myself to consciousness, wiping the sleep out of my eyes, I yelled for the wife. "Honey! Why did you let me sleep so late?"

Her voice came up the stairs. "You looked so peaceful, I didn't want to wake you!"

"When we're in heaven, I'll have all the time to sleep in the world!" Shaking myself awake, I plopped bare feet on carpet and pushed off the bed. "You should have got me up!"

I quickly showered and shaved—did not want to be grizzled for our Lord—and pulled together my traveling clothes. Something comfortable for the drive, easily changed when I got to Lake Michigan. I did not have time to figure out the hows and wherefores for boating there, but I could figure it out once I got there. Surely, a big city like Chicago would offer all the amenities a boating man would need.

Jesus held court on Galilee. I would hold court on Lake Michigan.

Over breakfast—

(At least the wife thought to make me a hearty breakfast: fried potatoes, eggs, bacon *and* sausage, waffles, and French toast. "We might as well eat it now," she said. "After the Rapture, it's all going to go bad.")

—I looked over my to-do list. I had already lost precious man-hours, slept away like…well, those hours were gone. This was what I had planned:

1. Make list
2. Eat hearty breakfast
3. Make videotape for the neighbors
4. Have man-to-man with the boy
5. Listen to the girl play her clarinet
6. Make peace with Dad
7. Lunch with the boys at the office
8. Tell off boss
9. Go boating

I had planned to make a list of an even dozen—it's a holy number, you know—but even at nine it ended up as a bit of a stretch. "Lunch with the boys at the office"? I wasn't sure what I was thinking when I wrote that. I had no intention of even showing up at work today.

Checking my watch, though, I saw that I would have to strike most of the items off. They were nice thoughts, but there just wasn't enough time. According to my online map, it was 507.5 miles to Chicago and Lake Michigan, with an estimated travel time of 7 hours and 51 minutes.

Mixing together the fried potatoes with the runny egg yolk, I looked over the list again and made some hard choices.

⸺ ⸺ ⸺

1. Make list

Well, okay, that was a given. I am not even sure why I bothered to make it an item. (I think it was to try and make it to the full twelve, but it did not work.)

I scratched the item off the list.

— — —

2. Eat hearty breakfast

The wife may have goofed big-time letting me sleep through the alarm, but at least she took care of me here. Sure, it was her way of cleaning the fridge before the trumpet sounded, but it also meant I finally got to have sausage and bacon together. I deserve sausage and bacon.

I scratched the item off the list.

— — —

3. Make videotape for the neighbors

This was my final chance to preach to the neighbors. Explain to them what had happened when a sizable percentage of the world's population—best-case scenario, of course—suddenly disappears off the face of the earth. I had seen the classic end-times films, so I knew all the crazy theories that the world leaders would try to foist on an uneducated populace.

Looking at item number three, I felt a twinge of guilt. I should have spent more one-on-one time with the neighbors. I should have reached out. Should have offered to help when they needed help, should have offered friendship and advice. Should have been there for them.

But now the time was gone. The videotape was my last chance to explain the spirit of the world to them, my last chance to offer them the same rescue that was coming for me. After I was gone, they could find this videotape—my last will and testament, more or less. My last words to them.

I checked my watch. I scratched the item off the list.

— ⌒ —

4. Have man-to-man with the boy

A pang hit me right in the heart when I looked at this item. I almost stopped chewing. Was it possible to connect with my son at this late hour? Was it possible to finally straighten him out once and for all?

Ah, well. Scratch.

— ⌒ —

5. Listen to the girl play her clarinet

Did she even still own the clarinet? I tried to remember the last time we'd gone to see her in the school band for one of their "concerts."

Scratch.

— ⌒ —

6. Make peace with Dad

He'd had his chance. Scratch.

— ⌒ —

7. Lunch with the boys at the office

Scratch.

— ⌒ —

8. Tell off boss

I checked my watch. It was almost noon. With hitching up the boat and all, packing snacks for the trip, I would not be on the road for another hour. Which put me in Chicago at maybe seven o'clock, maybe eight, depending on traffic. Towing the boat, it could be even later. How late would Lake Michigan be open? How long would it take to find wherever they allow boats in?

But I looked at item number eight again and smiled. I sopped up the last of the yolk with a slice of French toast—another combination the wife normally forbade—and pushed aside my breakfast plates. Went to the phone, wiping my hands on the paper towel.

Punched in the numbers for the office, asked for ol' Sherman himself. The boss came on the line and I let him have it.

You do not even *want* to know what I said. But it was bad.

If Sherman and I met up again in heaven, we could straighten it out. Not that I expected any chance of *that*.

And, in something like eighteen hours, give or take, it was no longer going to be my problem.

Which, of course, left item number nine…

— ᵔ —

9. Go boating

— ᵔ —

Throwing stuff together as quickly as possible, I tried to find the wife to kiss her goodbye, but there was no time. I grabbed my bags and trudged through a den full of clothing and shoes, all strewn about—she must have spent the night trying everything on at least one time.

By two PM, I was on the road. Followed the directions printed off the Internet—US 36 East, I-72 East, I-55 North—cutting across the width of Missouri and then across the northern part of Illinois. Tried not to stop any more than I had to, just for gas and drinks and candy bars.

I hit a pocket of afternoon rush-hour traffic, which slowed me down. By the time I got to the Chicago city limits, it was almost ten PM. I had no idea how to find Lake Michigan now, much less whether it was even open this time of night.

Wishing I had given a more specific request than "go to Chicago"—the giant lake was right there on the screen, it had seemed so simple then—I stopped at a station and bought an Illinois map. By the light of the truck cab, I sent up a prayer for guidance as I tried to decipher the veins and capillaries of the Chicago streets. Just because something went toward the lake did not necessarily mean it was a place you could tow a boat. What if I got lost? What if I ended on some little side street with all the cars parked along the sides and it was too narrow for my boat? What if I got on a busy street and all the cars darting around me somehow forced me to take an exit I didn't want?

I decided the best thing was to pull in to a motel for the night. Surely the lake would be open before daybreak. If only because fishermen—as I hear it—do all their best fishing before the sun comes up. Surely I could at least be out on the water by 5:51 AM tomorrow morning.

Finally found a vacancy at the third motel I tried. It was not a fancy place. When I tried to wash my face in the sink, the water was black.

My last night of freedom, I lived it up. I checked in with the world, checked in with how they pursue their worldly pleasures.

But I did not partake. That's not the same, right? There's no penalty for that, right?

I stood outside that strip-club establishment. And prayed. I stood outside that gambling establishment. And prayed. I stood outside that gas station that sold alcohol and adult materials. And prayed.

Yes, I thought about it. I struggled with it. I was almost to the door one time, and did not have the nerve to face anyone. I did not want anyone to see me.

Silly, isn't it? I mean, I was like eight hours from home. Who would see me here?

Back at the room, I put in for a wake-up call at 3:30 AM. About two hours from then.

— 53 —

I did not plan to sleep—I was not making *that* mistake again—but the wake-up call was my backup plan.

I looked for a Bible in the nightstand, to no avail. A little voice said I should have packed one for the trip. A little voice said I should call home and tell the wife where I was.

I ignored the little voice and turned up the TV. There was no religious programming, so I ended up watching some movie. Some Asian guy who worked as a hired killer apparently couldn't go through with his job—I think it is called a "contract"—and now the Chinese mob boss calls in some replacements to finish the job. I didn't know what I was watching, but there was a scene in a church, which was nice. I only caught the last few minutes, then switched around until I ended up on some television program about lifeguards. It had a lot of scenes shot in slow motion. Or was I just getting that exhausted?

The call came at 3:30 AM. I was so dazed, I don't actually know whether or not I had been asleep. Either way, I dragged myself to the sink, threw some black water in my face, and was on my way to Lake Michigan by 4:00.

I was in traffic at 4:30.

I was in traffic at 4:47.

I was in traffic at 5:23.

I was in traffic at 5:47.

— — —

I was pounding the dash. Where were all these people going? Didn't they know this was the beginning of the end? Shouldn't they be home praying? Home atoning? Home sacrificing? Doing whatever it took to—

— — —

5:50

— — —

I activated my blinker and pulled to the side of the road. In a matter of seconds, my Chevy Avalanche, towing my Bayliner 192, would be driverless. It was my final act of mercy on these people to at least leave the vehicle idling at the side of the road.

Because if I were on the road at 5:51, the Rapture would suddenly pull drivers and pilots and riders and all manner of people from all over the world up into the skies. In the twinkling of an eye, we would vanish.

— — —

5:51

— — —

Any second now. Any second. All over the world, unmanned breakfast skillets catching fire, unmanned jetliners suddenly crashing into mountains, unmanned cars careening off the—

— — —

5:52

— ~ —

Hmm. Owing for time differences, it should be any second now.

— ~ —

5:53

— ~ —

I held my breath.

— ~ —

5:54

— ~ —

I let my breath out. I was dizzy.

— ~ —

5:55

— ~ —

It was 7:06 when I began to have my doubts.

⁓ 54 ⁓

Ross Cleaver pushed aside his plate and stretched out his legs under the diner table. "We gotta make ourselves a plan."

Lamb leaned back in the other side of the booth. "A plan?"

"A plan of attack."

"A plan of attack?"

Cleaver nodded. "A strategy."

"A strategy?"

"Just shut up." Cleaver reached for the napkin dispenser on the table, pulled out a napkin, and worked at smoothing out the wrinkles. Lamb watched the ritual with curiosity. Cleaver, satisfied the sheet was flat and ready for his notes, snapped his fingers. "Utensil."

Lamb frowned, handed over a fork.

Cleaver gritted his teeth. "Writing utensil." To Lamb's bewildered look: "A *pen*." The other man nodded and jumped from the table, scrambling for the front counter. A few seconds passed before Cleaver had his pen. He scribbled to make it write, causing a tear in the napkin.

He stretched it out to make it taut, tried writing again: BARTON. LI. PARFREY. MURDOCK. LAWSON. STUBBS.

Lamb hovered. "What're you doing?"

"Shut up." Sticking out his tongue, Cleaver finished scrawling the list. TOBIN. RIVERA. HAUS. When he was done, he went back to the top and put a checkmark by the top name. Then he sat back in the booth. Pleased. "There. These are the candidates for City Council."

Lamb furrowed his brow. "You remembered all those names?"

"Yeah." Cleaver smiled, folding the napkin twice and sticking it in his shirt pocket. "I got what you call a 'phonographic memory.'"

"I think it's called—" Lamb stopped dead at Cleaver's glare. Took a convenient sip of water.

Cleaver, elbows on table, locked his fingers together. "There are like a dozen different people trying to get into the city council. We just gotta sidle up to alla them and make friends. See?"

Lamb, still sipping his water to keep his mouth occupied, nodded. There was spillage.

Cleaver ignored the mess. "We have the list. We find each of them. We talk to them. We..." He smirked to himself. "We get them in our pocket."

"Shouldn't we take more notes?"

"I got this list."

"No, I mean, shouldn't we write down more than their names?"

"What else would we write down?"

Lamb paused. Shrugged. "Where they are, where they live, where they work..."

"Details, details." Cleaver looked out the window, regarding the people walking by. Wondered if they were registered to vote. "And it's like the boss says, get 'em in our pocket. And when the election comes and goes, we keep the winner and drop the rest."

"Won't that be suspicious?"

Cleaver frowned. "What?"

Before Lamb could explain himself, the waitress was there with the check. "That all for you gentlemen?"

Cleaver grinned. "Yes, ma'am." He patted the pocket on his shirt. "We got all we need right here." He leaned forward, the grin turning ugly. "Less'n you got any suggestions?"

She glowered *As if,* ripped the check out of the book, and slapped it on the table. Without another word, she turned and whisked away.

Cleaver looked toward Lamb. *"Don't you say a word."*

— 55 —

Coming downstairs in his T-shirt and sweatpants, Griggs stumbled into the kitchen and fumbled for the light switch. It was early. Maybe 4:30 AM, give or take. He needed his morning coffee to know for sure.

He was going to once again attempt to make it himself. In the past few weeks, he had taken it upon himself to learn how to make the morning coffee. No more waiting for Carla, no more bothering Carla, no more giving Carla a hard time until she got up early with him and made the coffee.

He felt good that he was giving Carla a few more minutes of sleep. All these years of nudging her awake, asking her to keep his crazy hours to make the coffee, it had never occurred to him to just make it himself. It had only finally dawned on him during one of their counseling sessions.

So here he was, 4:45 AM, give or take, making the coffee. It was not much, but it was something. He liked to think he was making progress. As a husband. As a human being.

Grasping desperately for some semblance of consciousness, he shook his head vigorously and breathed deep. He needed his caffeine. He needed it bad.

He grabbed the coffeepot off the counter, set it on the square tile. He never thought to ask Carla, but the tile must have some special insulating properties. Whatever. It was somehow part of the routine, and at this time of the morning, the routine was what mattered.

He paused for a second, leaning on the counter, trying to remember the next step. *Ugh. Early.* Carla always asked why he got up so early, but it was ingrained in him. His father had always said…had always said…something about the importance of getting up early. Griggs could not exactly remember what it was now, what his father had always said about the importance of getting up early, but it must have affected him very deeply. Because he was up. In a way.

He went to the cabinet and pulled out a coffee mug labeled *I HEART KC.* He went to the tap and got four and a half cups of water for the pan on the stove. He pulled the El Pico coffee can out of the fridge, measured eight spoonfuls (more or less), and put them in the weird sock device suspended in the top of the pot.

Griggs put the stove on high and stumbled to the kitchen chair and plopped down. Set the timer and waited. Ten minutes for the boiling water. Put boiling water in sock so it can drain through into the coffeepot. Five minutes for the coffee.

Sitting at the table, waiting, Griggs yawned. Stretched. Decided against flipping on the morning news. He was sure there would be enough trouble when he got to the office. No point in hearing the doom and gloom of the day any sooner than that.

"Each day has enough trouble of its own," Griggs grumbled in a cracked morning voice. Quoting something Charlie often said. Knowing the kid, it was probably literary. Or from *Star Trek.*

Waiting for the timer, he tried to map out his day. The joint task force was figuring out how to get deeper into Massey's business. How to watch him, how to tap him, how to get his plans on record. His organization was clearly trying to muscle in on a lot of real estate, but for what purpose? To build massage parlors? Strip clubs? His own chain of casinos? What was the man trying to do?

Sure, following something like this wasn't as glamorous as some of the task force's cases. But you couldn't have a gang war every day.

Thank God.

Thoughts of work drifted out of his mind as Griggs looked across the kitchen at the machine collecting dust in the corner. Some sort of fancy coffeemaker. He never quite understood why Carla insisted on using the weird sock device when they owned this fancy coffeemaker machine right here. Never quite understood why it did not work.

All he knew was, it was a gift from his father. It was missing some essential part, a filter or something. Griggs did not remember the details. All he knew was, Carla had called the manufacturer and their lousy customer service refused to make it right. And without that essential part, the machine was, for all intents and purposes, useless. A very large, very unwieldy, very expensive paperweight.

But Griggs refused to part with it. Refused to let her throw it out, sell it, give it away. She never really understood his attachment to it. It was a daily reminder of his anger. His disappointment.

But it was a gift from his daddy. One of the last things he had ever gotten from the old man.

The timer went off. Rubbing his eyes, still struggling to hang onto consciousness, he pushed himself from the kitchen table. Went to the counter and pulled the sock, dripping, from the coffeepot. Set it in the pan on the stove. Tried the coffee.

Blech. Too weak.

He pulled the sock, dripping, back from the pan and put the sock back in the pot. Dumped his mug of weak coffee back in. Went to the fridge, grabbed the can of El Pico and put one more spoonful into the sock. Set the timer for another five minutes and let it all soak.

Elbows on the kitchen table, he struggled to think about work. Tried to focus on Massey. On the task force. On making the streets of Kansas City safe from the threat of organized crime.

But he couldn't stop staring at the fancy coffee machine collecting dust in the corner.

– 56 –

Hank Barton, candidate for City Council, Seventh District, on his third round of door-to-door. This time, he had one of the volunteers with him. It was such a lonely job. Each door was another opportunity for heartbreak. Another opportunity to be angry and sin not. Another chance to see that stupid booklet and try to explain to some well-meaning churchgoer that, yes, Jesus is coming back, but that doesn't mean you don't register to vote. He also had to explain to several people that his black eye was the result of an "accident."

And then there was that weird argument about the special election. The old lady demanded, "What are you talking about? It's not an election year."

"It is a special election," Hank replied. Struggling to keep his smile warm and friendly.

"It's not an election year."

"It's a...*special* election. It was on the news and everything."

"It's not an election year."

By the time they broke for lunch, Hank did not even have the heart to keep going. He turned to the young man helping him, Brad something. "Why don't we go back to headquarters and see how things are shaping up?"

Hoping the doubt was not creeping into his voice.

— 57 —

I sat there at the side of the interstate for what must have been hours. Waiting. Just waiting.

The appointed time had come and gone, and I was still sitting on the side of the interstate in my Chevy Avalanche with my Bayliner 192 hitched to the back. And for all intents and purposes, traffic seemed to be moving normally. It was thick and it was slow, but every car seemed to have a driver behind the wheel.

For the first hour-and-change, I fought back my nerves with the hope that this was a misunderstanding. That when Reverend Daniel Glory had announced "5:51 AM," he had not meant "Central time." Maybe his calculations meant 5:51 in some other time zone.

After all, it would be 5:51 AM Pacific time in another hour. And then it would be 5:51 AM an hour later, in the next time zone, whatever that was. And then 5:51 somewhere else. And again somewhere else.

As the hours passed, the cracks in my hope grew into fissures.

I had no idea how many 5:51 AM's were left in the world—or at what point it simply became some other day.

What time zone was it in Israel? If only I could call and ask someone, but my cell phone had run out of charge. When it had needed charging before my trip, I'd figured, why bother?

None of the end-times prophets had prepared me for this. I punched all around the radio, searching for news, searching for information, for any clue as to why I was still here. Why traffic was still moving like normal.

Where was the chaos? Where was the judgment? Where was the shock and awe? Where were the gates of hell? Where was the Kingdom to come?

Now I was in a desperate need to contact someone. Anyone who could talk me through this. I was 500 miles from home with no cash, a single change of clothes, a credit card that was probably now maxed out, and no phone.

It took me almost another hour to get turned around and going the other way on the interstate—I was hardly in the mood to try out Lake Michigan now.

I went back to the motel. When I'd left that morning, I hadn't bothered to check out or even drop off the key. In the room, I collapsed on the bed. How long did I sleep? Hours? Days? I lost all track of time.

~ 58 ~

When I finally got back on the road, the drive back from Chicago certainly wasn't heaven. It was more like the Other Place. (Can I say that? Am I allowed to say that?) Exhausted, blinking to keep the road in focus, I backtracked the directions I'd printed off the Internet—I-55 South, I-72 West, US 36 West—through the northern part of Illinois and then cutting across the width of Missouri.

The whole trip, my spirit churned inside of me. Had the Rapture happened without me? Was I left behind? In the back of my mind, a little voice chided me for last night's activities. Had my check-in with the pleasures of the world disqualified me?

Still listening to the radio: sports scores. Weather reports. Wars and rumors of wars. No reports of abandoned breakfast skillets catching fire. No abandoned cars careening into traffic. No abandoned jetliners crashing into mountains.

What if it was a massive cover-up? What if the Rapture had happened and the radio news was forbidden to report it?

I wished my cell phone would work. Then I could call around. I could try to get into touch with some of the folks from church. See if they were still on earth. I could call the neighbors. See if any of them had seen or heard anything unusual. "Excuse me, neighbor, but did you see any people flying through the air this morning?"

The long, long drive gave me much time to think. I started to have my doubts that the Rapture was coming at all. What would I do then? I had burned my bridges.

Exhausted, confused, and famished, I pulled into a truck stop. About halfway into my drive back, somewhere outside of Springfield, Illinois.

Over a greasy afternoon breakfast, I considered my options. Whether to finish the trip back to Kansas City or to get onto the interstate and head to parts unknown. Back in Kansas City, I had the weight of the world waiting to crush me: my boss. The wife. The kids. Outrageous truck payments. Outrageous boat payments.

Those gangsters. As I sucked down my third cup of coffee, just praying for the caffeine to kick in, I shuddered to think what they might do to me now. It was one thing to laugh at them when I thought Jesus would cover my back. But the Lord had let me down, and I was the one who had to suffer the consequences.

In the end, I knew I had to go back to Kansas City. Face my fate head on. To tell the truth, I had nowhere else to go. Not towing a boat, especially. And I could not afford to ditch the boat at this point; as long as I had it, I could try to get a refund, or sell it, or something. Without it I was as good as dead.

So that was the plan: Get back home. A shower and a change of clothes would turn everything around. Then I would simply return the boat to the dealer and get my money back. And then I would calmly trade in or sell the truck and get whatever money I could out of that. And then I would pay off the mobsters and everything would be fine.

And then I would go face Sherman at the office and explain myself. Or start looking for a new job.

Sopping up the last of the egg yolk with the toast, I felt better. With some food in my stomach and a plan for the future, I felt like I could handle it.

After lunch, I discovered my card was, indeed, maxed out. Skipped out on the check like a common sinner.

～ **59** ～

Over the next few days, Ross Cleaver followed up on the list. Bill Lamb kept his mouth shut. Mostly.

Cleaver was not happy. Thanks to Massey's orders, he was too busy to follow up on other business. Too busy to collect on overdue loans. Too busy to work his insurance business.

Between chapters of his book on the ghost girl of Watseka, Cleaver tracked down each of the candidates for City Council, Seventh District. Each campaigning for the open seat in the special election.

Cleaver thought of the man who had vacated the seat, the friend of Mr. Massey's. A shame, the man going out like that. In the prime of life. What was his name?

Maybe the councilman shoulda been a client of Frozen Futures. Somewheres in the future, the doctors would look him up on the chart, say, "Hey, we can cure this guy now." Stick him in defrost, make him right as rain.

If only.

So these were the folks pushing for that empty chair. Elbowing each other on their way to the top.

Over the next couple of days, this was how the interviews turned out.

TRACEY LI: "I think you have me confused with somebody else."

WILSON PARFREY: "I'm here to serve all my constituents."

D. EDWARD MURDOCK: "Oh, I'm just his assistant. Mr. Murdock is out of town this week. Family emergency. Did you want to leave some sort of message?"

CHESTER ANDERSON: "I don't know what you're talking about. I'm not running for any office."

JAKE LAWSON: "Absolutely, sir. Absolutely."

JANET MODELL: "I'll have to pray about it."

RICKY STUBBS: "I think you need to compare notes with Mr. Massey. Otherwise, you wouldn't be here. Know what I mean?"

SALLY TOBIN: "You'll have to talk to my campaign manager. I think she's around here somewhere."

PEDRO RIVERA: "¿Que? Perdoname, pero usted tiene que inscribirse como todos los demas. ¿Recibió usted uno de nuestros avisos por correo?"

IRWIN PAL: "No *way*, José! You get out of this place *now!*"

NORMA E. HAUS: "My horoscope didn't say anything about *this*."

SAMANTHA CROTEAU: [Did not talk with the lady.

As soon as Cleaver saw the badge from the Kansas City Police Department, he excused himself.]

⏤ **60** ⏤

That afternoon, Detective Tom Griggs and Detective Charlie Pasch were at the batting cages. "Let me show you how it's done, Charlie." Griggs inside the cage, head down, elbows out. A baseball rocketed out of the machine. Griggs had his eye on it. SMACK! The ball shot up into the net.

Charlie, gobbling a hot dog, wiped mustard off his mouth. "Good one!"

"Ah." Griggs shook his head. "It's a foul."

"How can you tell?"

Griggs was already locking himself into position again. "By where it went."

"Oh."

It was a weekly ritual, coming out here during the workday, something that seemed to help Griggs think. He often told Charlie that things always came into perspective after swatting the stitching off a few baseballs.

Another baseball rocketed out of the machine. SMACK! The baseball shot up into the net.

Griggs seemed happier with this one. "That's how you do it!"

Charlie couldn't tell one hit from the other.

He did not even get his turn at bat. (Not that he was broken up about it.) The whole time they were there, Griggs kept asking him for the time. Once it hit two PM, Griggs said it was time to go. "We got someone to see."

In the car, Charlie noticed Griggs taking a different route. This was not the way back to the police station. "Where are we going?"

"Just making a quick detour."

"Uh-huh."

After a few more minutes, Griggs smiled over at the younger man. "See where we are now?"

Charlie shook his head. "Actually, no." The buildings looked familiar, but only just. "I have never been good with directions. It's why you usually do the driving."

"Not good with directions? But you're the wonder kid. You always know everything."

"Not useful stuff."

Griggs raised his eyebrows. "Some useful stuff." Encouraging tone of voice.

"Okay, some useful stuff." Charlie shrugged. "The Bible is obviously useful."

"Well—"

"But not a lot of practical stuff. But if you ever want to talk about comic books or *Star Trek*..."

"You shouldn't put yourself down like that."

"Put myself down like what?"

"Saying you don't know anything."

"I didn't say that."

"You said that."

"I didn't say that at all. Look—I am brilliant. I am a genius. I should win a Peabody Award for my police work."

Griggs squinted. "A what?"

"Never mind." Charlie chuckled. "I'm just saying that I have a healthy self-image. I do believe in myself. But I also have a realistic grasp of my weaknesses. Lying about them or having misplaced self-confidence would hardly be the smart thing."

"You think so."

"Yes, I do. Like now, for example—if I were under the mistaken impression that I knew where we were going and, say, I were the one doing the driving..."

"Yeah?"

"Well, let's just say we wouldn't be here."

"Where would we be?"

"Okay, I've sort of lost track of what we were supposed to be talking about. So let's just circle back to…where are we going?"

"I just thought we might have some lunch."

"I had a couple of hot dogs."

Griggs gave his partner a cryptic smile as they turned at the corner. "I was thinking of something a little fancier. More sit-down."

"Why are you being so mysterious?"

"Am I?"

― 61 ―

They pulled in at a restaurant: The Palm. It took Charlie a second to remember why it sounded familiar.

Then he realized why Griggs was making a stop here. "We're coming here to pay Massey a visit."

"And you said you didn't know anything."

"I didn't say that."

"I heard you say that."

"I didn't say that."

The argument continued until they got inside. As their eyes adjusted to the indoors, Griggs waved off the hostess at the front. "We're here to meet somebody."

"Oh. Well, if you would like to tell me the name…"

"We're here to see Massey."

"Mr. Massey?" She suddenly got nervous. "Does he know what this is about?"

Griggs gave a predatory grin. It always gave Charlie the creeps. "This is just a social call."

"If you would give me your name…"

Griggs pushed deeper into the restaurant, nodding for Charlie to follow. "We're just going to take a look."

The two men sauntered through the restaurant. Charlie felt all eyes on them as they went through. Being so public about their business was not his first choice, but sometimes Griggs got this way. He noticed several prominent businessmen at the tables, wait staff heading to and from the kitchen.

Fortunately, it was not a full house. Several of the tables were empty. The lunch rush had already come and gone. Charlie was not sure why Griggs decided to come at this particular time of the afternoon. Maybe he wanted to make sure there were fewer innocent bystanders around when he made whatever presentation to Massey.

And what were they doing here, anyway?

They went through to the back dining room. A uniformed man on a ladder was fixing the sprinkler. At the table in the back of the room, a dapper, silver-haired man was attended by younger men in suits. One of the attendants was lighting the older man's after-lunch cigar.

Griggs headed right for the man. "And how is the world treating us today?"

The men in suits standing around the table popped to attention. One of them placed himself between the older man and the newcomers.

The older man puffed heavily on his cigar, regarding Griggs. "I don't know you."

Charlie went for his badge and started to speak, but Griggs put up a hand to stop him. The other men had stiffened. As if they'd expected Charlie to pull a gun.

Griggs pushed past the guardian at the table and turned a chair backward. Sat down with the old man. "It seems to me the world is treating you pretty well."

The silver-haired man puffed on the cigar a couple more times. Considering the brazen stranger. Finally, he grinned. "I got no complaints. If you have business, Mr...."

Griggs just sat, grinning.

The old man let the questions hang for a second, then continued.

"If you have business, you need to make an appointment. We do everything in an orderly fashion."

Griggs rubbed fingernails on his shirt. "I hear you have interest in real estate."

"I always have an interest."

"But some of your interests are, shall we say, sudden. And unusual."

The guardian seemed impatient, moved toward Griggs to remove him. The older man stopped the man with a gesture. He seemed amused with the detective. For now.

Charlie nervously gauged the room. The men surrounding them. Calculating an escape strategy, if it came to that. What was Griggs doing?

The old man puffed the cigar a few more times. Finally, said, "Perhaps you should tell me your business, Mr...."

"Griggs." He went for his badge. As the men around the table once again stiffened, ready to jump, Griggs put his other hand up to tell them to relax. He very slowly, very carefully, pulled the leather case from his jacket pocket. Revealed the badge. "Detective Tom Griggs. KCPD." He nodded toward Charlie. "This is my associate, Detective Charlie Pasch."

All eyes turned toward Charlie. Who blushed.

The silver-haired man regarded Griggs with a look of bemusement. He did not seem to understand Griggs's approach any more than Charlie did. "And to what do I owe the pleasure of your visit, Officer?"

"Detective," Griggs corrected smoothly. "We just wanted to come by and say hello. We were friends of the Catalano family. And we just wanted to make sure you felt at home."

Charlie kept his frown to himself. *Friends of the Catalano family? Make sure you felt at home?*

The old man nodded, a twinkle in his eye. He bowed his head lightly as he said, "Ted Massey, at your service." He considered adding something, then seemed to change his mind and say something different. "We appreciate the consideration, gentlemen. But, you see, we were just on our way out." He made a gesture, and the men all moved into different positions as the older man rose from the table.

The guardian waved his hand toward the door, gesturing for Griggs and Charlie to see themselves out. Griggs took his sweet time standing up, then regarded Massey for a long, silent moment. He then flicked his eyes in different directions around him, as if taking in the others.

Charlie hoped Griggs wasn't about to start something. He couldn't help but send up a silent prayer.

Finally, Griggs nodded politely. "Thank you for your time, Mr. Massey. We'll be seeing you again."

The old man said nothing, puffing his cigar as Griggs and Charlie left the dining room. The two detectives went around the ladder, through the main dining room, headed for the exit.

Once they hit the parking lot, Griggs led Charlie briskly to the car. As they hit the road, Charlie could no longer contain himself. "What was that all about?"

"What?"

"Back there in the restaurant. What were you—"

"Just paying a friendly visit."

"Are you crazy?" As they reached the corner, Charlie's train of thought was cut off when he saw the telltale van parked across the intersection. He looked at Griggs, who was looking pretty smug.

Charlie sat back in the passenger seat, thinking. When Griggs got in one of his moods, he liked to keep to himself. Griggs didn't want to explain their visit to Ted Massey? Fine.

But Charlie knew that the van meant the entire conversation had been recorded by the FBI. And they were recording whatever Massey and his men had to say after the detectives had left.

～ 62 ～

The door opened on the third knock. "That's quite a shiner you have there, young man." The old lady peeked through the half-closed door at Hank Barton, candidate for City Council, Seventh District, standing on her porch in the cold. "I hope you look better than the other guy."

Hank tried a smile. Ouch. Still hurt. "My name is Henry Barton— you can call me Hank—and I would be honored to serve you on the City Council." He nodded toward his associate, the volunteer helping with the field campaign today. The young lady smiled and curtsied. An old-fashioned touch, but it seemed to impress many of the older residents who bothered to open the door.

He grinned broadly, continued, hoping to get inside. It was really hot out here. "I am on a mission to join with as many people as I can to become active in the affairs of our city and to participate in a respectful, transparent, and effective manner."

The lady blinked. Door still half closed.

At least she was still listening.

"If we could sit with you for just a few minutes, ma'am, I would love to discuss with you how together we can send a message to the whole council...so that our economy and our community will be free to develop and thrive."

There was barking from inside the house. The old lady turned and yelled toward the back. "Down, Shep!" She turned back to the folks on the porch, closing the door another fraction of an inch. Staring.

"If we could just sit with you for a couple of minutes," Hank Barton soldiered on, sweating, "we would love to explain how I am dedicated to preserving and enhancing District Seven neighbor-hoods, ensuring the safety of residents and creating an attractive and healthy environment that will encourage people to live, work, and shop in the district. We have an opportunity to start over in Kansas City. We can now all wake up to the new morning of Kansas

City and get ready for a great day. All of Kansas City must stand together, or we will fall together."

The door shivered a little, from some thing bumping against it from the inside. The old lady turned and yelled. "Hush!" She turned back to Hank and his young volunteer. "So you're some sort of senator?"

Wiping his forehead with a damp white handkerchief, Hank smiled at the woman, pretending he wasn't about to thoroughly repeat himself. It was hard. "I am running for City Council. I hope to be elected to the seat that was vacated by Council Member Lester Goode. The special election to fill the remaining two years of Mr. Goode's term. If we could just come in for a minute—"

The old lady frowned. "Little early for elections, ain't it?"

"There is a special election in a month to fill the seat of the late Lester Goode. We have a mandate from the people—"

"That your daughter or your girlfriend?" The old lady nodded toward the volunteer.

Hank Barton, candidate for City Council, Seventh District, flinched. "What?"

~ 63 ~

It was a long and exhausting drive back to Kansas City, but I finally got home late at night. Just dropped into the bed next to the wife. Still in my clothes. I must have been out like a light.

The next morning, I got up bright and early. I didn't see the wife anywhere, didn't hear or smell anything resembling breakfast. I showered, shaved, and put on clean clothes. Grabbed the cell phone off the charger. The wife must have put it there. My head was still buzzing from nerves and lack of sleep, but I felt far better now than I had in days.

When I got downstairs, I was able to catch the boy before he popped out the door for school. "I'm going to need your help with something this morning."

He slumped his shoulders, his backpack sliding down his arm. "I was just headed to school, Dad."

I'm sure I squinted at him. "How did you know you were going to have school today?"

He shrugged. "What do you mean? We have it every day."

I wasn't in the mood for a theological debate. Not this morning. "I know, but you're going to have to go into school late today. Your ol' dad needs some assistance."

He gave me a look. "I have to turn in my assignment today." He shifted his eyes toward the open door. "And my ride is already here."

"You can turn your assignment in later." I kept my voice relaxed. Considering the circumstances, I think I conducted myself rather fairly. "Now, go out and tell them you have a ride already. I'll give you a ride to school."

While he went to follow orders, I went into the kitchen. No sign of the wife or the daughter. No sign of breakfast. No nothing.

First order of business, I needed some juice. But of course, the wife had cleaned the fridge out for the Rapture, so there was nothing.

I combed through the cabinets until I found an unopened can of peaches in syrup. I was not a fan, but I was hardly in a position to choose anything different. I was digging through the drawers looking for a can opener when I heard the boy come in. "Do you know where the can opener is? Your mother has hidden it from me."

He gave a sigh and grabbed something off the counter. "It's right here."

I took the can opener with a smile. Tried to be pleasant. "Thank you." As I twisted the knob to cut open the can of peaches, almost dreading the eventual results, I started to explain our morning plans. "I need you to help me take this truck back to the dealer."

"Oh?" I couldn't quite place that tone of voice. Disbelief? Mockery?

"Do you know where your mother and sister are this morning?"

"Rachel stayed with a friend last night. She must be in school by now. Mom went to the mall. I think she was also…making some returns."

I decided to let his comment drop. The lid was now loose. I cut my finger trying to pull it out of the can.

"What about the boat?"

I wrapped my finger in a paper towel. "What about it?"

"Are you keeping the boat?"

"Not that it's any of your business, but I am also returning the boat. We'll park it in the yard for now and come back for it later."

"But don't we need the truck to—"

"Look!" I slammed my hand on the counter. Blood spattered. "I don't need you to understand this, I just need you to do this." I took the paper towel and tried to wipe the blood off the counter, but it just seemed to smear. "This is my story. Don't let anyone tell you different."

The boy grumbled something.

"What was that?"

"You are not the only story. We all have lives, you know."

"Look, just help me with this and then you can go take a vacation or something."

"Or maybe go to school?"

I flashed him my *that's enough* look. "No more of your smart mouth. Now help me park the boat and unhitch it."

I decided I really did not want the peaches and syrup, so I dumped the can in the dog dish.

"He's not going to eat that."

"Well, neither am I." We headed out through the garage to the front, where I had parked the truck and boat at the curb. I pointed to the truck cab. "Son, I need you to put the truck in gear and back the boat right over here for me." I motioned to the space between our garage and the Mendels's garage.

The boy scrunched up his face. "Really?"

"Yes, really."

"But I've never done that before."

I gave him my most reassuring grin. "There is always a first time. This is your lucky day." I motioned again to the spot between the two garages. "I am going to guide you in. Piece of cake."

The boy got into the truck and started her up. He put her in gear and craned his neck to look over his shoulder.

"Use your mirrors, son!" If I pushed him, I knew he could rise to the challenge. "Angle your truck the other way!" Just push. "You're going to jackknife! Pull up and try again!" He could rise to the challenge. "Your mirrors! Check your mirrors!" Just push.

It took a good fifteen or twenty minutes of trial and error. The boy finally pulled all the way out into the street. It blocked oncoming traffic, but he finally got the truck at the correct angle. Finally got the boat at the correct angle. Started backing it across the driveway and then the yard.

Through the whole process, I tried to figure out what I would say to the boat dealer. How to explain. How not to look like a fair-weather borrower, one of those people who "buys" a TV in time for the Super Bowl and then brings it back on Monday for the refund.

I certainly did not want them to think I was hard up for money. Did not want them to think I was not in control of the situation.

I was so wrapped up in my plans that I barely heard the crash. I blinked my vision back and was staring at my boat inside of the Mendels's garage. A lot of extra plastic and metal and wood scrunched up where the two had collided.

The garage door and the boat were ruined, and I only had one person to blame. "How could you do that?"

The boy leaped out of the truck. "I couldn't see! You were the one guiding me in!"

"I *was* guiding you in!" I was now inspecting the damage with shaking hands. "You did this on purpose."

"What?"

"You and your mother just like to see me suffer." I shook my head as I calculated the immense cost to repair the damage. To the garage. To the boat. To my life.

"How could you say that?" The boy's voice was trembling. Was he going to cry at a time like this? That was certainly no help.

I ignored it. I went to the truck bumper and unhitched the boat. We would have to extricate it by hand. Towing it could only make it worse. "Go move the truck."

"What?"

I yelled. "Move the truck! Try and be useful!"

I barely paid attention as he got in the truck, sobbing. Barely noticed when he shifted into gear. Barely heard the tires squealing. Barely noticed the truck rocket down the street.

All I knew was I could never get my money back on this boat. What would the mob say about this?

– 64 –

"Quite a shiner you got there." The shorter guy grinned at Hank Barton, candidate for City Council, Seventh District. Chuckled. "Hope you look better than the other guy."

Actually, the other guy had fared much better, but Hank didn't share that. Wishing he had left campaign headquarters with the others. *Don't worry, honey,* he had told his wife no more than ten minutes ago. *I'll lock up and meet you at home.* He wondered what the two men were going to say now. "What can I do for you gentlemen?" He casually glanced toward the exit. And toward the phone. Decided the exit was the smarter move. You could always phone the police from somewhere else.

"We just wanted to pay you a visit. See how you are doing." The shorter man nodded slowly, eyes wide. Words dripping with unspoken meaning. He made a motion toward Hank's black eye. "Like, who did this thing to you?"

"Wh-what?"

"We're friends, right? I know you want to do the smart thing." The shorter man breathed through his nose. "We don't take kindly to others butting into our business like this."

Hank casually leaned against the desk, which got him closer to the door. "It was a simple misunderstanding."

"Lissen, misunderstandings like this we don't need." The shorter guy looked over at the other one.

The tall gangly man had his hands in his pockets, was doing some weird hand movements that made his pants seem to balloon in and out. How did he do that?

The short guy growled, "Do you mind? The grown-ups are talking here." When the other man stopped and started to sulk in the corner, he turned back to Hank. "We need to be on the same team here, captain. We don't need outside parties muscling in on our...friendship." Chomping gum, he reached up and playfully slapped a hand against the side of Hank's head. "Huh?"

Hank didn't know what to say. Nodded. Trying to calculate the number of steps to the exit from the desk.

"Just give me a name."

Hank stopped nodding. "Um...I don't understand."

"Tell me who did this to you."

"I...it was nothing."

"Tell me."

"Seriously, it was just a—"

"*Tell me!*" The shorter man's voice bellowed through the office, rattling the windows. How could a man that size make that much noise?

Hank trembled. "The preacher at that Tribulation House church." Felt his mouth go dry. "Reverend Daniel Glory."

A strange look came over the shorter man's face. "Really?"

Hank nodded and tried to smile. Still hurt. "It was a simple misunderstanding."

"Uh-huh." Something was in his voice...

"No, really, there was a disagreement and then I got a little upset—"

The shorter man held up a hand. Face calm now. Dead calm. "Say no more."

"But—"

"We take care of our friends."

What did that mean?

"Mr. Massey is a man who takes care of his friends." The man motioned to his partner that it was time to go. As they headed for the exit, the shorter man turned back. Chomping gum. Grinning. "Which makes it important for us to *stay* friends, right?"

As they left, Hank Barton, candidate for City Council, Seventh District, felt his knees give way. He slid to the floor. Wondered what in the world he had just done.

Prayed to God it wasn't what he thought it was.

– 65 –

When the wife got home from the mall, I waved off her questions about the wrecked boat in the yard and matching hole in the Mendels's garage door. "It's too complicated to get into now."

"But...what happened?"

"I don't want to talk about it!" I cleared my throat. Tried again. "Honey, I have a splitting headache right now. I have to figure out what to do about this."

"Are you okay?"

I remembered it was the first time I'd seen her since the previous morning. I nodded, tried to play it cool. "Sure, sure. I..." There were no more words coming, so I let the sentence drop.

We exchanged weary looks, but had no words to describe the

past twenty-four hours. Or the fact that we were still here on earth. She hugged me, and I let her.

She cried a little, and I patted her on the back. She sniffled, pulling a tissue from her purse. "Where's your truck?"

"I'm sorry?"

"Your truck. What happened to your truck? It isn't there inside the neighbor's garage, is it?"

"No." I forced a chuckle. "The boy needed it to drive to school."

"Oh." She wiped her nose again, and put her purse on the table by the front door. "That was nice of you."

"I'm a nice guy."

She went into the kitchen to try to figure lunch out. When she left, I grabbed her keys and borrowed her car.

Spent the afternoon just driving. Drove for hours. Drove to the office. Did not have the nerve to go in. Drove to the boat dealer. Did not even know how to begin to make a deal on returning a boat with a garage-shaped hole in the hull. Drove by the school. Did not see my Avalanche anywhere.

I was at the end of my rope. My life was falling apart. I had lost my career. I didn't know where my son and my truck were. And I would no doubt be getting a visit from the mobsters in just a matter of weeks. When was my loan even due? I had barely listened to the terms when I got the money. I didn't think there would be any point.

I only had one person to blame.

I found Reverend Daniel Glory in his office at the church. His desk was littered with charts and graphs and scribbled formulas. "You've got to help me!"

Reverend Glory looked up from his papers. He was still his everyday smug self. As clean-cut as ever, his hair helmet in place, his strong jawline bejeweled with that toothy grin. "I'm working on it right now." He pointed to the scribbled formulas. The trash can was filled with crumpled previous drafts. "I think I have discovered where I misplaced the—"

I lunged across the office, fell to my knees by his desk chair. "You don't understand! I'm in debt up to my eyeballs!"

He didn't seem fazed. "I'm sure if you talk to the bank, they'll understand your—"

I grabbed him by the shoulders. "Not the bank! I borrowed the money from somebody else!" I shook him. "These are bad men! These are the people who break your legs!"

Reverend Glory gave me a look. How dare he give me a look at a time like this? "You did *what?*"

I stood up. I walked to the other side of the office. I tried to recover. Tried to reclaim myself. Tried to get my story back on track. "I entered into a business arrangement. Simple. Given the circumstances, it made perfect sense."

"Let me see whether I understand this." The Reverend pushed back his chair. Raised an eyebrow at me. "Let me understand here— you entered into some sort of exchange with...criminals?"

"It was a carefully thought-out decision."

"With gangsters?"

"We weren't supposed to be here."

"What do you mean?"

I couldn't help but bellow. "What do I mean?" I lunged again for the desk, started pounding on the various charts and graphs. "The Rapture was coming! We just needed to fasten our seat belts and be ready to fly!"

He gave me a smile. He said, "Look, son, I'll keep you in my prayers."

"What good is that? You have to do something! What good is prayer if you're not going to help me?"

"I know, but—"

"This is your fault!"

"Now wait a sec—"

"You did this!" I'm not sure what came over me. I suddenly had his lapels in my hands, but they were like someone else's hands. "You were the big man, with your charts and your graphs!" I was yelling, but it was like the voice was coming from someone else. "We trusted you!"

Reverend Glory yelled something and grabbed my wrists. His grip was strong—stronger than you would think—but I had the strength of a madman. I pushed back and kicked as hard as I could.

He cursed and threw a fist, which grazed me. I grabbed something off his desk and swung. He was on the floor before I even realized it was some kind of trophy.

He lay on the floor. Blood spattered on the side of his head where I hit him. He wasn't moving. Didn't seem to be breathing.

Oh God.

Oh God oh God oh God.

I was still praying when I heard a ringing noise. It took me a moment to recognize it as a phone. Another moment to recognize it as my own.

I looked at the ID on the screen. The wife. "What?"

"Where are you?"

I swallowed. Tried to sound calm. "I'm sorry I borrowed your car, but—"

"Clint is at the hospital!"

"What?"

"There was some sort of wreck and he was—"

"What happened?"

"I'm telling you what happened."

"What happened to the truck?"

"I don't know." Her voice cracked. "Clint is in intensive care. Can you come take me to the hospital?"

"It's going to be a—"

"Are you coming to the hospital to see your son?"

I looked down at the body on the floor. "I have something I have to take care of first."

She hung up on me.

~ 66 ~

Full of spunk and Fritos and lemonade, twelve-year-olds Gordon Cruz and Arthur Tarrant were headed for the wastelands. At least, that is what they liked to call it. It was actually a patch of pre-developed land given the all-okay sign by the local university, who had come through with their lab coats and their picks and shovels and given up on finding any genuine fossils.

Now the land was ready to be carved up and parceled out for houses and schools and a shopping center. The boys only knew it was ideal for playing superheroes.

Arthur especially liked pretending he was a superhero; it was his only connection to the genre. His folks did not let him read comic books, or even wear the shoes or T-shirts. They did not have a satellite dish either.

To date, he had managed to sneak only a few scraps of four-color heaven past parental lines. An issue of *Spider-Man* proudly labeled "Part Three of Six!" An issue of *Batman* with a swear word in it.

Gordon was the expert. He was the boy with the comic-book collection and the satellite dish. He knew the names of the super-heroes, he knew their archenemies, he knew the drills.

Arthur had wanted to be Hawkman today, wanted to pretend he had the cool beak mask and enormous wingspan.

Gordon insisted that Arthur play Hawkeye. Claimed that Arthur would have all the benefits of the cool beak mask and enormous wingspan, plus a sharpshooter's aim and bow and arrow.

Gordon, as always, was Doctor Fate. The golden-helmeted mystic with nigh-omnipotent powers.

Arthur made a face. "I don't think Hawkeye has the beak mask and wings."

"Of course he does."

Not that either boy was actually wearing a costume. In their street clothes, all the accoutrements of being a superhero were strictly in their imagination. But for Arthur, it was the principle of the thing.

Wishing he had grabbed more Fritos on the way out the door, he headed for the big, dead, split tree, a feat of engineering only nature could provide, big sprawling curves leading out of a split middle, low toward the ground.

Hawkeye was halfway up the second branch on the left, deemed the Weapons Locker, before he noticed Doctor Fate had not entered the complex. Arthur turned a freckled face and saw Gordon by the creek, poking at something with a stick. "What are you looking at?"

His friend looked up and wrinkled his nose. "Code names!"

Hawkeye sighed. "Doctor Fate! What are you doing?"

"I found something, Hawkeye!"

Arthur climbed back down out of the Hall of Justice. Trudged toward the creek. Heard the thin gurgling of water over pebbles.

By the time he reached the spot, Gordon—that is, Doctor Fate— was on his knees, working feverishly with a knotted stick to gouge into loose dirt around the edge of the creek. Stabbing, jabbing, digging out craters, shoving dirt and mud and whatever else Arthur could imagine was buried there off to the side.

There was something in the ground.

Arthur got down on one knee. "What is it?"

"I think it's a dinosaur."

Arthur frowned. "Wouldn't they have dug them all up?"

Gordon shook his head. "They didn't have permission to dig this far over." He motioned to the nearby fence, rusted barbed wire stapled to wobbly wood posts. "This property belongs to Old Man Haney."

Gordon returned to his project. Something white and shiny poked through. Gordon dropped the stick and reached for it.

Arthur tried to imagine what they would find.

Maybe the bones of a pterodactyl. He and Gordon could wire the skeleton together, wrap it in canvas or something, make a glider.

Maybe a rhinoceros. A huge skull with the neat horn on the end, use it as a kind of helmet. Take turns terrorizing bullies at school.

Maybe it was a pirate. Maybe when this creek was a raging river, cutting a swath through everything in its path, a pirate ship came through Kansas and deposited its massive treasure and left this poor man behind to guard it with his life.

Here. In Kansas.

Yeah. Right.

Arthur did not feel like playing Justice League crossover as one lone marksman who might or might not have a beak mask and generous wings. If he couldn't pull Gordon away from his prize, he might as well help dig. If it was treasure, his friend would have to share.

Arthur started looking for a tool of his own, went through several branches that were not sturdy enough or long enough to do the job. Finally, he found a shard of some rusted metal. Something that had broken off some kind of farm equipment.

Arthur went back to the spot, crossed to the other side of the hole, and got on both knees. Jammed the rusted metal into the ground, chipped earth from around the edges of the growing hole. Grabbed clods of dirt and threw them aside.

The two boys focused on their investigation, neither speaking, neither remembering they were supposed to be monitoring for injustice.

All that mattered was the dig. The hole. The history they were discovering. The history they were making.

Within a matter of minutes, they found something else.

Gordon and Arthur both jumped up, both breathing hard through their mouths, unable to speak. All they could do was stand there and gasp for air.

All they could do was stare down at the human skull.

⁓ 67 ⁓

I stared at the body—at Reverend Daniel Glory—for I don't know how long. Forever facedown on his precious charts and graphs and Bible maps. Never to prophesy again. Never to rise again. Not in this life.

Everything seemed to have stopped. It was like the entire universe had ceased spinning to stare at this one horrifying moment in time. Like God Himself had nudged the Milky Way to a stop and said, *Can you believe this?*

Everything moved in slow motion: the second hand on the clock, the blades on the desk fan, the beat of my heart.

I glanced down at the cell phone in my hand. The wife had called earlier, hadn't she? I vaguely remembered the conversation. I'd barely heard what she had to say. *What happened to the boy? What happened to my truck?*

I did not know for sure. All that mattered was what had happened in this office. All I could do was stare at the body on the floor. Facedown on the charts and graphs strewn about the office.

I was staring and yet not staring. Unable to focus through the headache. Through the nerves. Through the fear.

Worn out, I collapsed into the huge leather chair. I set the clunky trophy on the desk. I stared at it a few moments, struggling to process the chain of events.

There had been a disagreement of some sort between me and Reverend Daniel Glory. There had been a scuffle. I had simply, instinctively, grabbed something off the desk. This trophy. This award. I had picked up the award in my hand. What had happened after that was vague. I must have slipped. Somehow, Reverend Daniel Glory's head had connected with the object in my hand.

I squinted at the object. What was it even for? I tried to focus on the engraving. I finally made out the words *PROPHET OF THE YEAR, 1988.*

I slowly swiveled the chair around a couple of times. Ran my fingers through my hair, tried to collect myself. Considered my options.

I could call the police. Report the incident. Wait for them to arrive. Tell them it was an accident.

That's right, officers, Reverend Daniel Glory and I got into an altercation. There were some heated words, which led to fisticuffs. Somewhere in there, he slipped, I slipped, who can remember, and I clobbered him in the back of the head with this object. By accident.

What is it called when it's an accident? Is that still called a "homicide"? Or do they call it "manslaughter"?

— — —

Okay. I could call the police. Report the incident. Wait for them to arrive. Tell them it was self-defense.

That's right, officers, Reverend Daniel Glory attacked me bodily and threatened to commit great bodily harm. Tried to kill me, officers. I did the only thing a man in my position could do—defend myself.

Yes, sirs, he is an award-winning preacher. In fact, here is his award right here.

— — —

Okay. I could call the police. Report the incident. Wait for them to arrive. Tell them Reverend Daniel Glory was like this when I got here.

That's right, officers, I came to have a private prayer session with Reverend Daniel Glory. He was dead when I got here. Perhaps he was overcome while in fervent prayer and fell on this object on top of his desk.

Of course, I would have to explain how that could happen.

Would they understand? Would they believe? The world often ridicules what it cannot understand.

— — —

Okay. I could call the police. Anonymously. I did not actually have to be here when they showed up.

Was there any evidence I had been here? Were my fingerprints all over the office? Actually, I was one of the deacons in the church—all our fingerprints would be all over the office. In fact, it would be strange for my fingerprints *not* to be there.

I took a deep breath. I did not want to overreact. Did not want to overthink this. If I removed all evidence of my presence in this room, that might be the vital clue that did me in.

— — —

In the end, I did what any man in my position would do. I ran. Fled. Determined to get as far away as possible as fast as I could.

I did not bother to lock up the church. I just made sure there was no one around, headed straight through the lobby and out to the parking lot, got in my car and drove away.

– 68 –

Cleaver grunted, "Just wait outside." The car racing down the road.

Lamb, staring out the passenger window, turned and blinked. "What?"

"I'm going to go in and talk to the man and you're going to just stay in the car."

"We're not even there."

"When we get there, I'm going to go inside, and you're going to stay outside."

"Whatever."

"What's that supposed to mean?"

"It means 'yes.'"

"It doesn't sound like 'yes.'"

"It just means 'yes.'"

"It better." Cleaver pulled into the parking lot. As he headed for the front door, he glanced to the sign announcing *TRIBULATION HOUSE*. He kicked at the sign, then went and savagely pulled the door open. These church people had given him too much trouble.

— — —

Lamb tried waiting. In the car. Really, he did. But something inside made him want to demonstrate his bravery. Cleaver didn't scare him. And Lamb would prove it.

He decided to wait outside the car. Maybe take a walk. Maybe go to some of the locals and check up on their protection—that is, their insurance.

He just had to remember which ones were actually on the list. For all his two-fisted negotiating technique, Cleaver was not that good at his job. Lending out money and not collecting. Taking "no" for an answer.

Yessir, Lamb just might have to have himself a talk with the big boss. Report to Mr. Massey that Cleaver was not really working out.

And then who would be the strong man? Who would be the one punching the other guy in the face? Bill Lamb, that's who.

He leaned against the car casually, striking his best pose. He tried cleaning his nails with his teeth, like he saw Cleaver do. Yeah, acting tough could work.

And then Lamb would be the—

"Get in the car." Cleaver was suddenly on the sidewalk, headed his way.

"How'd it—"

"Get in the car."

As they peeled out of the parking lot, Lamb asked, "So what did—"

"Not now."

"What did he say?"

"He wasn't there."

They drove on in silence. A few miles down the road, Cleaver pulled into a gas station. "I gotta make a call."

"Use my cell."

"No." Something strange about Cleaver's voice. "Gotta use the pay phone."

～ 69 ～

How long did I drive around? I don't actually know. It couldn't have been too long. I tried to relax. Tried to slow down my breathing. Tried to slow down the pounding of my heart.

I had fled the scene of a man's death. Was that wrong? If it was an accident, did anyone really need to be around? Someone would eventually show up at the church. For a meeting. For prayer. For maintenance.

Someone would find the body of Reverend Daniel Glory. Come to the only realistic conclusion: It was an accident. They say that millions of people die from falling in the tub every year. Surely there was a similar precedent for people falling in their office.

It is obvious what happened. The Reverend Daniel Glory, eaten up by guilt that Jesus had not come back on schedule, was recalculating his numbers. He had all these papers strewn about all over the floor. He slipped on one of these Bible maps and hit his head.

Probably on this prophecy award sitting on top of his desk. Open-and-shut case.

There was no reason for me to hang around. Just in case the authorities felt the need to pin this on some innocent scapegoat. No reason for me to get involved. I was an innocent bystander.

As I drove through the thickening evening traffic, I was vaguely glad to be in my wife's beat-up old car. It blended into traffic very well. My shiny red truck would have been a beacon, pointing everybody right to me.

During that drive, I prayed long and hard. *Lord, how could you let me down like this? First, you failed to show up on schedule, and now you failed to intercede when Reverend Daniel Glory attacked me. You saw it, Lord—I had no choice. It was him or me.*

I honestly don't know how long I was gone. I don't know how long I prayed for deliverance.

But it finally dawned on me: the security camera. Back at the church. In that little control room, there was a video recording of me picking up that award and smacking Reverend Daniel Glory in the back of the head.

I had to go back. Had to cover up my presence at the scene of the murder. I was relieved that I had not already called the police. With any luck—with God on my side—I would be able to slip back in before anyone noticed what had happened.

The whole trip back, I continued praying. Continued praying for deliverance from this temptation. Praying for victory over the ol' devil and his plans. *All things work together for good,* I told myself. *What the devil means for harm, the Lord means for good.*

These were the promises I was clinging to. I knew if I just held onto the promises, everything would be okay.

When I got back to the church, I don't think all that much time had passed. There was nobody parked in front. The front doors were locked, so I used my keys to get in.

Inside, I listened to make sure it was safe. Reasonably sure the place was empty, I crossed the lobby and went straight through the sanctuary, all the way to the little room at the back. The door was locked and I did not have a key. I took a music stand and whacked on the doorknob until the lock broke.

The small room was even more alien than I remembered. It took me a few minutes to reorient myself, analyzing the sound board, the banks of screens, the various boxes and wires and plugs. Trying to reconstruct what cute little Sandra Robertson had told me when she gave me the guided tour.

The various video screens were on, cameras silently absorbing every move all over the church. Right now, they were recording empty rooms. Everything neat, everything orderly, everything in place.

Except in the office of the Reverend Daniel Glory. On the tiny screen, I saw the body lying there on the charts and graphs and magazines. Staring upward. Toward the ceiling. Toward heaven.

The screen was too small to see, but I was sure his eyes would be glazed by now. Dead. Seeing but not seeing.

I needed to find the recording device. Needed to remove the video recording of the events in his office.

I held my breath and listened. At first, all I could hear was what must have been the air conditioner. Eventually, a whirring sound revealed itself. I finally tracked the sound to the recording device. Everything that had happened in Reverend Daniel Glory's office was on one of its tapes. When the police finally showed up, it would reveal the identity of the murderer, quickly and clearly.

I looked for switches or buttons, but just could not figure out how to stop the machine. I also had no way of knowing which of these tapes were recording the events in that office. Impatient, I grabbed a screwdriver and began prying the tapes out. One by one, there was a cracking of plastic and a grinding noise in the machine and then a tape broke and was on the floor, in pieces.

I removed all six in this fashion when I heard a beep—someone had entered the church. Holding my breath, I looked on the bank of screens. In the lobby, two uniformed police officers had entered. Guns drawn.

I had not called for the police. I had not set off the alarm. *How did they know? How could they know?*

Gathering up the streams of videotape and fragments of plastic casing, I stuffed them in an offering bag. The monitor showed the officers headed around the side of the sanctuary, for the stairs to the offices. The sanctuary was safe. For the moment.

Offering bag in hand, I snuck out. Got to the car. Drove away. Clean.

Finally, the Lord answered at least this prayer.

⟍ 70 ⟋

It was a few hours before Detective Tom Griggs and Detective Charlie Pasch arrived at the scene. The Last Church of God's Imminent Will. The office of the Reverend Daniel Glory. Pinned to the chest of the deceased, a note: *THIS IS WHAT HAPPENS WHEN YOU CROSS THE MOB.*

Griggs was pacing. He always paced at the scene of the crime. Waiting for the technicians to get their evidence, waiting for the photographer to get his photos, waiting for the word on what to look for or who to chase.

Charlie was the curious one. Always looking around. Always asking questions. Always driving the techs crazy.

When Griggs and Charlie got there, the uniformed policemen had blocked the church off to outsiders. The techs were already in the office examining every fiber, every particle that seemed out of place. They came in and found the man flat on his back, looking toward heaven with dead eyes.

With the note, there was the suggestion that organized crime was involved. Detective Utley and his homicide squad had pushed the case over to Griggs and the joint task force. Which Charlie found kind of weird—Detective Griggs and Detective Utley never

184 — Chris Well

got along; they always fought over jurisdiction. Essentially fighting to have more work to do.

Maybe Detective Utley had got smart. Realized he didn't need to fight so hard to make more work for himself.

When Griggs saw the note for himself, he said, "That's peculiar."

"What?" Charlie was distracted by the charts and graphs strewn on the floor around the body.

"This." Griggs pointed to the note, careful not to touch it, careful not to contaminate the evidence. "The mob wouldn't leave a note like this."

"Oh, yeah. I see what you mean."

Griggs had spent his pacing time trying to figure it out. If the mob had killed this guy, they would not have left a note. In fact, if the man's death had been some sort of message, the death itself would have been the message.

More likely, the real killer was not in the mob, but was trying to point the finger away from himself or herself. But of course, that brought the risk of getting the mob after you too.

Griggs wished Charlie would turn his *Star Trek*–like mind to the problem. But the kid was mesmerized by the various papers around the body.

"Look at this," Charlie said. Now he was by the desk, looking at some lump of metal and plastic on a wooden base.

"Some kind of trophy?"

"It's an award." Charlie pointed with a pinky, careful not to touch. "The engraving says...*Prophet...of the...Year...1988.*"

"Prophet, huh?" Griggs snickered. "I guess he shoulda seen this coming."

The kid frowned. "A prophet doesn't claim to be psychic. This is different."

"Sure."

"Although I can't imagine a genuine prophet would be in any kind of organization that hands out awards." Charlie squinted more closely at the trophy. Turned to one of the techs. "Hey, I think I see blood."

The man came over and shined a tiny flashlight on the trophy. Without uttering a word, he grabbed it with tongs and inserted it into a plastic bag.

Charlie turned his attention back to the charts and graphs on the floor. "These must be related to the end times."

Griggs stopped his pacing. "How do you figure that?"

"I think he was trying to study the biblical prophecies as they relate to the end of the world."

"For all the good it did him."

"One thing does not have anything to do with the other." The kid turned his attention to the shelves of books. "A lot of end-times books here, too." He found a series of identical thin spines, all labeled *107 Reasons Jesus Is Coming Back in 2007*. Charlie gasped. Whirled around. "I know who this guy is."

"Of course," one of the techs said. "The victim is a Daniel—"

"Reverend Daniel Glory," Charlie cut in, eyes widening. "He claimed to have calculated the exact day of the Rapture."

"Right," the tech nodded. "It was in the *Kansas City Blade*."

Now Charlie was pacing too. "He said that Jesus was coming on October 17."

Griggs was intrigued. "What, last Wednesday?"

"Five days ago." Charlie nodded, looking down at the markings where the body had been. "He was, of course, wrong."

"Of course?"

Charlie nodded. "The Bible says that no man will know the day or the hour. Even Jesus Himself does not know the day or the hour of His return." He went over to Griggs. "History is littered with false prophets and heretics who thought they could pinpoint the return of Jesus."

"You mean, like the Y2K scare?"

"Not exactly. There have been false claims going all the way back to the church of the Thessalonians."

"Who are they?"

Charlie shrugged. "They are the Thessalonians."

"Oh, that clears everything up."

"It was one of the early churches. The apostle Paul wrote letters to them—two of them are in the Bible. One of the letters chided the Thessalonians for believing the false reports that the Second Coming had happened. And that was, what, like 50 AD? And then every few years since then—at least once in every generation—someone has risen up and claimed they were the 'last generation.'"

"Uh-huh."

Charlie knelt by the charts and graphs. "What is this?"

"Why, what did you find?"

"This looks like some sort of schematic..." Charlie was squinting, fighting the urge to grab the sheet. He didn't want to move anything before the forensics team said it was okay. "...for the Sphinx?"

"What, in Egypt?"

Charlie looked up, puzzled. "I think so." He looked down at the papers on the floor again. "He seems to have based some of his research on this. I don't know that I think much of that notion."

Griggs deadpanned, "I'm sure the deceased is all broken up over it."

"Wait a second." Charlie stood, an idea hitting him. "Let's hit control-alt-delete."

"What?"

"Let's rethink this a second. We may have found the killer's motive right here."

"How do you figure that?"

"Glory claimed he knew when Jesus was coming back. He made a big deal out of it. He wrote a book. His church held their special Tribulation House event."

"And he was wrong. So?"

"He turned out to be wrong—and before the week is out he's lying dead in his office, on top of a bunch of his charts and graphs." Charlie stood and looked at Griggs. "I think there's a connection. There almost has to be."

Griggs stood over the spot, staring at the charts and graphs.

They made no sense to him, but the kid usually knew what he was talking about. "Maybe. But then what about that note?"

"Trying to cloud the investigation."

"Yeah." Griggs frowned. "But why leave a note at all?"

"Hey!" A tech came in from the hall, another object in a plastic bag. "Letter opener. Appears to have blood."

~ 71 ~

Forensic artist Bailey Andrews woke up when one of her cats pranced across her face. "Scat, cat," she grumbled in a weary voice, shoving the tabby off the bed.

It was one of the less charming habits her cats had developed. Not nearly as brilliant as the trick where they walked on their hind legs like people. The cats could only take a few steps at a time, of course, but it was still pretty impressive.

Rubbing the cat out of her eyes, Bailey robed up, stuck bare feet in fuzzy socks, and shuffled for the kitchen. As she headed down the hall of the apartment, she heard the gurgle of the coffeemaker and the chipper voice of her roommate, Julie Lennox, singing some chipper morning song.

Blech. Julie was the morning person. Bailey considered mornings a necessary evil.

As she rounded the corner into the kitchen, she heard the chipper voice directed at her. "Well, good morning!" Southern accent, Southern charm. *Blech, Blech.*

"G'morning." Bailey could barely open her eyes. She wondered how much of it was a result of the cat. She tried a follow-up statement, but all she could manage was, "Blech."

"Here." Julie pulled the pot out of the coffeemaker, poured steaming hot blackness into a mug, and handed it over. "This is fresh."

Bailey accepted the mug with all the smile she could muster. "Blech." Headed for the plastic bowl with all the packets of coffee additives—nondairy creamer, sugar, sugar substitute, chocolate mix, the usual—and grabbed a handful of sugar packets. She ripped off the corners of three packets at once and dumped most of the contents into the mug.

As usual, spillover during the process left a pile of crystals on the counter. Bailey ignored the mess, grabbed the canister of off-brand nondairy creamer, and dumped it liberally into the mug. She couldn't find a spoon, so she grabbed a knife and stirred.

"Oh, dear," her roommate said in that singsongy voice. Julie wet a paper towel under the faucet and began wiping the counter. "This will draw ants."

"Naw," Bailey replied with a smirk. She slurped from the cream-and-sugar-substitute goodness. "I'm sure the cats would have licked it up."

Julie made an awkward smile. "Just the same, cleanliness is next to godliness."

"Sure." Bailey slurped again, headed for the dining-room table. Just to be a pain, she added, "That's why Jesus was born in a barn." Hearing the dramatic sigh from the kitchen, she plopped into the wooden chair and stretched across the table for the morning paper.

She missed her Chicago newspapers. The Topeka paper was fine, especially in this age of Internet and telecommunications, where every paper had access to more or less the same information. But it was just one more daily reminder that she missed her friends and family back in the Windy City.

Of course, the job offer that had brought her to Kansas, the chance to be the first forensic anthropologist to set up shop in Braxton County, had been too good to pass up. It had meant leaving behind her friends and family, but it was all about the advancement. All about the adventure.

Her first letdown was that her new roommate, nice as she was, refused to watch her *Alias* DVDs. "Too vulgar" was the verdict. Apparently, Julie had never actually watched a single episode of the spy series—but judgment had already been passed. And one thing Bailey had learned about her roomie was that once Julie passed judgment, Julie moved onto other things.

Her roommate joined her at the table. They split up the paper between them—Julie read the local news and wedding announcements, Bailey read the national news and obituaries.

As Julie snapped open her section, Bailey took another swallow of her coffee, then set the mug down. "How was dinner last night?"

"Oh." The other woman carefully sipped from her mug, careful not to spill on the paper. "Virden picked out a great restaurant. They had buffalo on the menu, but I didn't have the nerve to try it."

"Did he pop the question?"

Julie flashed dagger eyes. "No." Looked down at the paper again.

Bailey quickly pulled her mug up to her mouth to hide the smirk. "So, what is buffalo? Isn't it just another kind of cow?"

Julie shrugged. "I don't know. I just don't like trying out strange meats."

"But if you eat beef, and it's just another kind of cow…"

"If it was a kind of cow, it would be 'cow.' Or 'beef.' The fact that it has a different name is enough difference for me."

Something about the Southern accent made the argument more emphatic. Bailey wondered how it would have sounded with a British accent.

She turned to the obituaries. It was a morbid pleasure, but it probably went with the job of forensic artist. She heard a southern drawl ask, "Why is it 'cow' and 'beef'?"

Bailey looked up from the obits, blinking. "What?"

"Why is it a 'cow' when it's on the hoof and 'beef' when you eat it? What's that all about?"

Bailey smiled. "The way I heard it, it's from England in olden times. The lower class spoke Anglo-Saxon, so when they raised the stock, they called them some older form of the word 'cow.' The upper class spoke French, so when it was served for dinner, they called it something like 'beef.' "

"Huh."

"Therefore, our modern words 'cow' and 'beef' come from the original Anglo-Saxon and French, respectively." Bailey was grabbing her coffee for another hit of caffeine, when the phone rang.

Her roommate jumped for it and answered. "Good morning, this is Julie." In that cheerful morning voice. *Blech.*

Bailey had just found her place in the newspaper again when she heard Julie say, "Just a minute." She looked up as Julie handed the receiver over. "It's the sheriff."

⁓ 72 ⁓

Back when I drove away from the church, I knew I had to get rid of the evidence. The offering bag full of stolen surveillance tapes. The tapes inside the bag were probably damaged and no longer viewable; smashed and exposed to the elements, it occurred to me that they would no longer serve as evidence. But the fact I had them in my possession could be a problem.

Maybe I was being paranoid. But I didn't want to take any chances.

I was on the road for about five minutes before I turned into a subdivision, looking for a ditch to dump the offering bag in. Unfortunately, I could not find a good ditch. Every ditch was either too close to someone's house or in a too-busy area.

What next? Maybe, I thought, I could take these tapes and throw them in the dump. But where was that? All these years I'd lived in Kansas City, and it had never even occurred to me to think where all the trash ended up.

I finally ended up at a dumpster behind a strip mall. I threw some of the tape and fragments of plastic in there. Deciding it would be wise not to leave all the tapes together, I eventually ended up at six different dumpsters. Behind fast-food restaurants, behind discount stores, and even one behind a Catholic church.

Then it was time to figure out some sort of alibi. It would only be a matter of time before the authorities would come looking for me. I had seen the detective shows on TV. A man can breathe in a room and they can analyze the particles and say who was in the room and what he ate for lunch.

Sure, I could tell them how it really happened. But, as members of the world's system, the "principalities and powers" that Paul wrote of, they would not be inclined to believe the truth about what had happened.

This was my story. I did not want the authorities to come in and rewrite it to fit their needs.

I drove around a while before I pulled my wife's old beat-up car off to the side of the road. It struck me that I had spent a lot of time at the side of the road the past few days.

But it was not my fault. I had been pushed there. By God. By Reverend Daniel Glory. By gangsters. It was not my fault.

I just needed to get somewhere and convince them I had been there a long time. Convince them I had been there during the time of the accident with Reverend Daniel Glory.

At the side of the road, I kept checking the radio. Waiting for a news report that the Antichrist had taken over somewhere in the Middle East. That a worldwide union of ten kings had been formed. That credit-card numbers had been revealed to be the mark of the beast. Any evidence, any word, that these were the end times. That I was not the victim of some cruel hoax.

But the radio was devoid of any prophecy-related news bursts.

⁓ ⁓ ⁓

"You write your own story," my father always said. "Don't let other people write it for you." For all the good it did him.

I thought back to that time when I was twelve. Home alone with my brother, who was nine. My mother and father out at the movies or something. Maybe they went to some musical concert. I don't quite remember.

As soon as they were gone, my brother and I took the opportunity to explore forbidden parts of the house. My brother got into the closet and found a shoebox full of bullets. He couldn't find my father's gun, so he spent the better part of the night just playing with the bullets. Using them like immobile action figures.

I got into my parents' bookshelf. Their books were "off limits" to us, so you knew they had to be good. I climbed up the rickety shelf and pulled down some of the paperbacks. Sidney Sheldon and Judith Krantz and Robert Ludlum. I didn't know what these books were about, but if they were off limits to a kid, it was time for me to become a man.

I didn't even hear the living-room window break. Didn't hear the man enter our house. My nose was in one of the books when the man appeared at the door to our parents' bedroom. He locked me and my brother in the closet.

We shivered in the darkness while we listened. Listened to him throwing things around. Opening drawers, slamming them shut, breaking things. After he was out of earshot, we could only imagine what he was doing in the rest of the house.

Several hours passed before our parents returned. When we were sure it was their voices we heard, we screamed for them. Our mother opened the door. When she saw us huddled in the back of the closet, she shrieked and threw her arms around us.

My father was not so glad to see us. "I can't believe you allowed this to happen," he lectured. "I'm very disappointed in you."

— — —

I shook off the memory, flipped around for radio stations. Tried to find any word about the end times. Any clue. Any hope.

There at the side of the road, I broke down and cried. I admit it. I am not proud, but there it was.

— 73 —

Ross Cleaver and Bill Lamb were in the car. Sun beaming through the windshield. Cleaver glowering, eyes on the road. Lamb nursing a fat lip. "You din't have to hit so hard."

Cleaver didn't look away from the road. Passed some old lady in a Kia. "A man tells you to shut up, you best shut up." He pressed the cigarette lighter.

Lamb turned to look out the passenger window. Huffed like he was going to cry. Whined, "Just trying to do what Mr. Massey says." He shook his head. "He says we gotta talk to some politicians, I just wanna talk to some politicians. He says we gotta get that church off the property, we gotta get that church off the property."

Cleaver leaned toward the steering wheel, hit the gas to make the yellow light. "We are."

"I don't see us talking to no politicians." Lamb mumbled. "I don't."

"What are we doing, huh?" Cleaver gripped the steering wheel with white knuckles. "What are we doing right now?"

The man answered in a low tone. "Going to your ex-wife's house."

"And after that, dum-dum?"

Lamb huffed again. "I don't know about after that." The dummy got some nerve, his voice started to rise. Sat up in the passenger seat. Not enough nerve to make eye contact, talked into Cleaver's elbow. "All I knows is, Mr. Massey told us not to go to your ex-wife's house. And then your ex-wife told us not to go to her house."

"So?"

"So, here we are going to her house."

"Look, dum-dum, that is my house. It was paid for with my money. I am not going to shirk my manly responsibilities."

Lamb turned back to the passenger window. Murmured something to the passing cars.

"What was that?"

"Nothing."

"What did you say?"

"I didn't say anything."

Cleaver flashed angry eyes at Lamb, then turned back to the road. "Better not have."

The two rode in silence for a good five, ten minutes. It was the longest Cleaver remembered the dummy not talking. Until the dummy broke the silence. "How come we don't just burn it down?"

"What?" Cleaver shot a frown at the other man. Wrinkled his brow. Reached for the car's cigarette lighter and pushed it in. "What would I do that for? I'm trying to fix the place up. Why would I want it burned down?"

"It just seems like it would make everything go a lot easier."

"Do you ever think with that brain?"

Lamb thought over the question. "Yes."

"You could never tell by listening to you shoot your mouth off."

"Why do you always call me a dummy? I am not a dummy. I have what is actually a very reasonable idea. We burn this church down, and then they have to move. Don't they?"

"You're talking about the church?"

"Yeah."

"Why didn't you tell me you were talking about the church?"

"I did."

"No, you didn't." The cigarette lighter popped out, Cleaver pulled a cigarette from the pack on the dash, lit it with the glowing coil. "We were talking about my house. And we are not burning my house down."

"I don't think it's your house."

"Do I gotta—"

"But why don't we just burn the church down? Or show up some night with a bulldozer?"

Cleaver took a drag from the cigarette. Turned and gave his

partner an amused look. "A bulldozer? You got yourself a bulldozer in the garage at home?"

"I'm just saying, I don't know why we gotta finesse with these people when all we wanna do is make them go away. Working the insurance racket makes no sense."

"It don't matter if it makes sense to you. All that matters is it makes sense to me." Cleaver drove on in silence a few more minutes. Mulling the man's suggestion over. He would never tell the dummy out loud, but the man might be onto something. Cleaver just wanted to squeeze a few bucks out of the church, and those weirdos just kept giving him the runaround. Talk to the board of directors. Talk to Jesus.

But maybe the dummy had something.

Cleaver put the thoughts out of his head as they reached his destination. Pulled up to the curb out front of Enid's house. He heard the dummy ask, "How you getting in?"

"What do you mean?"

"She took your key, right?"

Cleaver grinned. "I got a key."

"But she took your key."

"I got another one."

"How did—"

"Do I gotta pop you another one?"

The dummy shut up.

Inside the house, Cleaver was going through Enid's mail when he heard the sound of the TV in the next room. The dummy was probably looking for cartoons. Cleaver flipping through the stack he had pulled out of the box. Bill, bill, magazine, bill. He'd found one interesting piece of mail, when the dummy shouted for him.

"Hey! Ross!"

Cleaver headed for the living room, found the dummy standing in the middle of the room, pointing the remote at the TV. Jaw open. Cleaver growled, "This better be good."

"Look."

Cleaver turned to see a picture of Reverend Daniel Glory. The newsgirl reporting that the man had been murdered. A note pinned to his chest: *THIS IS WHAT HAPPENS WHEN YOU CROSS THE MOB.*

Lamb turned and frowned. "What did you *do?*"

— 74 —

"We just want to ask you a few questions." The two men at the campaign offices of Hank Barton, candidate for City Council, Seventh District, showed their badges. The man who spoke to him was a Detective Tom Griggs. The younger man was a Detective Charlie Pasch.

Hank slowly rolled up his sleeves, smiling doubtfully at the two men. "Of course, officers." Seemingly in a daze, he motioned for his office door. "If you wish to come this way, gentlemen, we can have some privacy."

As the two men took the chairs in front of his desk, Hank closed the door behind them. Listened for the click. Holding his breath. Wondering what to do, what to say. *Lord, give me the words.*

He had seen the papers that morning. *LOCAL PREACHER SLAIN, MOB SUSPECTED.* Had read the whole report. Had felt the punch in the gut, the hollow feeling. He had fought with this man. Had argued with this man. Had wished harm to this man.

Had discussed this man with the mob.

And now he was dead.

Hank Barton, candidate for City Council, Seventh District, had wrestled with his conscience ever since then. Wrestled with the right thing to do. How to share what he knew without being linked to the crime. Wondered whether—

"Mr. Barton?" Detective Griggs, waiting patiently in one of the guest chairs.

Hank turned from the door, smiled. "I'm sorry. I was just trying to remember something." Headed for his side of the desk. "Running for office means a lot of little details, you know, trying to make sure you remember every last thing."

What he didn't say: *I have something I'm too scared to tell you.*

"Of course." Detective Griggs leaned forward in his chair, resting elbows on wooden armrests.

The younger man, Detective Pasch, had flipped open a notepad. Testing his pen. It reminded Hank of the journalist, the one who'd done a number on him. Which reminded him of the story, the one that had sent Hank storming into Reverend Daniel Glory's office. Which reminded him of the argument, the one in front of witnesses. Which reminded him of the fight—actually, the two punches, his hitting air, Reverend Glory's connecting in a solid right cross—the one that led to the black eye.

Which reminded him of the conversation with the mob. *Who did this to you?* He'd told mobsters it was Reverend Daniel Glory, and then they'd killed him.

Hank Barton, candidate for City Council, Seventh District, shared none of this with the officers. Just answered the questions as minimally as possible—yes, he had had an argument with the deceased; no, he had not seen him since that time.

All the while, fighting the little voice. His conscience? God? All the while, just wishing the whole inconvenient mess would just go away.

As the officers left, Hank Barton, candidate for City Council, Seventh District, wished he could just crawl into a hole somewhere. He didn't deserve the people's vote.

～ 75 ～

Ross Cleaver and Bill Lamb were in the back of The Palm, in the kitchen. Giving their report to boss Ted Massey. Around them, men and girls in white smocks bustling around them, tracing paths back and forth to the freezer on the tile around them. The air filled with the sizzle of grilling meat and the crackle of fires barely under control.

"This messes up everything." Mr. Massey pacing, puffing angrily on his cigar. Throwing ashes this way and that. "You sure you didn't whack this guy?"

"Of course we didn't." Cleaver trembled. He had never seen the boss this furious. "I'm telling you, boss, he was dead when I got there." Cleaver nodded toward Lamb. "Ask him."

Lamb's eyes widened. "You said the preacher wasn't there."

"No, I said I couldn't talk to him."

"No, you said—"

Cleaver shut the man up with a glare. "The preacher was dead when we got there."

Lamb shook his head vehemently, like he expected it to rattle. "I don't know nothin.'"

Massey whirled on the man, turned and jabbed the cigar toward Lamb's face. "You telling me you din't see nothin'?"

Lamb shrunk back to avoid glowing ash. "Not a thing, boss."

"We have no idea who whacked the preacher," Cleaver pled.

Massey turned and glared a second at him, then turned back and resumed pacing and puffing. A member of the kitchen staff had to navigate around him to get some plates.

Off to the side, Massey's bodyguards stood silently, like slabs of beef. Behind the dark glasses, Cleaver couldn't tell whether they were as freaked out as he was or if they were sleeping.

Massey mumbled to himself aloud, Cleaver unsure whether they were supposed to listen or leave the boss to his thoughts. "We need that property. But with this Reverend suddenly out of the picture under mysterious circumstances, it makes it difficult to grab it."

Cleaver coughed into his hand. Leaned forward on one foot, asked tentatively, "Actually, boss, wouldn't this make the deal easier? I mean, now that this guy is out of the way, we should just—"

Massey spun around, enraged. "That church property is now gonna be tied up in some legal trap!" He stopped and sighed, shaking his head. "When the Reverend was in charge, we coulda squeezed him to give us the deed and we'd be done. Now that the ownership is in question…"

"How could the ownership be in question?" Cleaver kept his voice low and respectful. "I would think it—"

"Nobody pays you to think." Massey puffed on his cigar again. "Don't try to understand the complexities of real-estate law, Ross." Puff, puff, thinking. "You…didn't already get the deed signed over, did you?"

Cleaver struggled with an answer. Lamb shot his mouth off, "Not yet, Mr. Massey, we were still working the—"

Cleaver jumped in. "Working the board of directors!" He was not one-hundred percent sure what the dummy was about to divulge, but he was one-hundred percent sure it would have been trouble. "We did not want to press on the Reverend as long as the control of the church decisions, um…"

Massey clicked his heels together and bowed slightly. "So, the answer is no."

"Um, no." Cleaver wished he could crawl into a corner and wait the storm out. He wondered why the boss would feel comfortable airing private business in the kitchen here, but none of the staff seemed to pay attention. "We were still following your orders to the letter when this unfortunate incident occurred."

"If you had been following my orders, then we would have the property." Massey puffed on the cigar, blew smoke rings. He watched them, chuckling, seemed to have a moment of joy. Then his eyes narrowed again at Cleaver. "And then when someone came in and whacked this guy, we wouldn't be in this mess."

"Yes, sir." Cleaver tried to think of a way out of this predicament. This Lamb guy riding around with him, offering his stupid suggestions, making his stupid comments, it just made him nervous.

It threw him off his game. If Lamb didn't seem to have some connection to the boss, some hidden card up his sleeve, Cleaver woulda polished him off long ago. Left him in a ditch somewheres.

Massey was pacing again, puffing and thinking. The bodyguards did not speak, did not move. Even the dummy was silent. Waiting for what the boss would say next. All Cleaver could hear was the sizzle and the crackle and the kitchen help yelling orders at each other.

The old man stopped pacing, looking off to some indeterminate place. When he finally spoke, he sounded strange. "I don't get the note." Puzzled.

Cleaver coughed again. "What about the note?"

Massey shrugged, raising eyebrows. "Why the note?"

Cleaver nodded, not following. "I don't follow you."

"When you kill a guy, who leaves a note? This *WE'RE THE MOB, LOOK AT US, WE KILLED THIS GUY.* Why the note?"

The bodyguards weren't about to start talking now, and who knew what the dummy might suggest, so Cleaver floundered, "What difference does it make who did it? Maybe there were some other guys moving in, trying to conduct business with the preacher?"

Massey shook his head. "No, no, no. That's no good." He folded arms, now gesturing with his cigar like it was a pointer. "Why would they call attention to themselves like that?"

Cleaver coughed again. What was in those spices? "Maybe they thought the note would scare the rest of the church into leaving."

Massey squinted. "You think so?"

"I would count on it."

"Why would you be so sure of such a thing?" There was suspicion in his voice.

Cleaver changed gears. "Or, you know what? Maybe it wasn't the mob."

"Okay, I'm listening."

"Maybe some other party was involved, whacked the guy, and then put the note down there to point the finger somewheres else."

Massey gave Cleaver a scary grin. "Like who, for example?"

"Maybe a broad." Cleaver croaked, felt his throat closing up.

What was in those spices? He cleared his throat, cleared it again. "A business partner." Cleaver snapped fingers. "A member of the church."

"Yeah?"

"Yes, sir," Cleaver nodded, grinning. He had it now. "The preacher man, he was getting a little friendly with a lady in the congregation, see? And her husband finds out, comes into the man's office, confronts him, the preacher man shoots off his smart mouth, *badda-boom,* the husband takes care of him."

Massey shrugged. "And the note?"

"The husband knows he's the first guy they're gonna go after, so he writes up this note." Cleaver found his heart racing. His breath picking up. He could see the light at the end of the tunnel.

Massey paced a couple more rounds, puffing, considering. Finally, he stopped and jabbed the cigar toward Cleaver. "Go figure this thing out."

What? Cleaver sputtered, "S-sir?"

"As long as there is this big question mark over the deceased, nobody is going to take possession of that property." Massey chewed on the end of the cigar, grinning, nodding. Pleased. "Yeah, I like it. You and Lamb go make the investigation, ask around, go make like *Murder, She Wrote.*"

Cleaver squinted. "So, you want us to…?"

"We can't wait on the cops. We got to solve this murder ourselves."

– 76 –

Checking the directions she had scribbled on the scrap of paper, Bailey Andrews was on the highway, driving to the site where two boys had allegedly found human remains. By all reports, already skeletonized. That could make things tough.

Bailey cranked up her Christian music CDs for the drive, Smokie Norful and Natalie Grant and Hawk Nelson. About forty minutes into her journey—the turnoff should be any time now, off to the left—her cell phone began ringing. She reached for the knob on the car radio, turned down the music. Checked the rearview mirror and to the left and right to make sure she had her bearings. Then she glanced over to the passenger seat, grabbed the phone and looked at the caller ID.

WALTER WARING.

Blech.

Poor Walter. Poor, deluded, creepy Walter.

Back home, Bailey and Walter had sometimes run in the same circles, especially with the church group. A group of ten or so hitting the bowling alley, going to the movies, getting group rates on tickets for Christian music concerts.

She and Walter were only mutual friends. He had on occasion worked up the nerve to try to maneuver into a closer friendship with her. Bailey did not want to hurt his feelings, so she tried not to shoot him down directly. However, she had given several hints that she had nothing more than a vague but completely platonic interest in him.

Walter could not take a hint. More than one of her male friends had explained that men do not understand hints—unless you *say* something to a male of the species, then you have not actually communicated it in any way, shape, or form. Bailey was not sure she was ready to believe men were so simple, but Walter was certainly acting like Exhibit A.

When Bailey had left Chicago without so much as a goodbye to Mr. Waring—or even inviting him to her going-away party—she had hoped that would give him the vital, undiscovered clue. But if the stream of e-mails and letters and phone calls from him were any indication, the clue had not, in fact, been received.

She set the phone back on the seat, making a mental note to

TRIBULATION HOUSE — 203

program the phone to give the man his own special ring. So she could avoid picking up a call from Walter on sound alone.

Then a pang of conscience struck. Realizing she was close to her destination, which came with the ready excuse, *I've got to go, I'm at a crime scene,* she grabbed the phone again. Sighed. Flipped it open. "Andrews." Tried to sound harried. Which was not far from the truth.

"Hey! Um. It's Walter."

"Hi, Walter. I can't talk long. I'm driving to a crime scene." *Take a hint, Walter.*

"Oh. Well. I just wanted to know how things were going in Kansas."

"Pretty busy. Crime scene and all." *Please give up, Walter.*

"Yeah." Pause.

Bailey checked her scribbled directions again. "So, did you call for any particular reason?" *I moved away, Walter.*

"Um. Just wanted to stay in touch is all. The gang all rented movies the other night, and we missed you."

"Uh-huh. Well, I'm going to be at the crime scene any second now." *Please get on with your life, Walter.*

"Sure."

"So I should probably go." *Gotta go, Walter.*

"Okay."

"'Cause, you know, 'crime scene.'" *Seriously, Walter. Gotta go.*

"Uh-huh. Well, take care of yourself."

"Thanks, Walter. See ya."

"Goodb—" Cut off by the flip of a phone.

Bailey slipped the cell phone into her jacket pocket. Looking at the road again, checking her scribbled directions again, Bailey found herself thinking about her friends here in Kansas. Or to be more exact, her lack of new friends here in Kansas.

Bailey saw the turnoff, the official vehicles parked along the side of the road, and all thoughts were now on the job. She wanted to be focused, wanted to be alert.

She was struggling to not get jaded by the work. That was one of the unspoken hazards of the "dead circuit," as one of her co-workers called it—the more you work with corpses and dead flesh, the more a mental self-defense mechanism kicks in that gives you emotional distance. You begin to share the gallows humor. It's the only way to remain human.

But one wrong word in front of a close friend or family member—to whom the deceased is not a statistic, but was once a living, vital, valuable human being—and you're reminded of the immense waste and loss of human life. After one particularly humiliating, shameful incident in front of a child at a crime scene, Bailey had vowed to never forget that fact.

She pulled down the sun visor for a reminder. She had taped a piece of white paper on which she had magic-markered:

> WHOEVER SHEDS THE BLOOD OF MAN, BY MAN SHALL HIS BLOOD BE SHED; FOR IN THE IMAGE OF GOD HAS GOD MADE MAN—GENESIS 9:6.

She clung to the words as she pulled the car onto the dirt next to the state trooper's car.

Image of God.
Image of God.
Image of God.

～ 77 ～

Ross Cleaver spent most of the day in a daze. The boss had told him to find the murderer who was framing the mob. All that on top of his previous responsibilities to get the church moved and get the city council in his pocket.

This was hardly a job for a major player like Ross Cleaver. What did he look like, Matlock? It was his job to be the tough guy, not do all the sissy detective work. There was a way to solve problems, and this wasn't it. A guy gets in your way, you mow him down. Whatever it takes to make him not be in your way no more.

Let someone else ask the questions. Let someone else sort out the bodies.

But here he was, sitting at the zoo. Sitting on a bench. Trying to figure how to make this work. He barely had time to even think about his own business operations. About his towing company. About collecting on debts owed to him.

Staring downward, Cleaver focused on stirring his iced tea. Stirring, stirring, stirring.

His associate, Bill Lamb, chewed his hot dog with his mouth open. The dummy had mustard on the side of his face. "Okay, who do we got?" he mumbled out around his bite, then gulped. "Huh?"

Cleaver looked up from his tea, startled. "Wha—?"

The dummy wiped the mustard off with his sleeve. "What have we got? What comes next?"

"I don't know." Cleaver pulled the spoon from his tea, set it on the wooden bench. Wondered if this was what shell shock was like. "We got to talk to some political guys," he mumbled, staring at the tea dripping off the spoon onto the cracked wood. "We gotta..." He trailed off, reached out, and stuck his index finger in the puddle of liquid.

Lamb finished his plastic cup of beer. Crumpled it in his hand, made a face pretending he was using superstrength, threw it under-handed into the trash barrel. "Now," he said, wiping his hands together, "we're supposed to get all Scooby-Doo."

Cleaver squinted at him. "Huh?"

"You know, drive around in the Mystery Machine, go around solving crimes. Solve the murder of that preacher guy."

"This ain't TV."

Lamb deflated. "Yeah."

Cleaver perked up. Something the dummy said..."Say, who would benefit from the death of this preacher guy?"

"Well, the note said—"

"Forget the note! Think about what this guy was all about—he was spouting this 'end of the world' stuff, right?"

"Right. So what?"

"So what business that would be a competitor do we know of?"

"You mean, like another church?"

"No. No." Cleaver tried to figure out how to lead him. Make the dummy think he was onto something. "I'm just saying, if this preacher guy is telling people there ain't no future…what business do we know of that is all about people *being* here for the future?"

"Like some other religion?"

"Listen to me." Cleaver leaned in. "The *future*."

"Right."

Cleaver sighed with drama. "What company predicates its entire business model around people being here for the *future?*"

"Um…"

"You know…ice cream…"

"Oh! Uh…that place! That place your ex-wife works."

"Right," Cleaver grinned. "Frozen Futures." He rapped his knuckles on the picnic table, stood to go. "We go to Frozen Futures, we're gonna find our killer."

"You think so?"

"I know it." Headed for the car, Lamb following, Cleaver couldn't help but grin. This was perfect. Solve two problems—get the boss off his back, and give Mikolaczyk a shiv in the ribs in the process.

Kill two birds.

— 78 —

Another house. Another knock on another door. Another tentative greeting for Hank Barton, candidate for City Council, Seventh District.

Another person not registered to vote. "But these are the last days, so why bother, right?"

"You do know that Reverend Glory's deadline has already come and gone, right?"

"Doesn't mean I should register to vote."

Another fake smile from Hank Barton, candidate for City Council, Seventh District. "Thank you for your time."

On to the next house.

— 79 —

The FBI/Kansas City Police Joint Task Force against organized crime was called to order. Detective Tom Griggs sat back in his desk chair. Baseball in hand, rubbing his thumb on the stitching.

Charlie watched. Bit his lip. A baseball like that should be in a glass case.

Special Agent O'Malley, chomping gum like a cowboy, was sharing the results of their tap on suspected crime boss Ted Massey. "I'll admit, when we started our watch on Massey, I thought it was going to be tough."

Griggs leaned back and set one foot on his desk. "How do you mean?"

"All we had was speculation and hearsay. Massey seemed to keep his counsel to himself. In public, all of Massey's conversations with his friends, family members, and employees—as far as we could ascertain through our previous means—were about legitimate business. We were worried we would never get close enough to find the difference." O'Malley grinned. Pointed at Griggs. "But that sprinkler job was a work of genius."

Griggs smiled. Shrugged. "I knew it was worth a shot."

Charlie frowned. "What are you talking about?"

Griggs leaned forward and gave Charlie a patient look. "Do you remember when we paid Mr. Massey a visit?"

"Sure." Charlie thought back to the weird trip to The Palm. Griggs had been so secretive. Acting so loopy. Demanding a meeting with a reputed crime boss. The entire conversation had been so vague, it begged the question, why bother? Then the lightbulb went on. "The guy on the ladder!"

O'Malley nodded. "That's right. It was so simple that Massey never expected it. When you guys barged in there, Massey was so focused on Griggs—trying to figure out what a Kansas City cop was doing there—that he never thought to check the sprinkler after our men finished 'fixing' it. We installed listening devices in the back dining room, the kitchen, and the back office."

"Sometimes the simplest things work best of all." Griggs sat up. Set the baseball on the stand. "So, now you have your listening devices in place. What has it got you so far?"

Special Agent Harper pulled a large fold of paper from a case. "Now that we hear some of the back-room discussions, we know that Massey has several low-rent mobsters working the streets for him. It is exactly like we suspected—he is pushing certain pressure points to get local businesses to move. In particular, around this area." She spread the map out on Griggs's desk. Pointed to a red felt-pen circle. "It's a depressed area. Even without the problem of organized crime, the business district is struggling already."

"Yeah." Charlie leaned in, looking at the map. "Several businesses around there are shut down or wheezing."

"So what does that mean to Massey?" Griggs absentmindedly grabbed the baseball again. "If his goal is not to bleed protection money out of them, then why is he going to the trouble?" He started rolling the ball from hand to hand. "Even if he wants that property, why can't he just wait them out? Buy them out? He's a major businessman. Why take the risk with a lot of low-rent muscle?"

Harper pointed to another line on the map. "There is some major construction coming through that area. The mayor is coaxing a big developer to come in and build a major shopping center." She looked up from the map. "The most likely place to build is right there in the middle. If Massey sits back and waits, there is the risk that this development deal will go public."

"And everyone who owns property along there suddenly becomes rich." Charlie grinned crookedly. "If they develop that district—shopping centers, strip malls, restaurants—it would be worth millions to anyone even adjacent to it."

"That's right, Charlie-boy." O'Malley set a stack of printouts on the desk. "By the way, the transcripts make for some interesting reading."

Griggs grabbed some of the papers and started skimming. "Anything in here about the Reverend Glory case?"

"Actually, you'd be surprised." O'Malley recounted Massey's orders to two of his thugs, a Ross Cleaver and a Bill Lamb, demanding that they go out and solve the murder for him. When the FBI man finished the story, he chuckled. "So if they solve the murder, that could save you guys a lot of work."

Griggs chuckled. "Funny."

Charlie grabbed his notebook, started flipping through it. "I still think it's significant that Glory made such an arrogant prediction. One that failed to come true."

"You said it yourself—it happens all the time." Griggs exchanged an amused look with O'Malley.

"Sure," Charlie said, finding his place in his notebook, "AD 950 in France. A man named Adso of Montier-en-Der predicted the rise of the Antichrist, which he said would happen when the line of the French kings failed.

"AD 1200 in Italy. Followers of a mystic named Joachim of Fiore believed the new millennium would begin somewhere between the years 1200 and 1260.

"There are also false alarms in 1600, 1666, 1736, 1844, 1908, 1925—"

Griggs cut him off. "But those were all a long time ago. People are more sophisticated now."

Charlie sighed. "In 1988, former NASA rocket engineer Edgar

Whisenant thought he had the date figured out. He printed up a pamphlet and sold millions of copies. He was wrong.

"In 1992, a man in Korea named"—Charlie squinted at his notes—"Lee Jang-rim convinced his followers the Rapture was coming, but only for the extremely faithful. Reportedly, some women had abortions to make sure they weren't too heavy to be lifted up to heaven. The man bilked his followers out of some four million dollars."

O'Malley rolled his eyes at Agent Harper. Chomped gum more loudly.

"The Tokyo subway gas attacks in the mid-'90s were engineered by a cult that believed its leader was Jesus come back in the flesh.

"In 1997, a church leader in St. Louis claimed—"

"We get it, Charlie," Griggs sighed. "We get it. A lot of people got it wrong. Which, if Glory is just one more in a long line of wrong people, makes it less likely—"

"But whenever one of these fringe groups latches onto their personal plans for Jesus, they get a little excited about it."

"Excited?"

"I'm trying to be polite. But these are the sorts of people who went out in 1999 and dug bunkers and stocked up on cans of beans, waiting for Y2K to shut down modern civilization."

"Why, was that in the Bible?"

"No," Charlie said. "And neither is October 17. But that doesn't stop the fringe from thinking the universe revolves around their plans."

Harper spoke up. "So you think that one of Glory's followers got caught up in all this, and went berserk after it didn't happen?"

Charlie nodded. "Maybe."

O'Malley winked at Charlie. "So, Charlie-boy, you're one of those church types. How did you avoid getting caught up in all the hysteria?"

"Because the Bible says not to get caught up in a lot of conspiracy theories. When Jesus comes back, I want to be doing the work, not ignoring it. I don't want to get caught with my nose in a bunch of charts and graphs."

Griggs stood. "I think Charlie has the right idea. Let's get back to work."

— 80 —

Inside the studio, forensic artist Bailey Andrews was surrounded by sculptures and paintings in various stages of being finished. Bailey was standing in front of a small table, where a white skull was perched on a metal stand. She looked up as the door opened, then she smiled. "Hi, Julie."

"I just wanted to see what it looks like."

"What?"

"Your work."

"You got a strong stomach?"

"Uh-huh." Julie stepped slowly toward the skull that had Bailey's attention. "I watch TV and stuff."

Bailey's eyes were on the skull. "It's not quite the same." She was hunched over, hands on her knees, gazing intently.

"What are you doing?"

"It's called facial reconstruction."

"No, I mean, what are y'all *doing*."

Bailey stood and rubbed her eyes. The distraction was okay. She needed a break anyway. "In a case where they find the remains of some unidentified person, but there is not enough soft tissue remaining for recognition or image enhancement techniques, we use something called facial reconstruction."

"You're going to, what, build it a new face?"

"Maybe. The two methods are two-dimensional drawings and three-dimensional clay models. The drawing would be created by working from photographs of the clean skull with tissue depth markers placed at various anatomical points." At the various points, she pointed a pinky, without touching the skull. "Or we may create a clay model, creating a plaster cast of the skull. Then we build on facial muscles and a final layer to represent the skin. Right now I'm using sculpture to create a three-dimensional facial reconstruction."

"And what does that do?"

"We use it to help authorities identify skeletal remains. I am going to construct the facial features based on the underlying cranial structure. It's called the Gatliff-Snow Method."

Julie's gaze wandered around Bailey's studio, which was filled with paintings, sculptures, and numerous other objects and pieces of equipment. Not much there she could identify.

"What's all this other stuff?"

"I do a lot of different things besides facial reconstruction."

"Like what?"

"Well, I might be asked to take a fugitive's photo and age-enhance it, I might be—"

"What's that?"

"You know, a fugitive who has been on the run for several years, the official photograph is no longer going to look like him. So I create a sketch to indicate how he would have aged. And what he looks like now."

"Oh."

"I could also reconstruct a traffic accident, I've been asked to—"

"How did you become a...a...person who does this kind of stuff?"

"When I was a kid, I was an artist."

"Artists don't usually go into crime-fighting."

"I wouldn't call this 'crime-fighting.' Unfortunately, I rarely stop a crime before it happens. All my work is about coming in after the fact and trying to bring closure to the victim's family. Try and give the police what they need to arrest the right person."

"But if the person killed once, you stop them before they kill again."

"Yeah, I guess you could look at it that way." Bailey looked at the skull on the metal stand again. *That isn't going to save you, is it? Who are you? What is your story?*

"How did an artist become what you do?"

"I went fishing a lot with my dad as a kid. My dad and my brothers."

"Fishing?"

"Right. Anyway, one time we were out on one of our fishing trips, we were out deep in this property, way back in the woods. And I found a body."

"Eww."

"It was an animal."

"Oh."

"But it was still pretty shocking. It was a horse. It had been decaying for some time. My dad told my brothers and me to stay away while he called the authorities—it turned out someone had shot the horse. My brothers didn't want to be anywhere near, but I found myself staring—just staring—trying to take in every detail. The way nature was participating in the horse's decomposition. The way everything was part of an order, part of a design."

"You saw God in a dead horse?"

"I don't know that I would go that far. Don't get me wrong— He was there, He's everywhere. But that's when I realized—I was seeing that horse like an artist would. Every bug. Every fly. Every maggot."

Apparently, the conversation finally hit Julie full force. Her gaze suddenly shifted to the human skull on the table, her face went white, and she ran from the room making a retching sound.

Bailey turned back to the skull. "I told her it wasn't for weak stomachs."

— 81 —

It was after children's church. At first, everything seemed to be proceeding as normal. Parents and children were lined up for the exit. Pastor Wallace was checking each child before they left, making sure that the sticker on the child's clothing matched the ticket being presented by the adult.

Charlie and the other children's church helpers were setting up for the second service. He was heading for the soundboard when he heard a shriek.

"Where is he? What did you do with my son?" The frantic woman ran up, dug sharp nails into Charlie's arm.

"What's the matter, ma'am?"

"My son isn't here! Where is he?"

"I-I don't know." Charlie flashed eyes around the church gym. He hadn't expected any emergencies. "What's his name? What does he look like?"

"Jack." Tense. Fearful. "Red hair, freckles. He was wearing a striped shirt."

Charlie looked toward the back of the gym, at the throng of kids by the stage. A sea of brown and white and Hispanic faces. Kicking himself for not being more familiar with their names. "You don't see him over there?"

"He's not there." The woman's voice trembled.

Charlie glanced toward the line of parents by the gym's front doors. The rest of the children's church team busily checking parents' tickets against stickers on the kids' clothing. Patiently keeping parents antsy from ducking through the wrong door, cheerfully helping those in line to be processed quickly as possible. No loose kids by the doors—certainly none that fit Jack's description.

Charlie rushed to the stage, the group of kids waiting to be claimed. They were playing with an assortment of balloons, bouncing them around. "Hey, kids! Is one of you Jack?" Just in case. Most of the kids kept their attention on the balloons, a few were polite enough to shake their heads. "Hey!" He waved his arms. "Did anyone see where Jack *went?*"

The kids kept at their game. Charlie was about to stop them, when a girl with braids pointed to the kitchen. "He and a man went that way!"

A man?

Charlie turned to the woman, who was right behind him. "Did you expect your husband to get him?"

"*Nobody* else was supposed to get him!" The woman's eyes went wide with horror. "If it was my husband...they said he would never find us..."

Charlies grabbed a nearby children's worker, and reminded her of the drill: 1) notify police officer and ushers; 2) close all exits; 3) check restrooms and odd rooms. He raced for the kitchen, burst through the door, taking a quick inventory. Nobody. The smell of bacon and eggs in the air, pots and pans from the choir's breakfast cleaned and drying in the rack.

Charlie held his breath and listened. The room was silent except for the drip-drip of the rack and low hum of the industrial fridge—

Click.

Charlie jumped for the fire exit. He hit the bar with his arm and pushed out into the open air. Squinted at the blinding sun. "Jack!"

To the left, toward the woods, he heard a small cry: "I don't wanna go!"

Lord, help me reach this child in time.

Shielding his eyes, Charlie stumbled across the pavement toward the woods behind the church. "Stop!" he yelled into the dense green. "Police!"

He burst into evergreens, listening for voices, for heavy breathing, for the crunch of brown leaves and dry pine needles. Charlie tried to imagine the perimeter of the woods. The church was behind him. There was a highway to his left—what direction was that, north? West? He had no idea. He vaguely knew a subdivision was somewhere ahead of him. Or was it off to the side?

He didn't know what else to do, so he started forward again, taking the natural path. No idea whether the assailant took it. As he picked up the pace, Charlie pulled the cell from his pocket and called 9-1-1. He gave his name and badge number, called for an amber alert, called for officers to surround the area.

All the while listening for telltale signs of the man and little boy. Watching for footprints, broken tree limbs, any evidence a person had passed this way.

He reached a clearing, sun streaming down on a circle of grass and wildflowers. Stopped and listened again. He heard a crackle of twigs behind him and reached instinctively for his weapon—remembering once again he didn't have—

A sharp pain on the back of his head. Charlie hit the ground like a sack of potatoes. *Don't lose it, Charlie,* he told himself.

Somewhere in the darkness, a voice yelled, "I won't go back!"

He struggled to feel his hands. *Don't lose it, Charlie.* Struggled to feel the grass. *Don't*—clutch the grass—*lose*—push against the grass—*it.*

Another sharp pain in his back. Charlie opened his eyes, tasted blood, used all his strength to roll over.

A tall man with stubble and greasy yellow hair towered over him, brandishing a large tree branch. "Why can't you leave us alone?"

The man lunged, swinging again. Charlie gritted his teeth and kicked out at the man's knee, hard. The man yelped and fell to the ground. Charlie, head still spinning, sat up and clutched the man's hair, swinging with his other fist. He knuckled the man in the face, not nearly as hard as he had hoped.

"Stay down," Charlie croaked, blood trickling down his lips. *Don't lose it, Charlie.* "You're under arrest." Charlie pushing up on his hands and knees, pushing up off the ground.

The man's eyes went wide with hate. He swung around to attack. If the man got his bearings, Charlie was dead—who knew what would happen to the boy. Charlie got on his right knee, grabbed the man's left elbow, and yanked. As the other jerked toward him, Charlie elbowed him in the head with all the strength he had left.

The man down, Charlie struggled to his feet. The world spinning. Charlie panting, spitting blood, trying to see if the kid was okay.

He saw stars as the world went black.

― 82 ―

The next stop for Hank Barton, candidate for City Council, Seventh District: The Kansas City Police Department. Detective Tom Griggs was in and available. "Step this way, councilor. Or, um, what do I call you?"

"Hank is fine."

The detective showed Hank the door to his office. Hank felt the world closing in around him as the other man closed the door and sat down behind the desk.

The detective shuffled some papers and set them aside. "What can I do for you, Mr. Barton?"

"I told you, call me Hank." He sat back, forcing himself to be cool. He forced a smile. The same expression that got such a workout on the campaign trail.

The other man was all business. "What can I do you for you?" There was something in the man's voice, some dark familiarity, but Hank couldn't place what it was.

He gulped and pretended to be brave. Took the leap. "When we spoke a few days ago, officer"—*look up from your shoes, Hank, make eye contact*—"I'm not certain I was entirely open with you."

"Hmm." The man behind the desk leaned forward. His face remained expressionless. "You're not certain."

Hank paused. Shook his head tentatively. "No, sir."

The man looked at him. "You are aware that this is a murder investigation."

Hank was looking down again. "Yes, sir."

There was a long pause, the man apparently waiting for Hank to explain himself. His heart was in his throat, so he could not.

Finally, the man asked, "In what way are you not certain you were entirely open with us?"

Look up, make eye contact, be brave. Fake it if you have to. "I *did* have a dispute with the deceased."

"Reverend Daniel Glory?"

"Yes."

The man seemed to be losing interest. "You told us as much in our interview." He began checking through his stack of papers on the desk.

"Yes, but..." Hank interlocked his fingers on his lap, fought the urge to fidget. Looking down at his shoes again. *When was the last time they were polished?* "...it was more than a simple dispute. It was a fight." He paused, looked up again. Looked into the eyes of the law. "I took a swing at him."

"Really?" the detective raised an eyebrow. But did not actually sound surprised. "You tried to hit a minister?"

Hank blushed. "I'm not proud. It was not my finest moment." He found his interlocked fingers twisting back and forth nervously, disengaged them and grabbed the wooden arms on the chair. "There was a story in the newspaper, and we had a disagreement...well, I suppose what led to the altercation is not entirely salient."

"You mean this story here?" The officer pulled a clipping from under a pile of papers. Held it up to show it. *CANDIDATE LISTENS TO VOICE OF GOD, THE PEOPLE.* He looked toward Hank, who nodded and went back to looking at his shoes.

"Yes, that is the one. I felt like the newspaper reporter had already gone out of his way to misrepresent my worldview, and then this two-bit so-called prophet had to stick in his..." Hank trailed off. Shook himself back to the present. "I'm sorry. I shouldn't speak ill of the dead."

The man set the clipping back down on his desk. Skimmed the story. "It seems you God types can never seem to get together on what you all believe."

Hank sat up straighter, something rising within him. "Officer, I cannot excuse my behavior, but you can't blame God for how some of his servants act."

The air changed in the room. The man behind the desk seemed to shrink back. "That's what Charlie was saying..."

"I'm sorry?" Hank frowned. "Charlie who?"

The detective recovered himself, shaking his head. Pushed the clipping back to wherever it must have belonged. "So far, Mr. Barton, you have not shared anything new." He leaned forward, a dark grin on his face. "What did you come to tell me?"

Hank felt his throat tighten up. His ears started to ring. He gulped and forced himself to forge ahead. "I know who killed Reverend Daniel Glory."

~ 83 ~

I needed to go for a walk. Just walk. Sitting in the car, I felt closed in. I didn't know where else to go, so I drove to the mall. I wasn't thrilled to be around a lot of people, but I needed to be able to just walk and walk.

I was getting pretty frantic. I needed to set up an alibi, some proof that I was nowhere near the Reverend when he died. But I had no idea how to do that. How do you do that?

Perhaps this was a proof of my innocence—the fact that I didn't know how to create an alibi. A common sinner would be able to snap his fingers and come up with a fake alibi eight ways to Sunday.

Ignoring the people around me, ignoring the storefronts, I tried to think up a place to go. Someone I could turn to. Someone who would vouch for my alibi.

I thought about the boat dealer. They owed me. I'd given them a lot of business. I'd spent a lot of money on that boat.

Ugh. The boat. The boat with the garage-shaped hole in it. What was I going to do about that? I could not very well return the boat for a refund now, could I? If only I had sprung for the insurance. But given the impending Rapture and all, it had seemed like a waste of money.

Ugh. The neighbor's garage. The garage with a boat-shaped hole in it. The Mendels would expect me to pay for it. What was I going to do about that? Maybe I didn't have boat insurance, but would my home insurance cover it?

Wait—insurance! Of course! That could solve my money trouble lickety-split. Money to pay off the mob. Money to pay off the neighbor's garage. Maybe a few bucks left over for my trouble.

I looked up to see where I was. An ice-cream place. I went in and spoke with the kid behind the counter. "Do you have a phone book?"

"A phone?"

"A phone book?"

"A whut?"

I tried to smile. Tried to be calm. "I need a telephone book. You know, with all the phone numbers in it?"

The freckled boy adjusted his cap. "We only sell ice cream here."

I had a little more luck at the next place I tried, a pet store. At the counter, a man and his son were purchasing a big snake. Ugh.

When it was my turn, I gave the woman behind the counter my friendliest smile. "Hi, this may sound weird, but I need a telephone book."

The lady frowned. It was not attractive. "A phone book?"

"Yes, may I borrow your phone book?"

"Did you try the phone booth? They usually have phone books."

I hadn't thought of that. "Do they still make phone booths?"

"Why wouldn't they still make phone booths?"

"Well, you know, everybody has cell phones now." I pulled my cell phone from my pocket. "See? Everybody has one."

"I don't have one."

"You don't have a cell phone?"

"There was always—"

I shook my head. "Wait—do you have a phone book? I need to borrow your phone book."

The lady shrugged and looked under the counter. She pulled

out a massive yellow book and plopped it on the counter. "Here you go."

"Thank you." I grabbed the book and started flipping pages. BATTERIES–BEAUTY. ELECTROLYSIS–EMBROIDERY GRANITE–GREASE.

Ah. INSURANCE. Now, what was the name of my insurance agent? I started looking through the various agencies. The various company ads. Finally found a name that looked familiar—and, checking the address, saw that it looked familiar too. This seemed like the guy. I looked up at the woman, now answering someone's questions about lizards. Ugh. "Can I use your phone?"

"But you have a phone."

"I know, but I don't know what the reception will be like in here." But she had already turned her attention back to the topic of lizards. Ugh. I picked up the massive yellow tome and made for the door.

"Hey! I still need that!"

"I'm just going over here." I went over by the door. I didn't know how good my cell-phone reception would be in here, so I went out into the mall. I paused by the pet shop's window, watched the puppies frolic in the display window.

Then I went to the set of benches. Before I had a chance to get situated, my phone chirped. I checked the ID in the little window. The wife. "Hi, honey, I am sort of—"

"Aren't you even coming to the hospital?"

"Honey, I am in such a—"

"Don't you even care whether your son lives or dies?"

"I have to do something. Just keep me posted on—"

She hung up on me.

I stared at the phone a second. Trying to remember what I was doing. Wait—insurance. Right. Get set up with the insurance company, they pay off the boat, they pay off the truck, I use the money to pay back the mob, I use the money to pay to repair the Mendels's garage. Everybody's happy.

I found my agent in the phone book again, dialed him up. Once we got past the pleasantries, he asked, "What can I do for you?"

"I need to get some insurance on a boat. Do you insure boats?"

"We sure do. Can you give me some details?"

"It's a 2008 Bayliner 192."

"Ooh. Those are nice."

"Tell me about it. It was sweet when I took it out on the lake. I just wish I could still use it."

"What do you mean?"

"The boy was backing it in the yard and smacked right into the neighbor's garage."

"Was there any damage?"

"Oh, it's pretty smashed up. I also have to pay for the huge hole in the garage too. Does the boat insurance cover that?"

"Let me get this straight—you want to buy insurance for something that's already been wrecked?"

"Exactly. So, if we can get this deal signed right away—"

"But we can't do that."

"What do you mean?"

"I can't write up a policy on that."

"Sure you can. You just said."

"Listen, if you wait until you need the insurance, then it's too late."

"How can it be too late? I need the insurance right now."

"But we can't do that."

"Look, are you going to help me out or not?"

"If you have already destroyed your boat, then we can't help you. You really should have insured it as soon as you knew you were buying it. Now it's too late."

I hung up on him. I had to think. I had to figure this out.

I owed the mob a large amount of money.

What was I going to do?

~ 84 ~

Detective Tom Griggs and Detective Charlie Pasch were in Griggs's office burning the midnight oil. Charlie had just finished telling Griggs about the big excitement at church.

Griggs said, "So what happened?"

"Well, they found us both in the woods there."

"You were both unconscious?"

"I wouldn't say I was unconscious..."

"You were unconscious, weren't you?"

"I was dazed, maybe," Charlie said. "I mean, the guy did club me in the head."

Griggs *tsk-tsked* the kid. Needling him.

"But I was able to subdue him."

"Right before you blacked out."

"I did not black out."

Sitting on either side of Griggs's desk, the two men were reading through transcripts provided by their friends in the FBI. Reading through reports, trying to connect the dots. One man was dead, one man was putting the squeeze on failing businesses, but they could not find the connection.

But it had to be there. It had to be.

Charlie looked up from the folder set in front of him. "What about that note?"

"Which note?"

"The one on the body claiming to be written by the mob. If Massey's boys killed the Reverend, why leave the note?"

"There were two people in that room." Griggs pulled up the sheet and looked at it. "Someone clubbed him in the back of the head with the blunt object—"

"The trophy."

"—and somebody stabbed him in the chest with the letter opener."

"It can't be one person?"

"Why wipe your prints off one object, and then leave them on the other?" Griggs shook his head. "No, there's something weird about this. If we find Cleaver and Lamb, maybe they can answer our questions."

"You know, it was not necessarily written by the mob."

"What?"

"The note."

"I know. We've been through that."

"No," Charlie said, sitting back in the chair, "I'm saying that the person who wrote the note was not necessarily claiming to be in the mob."

Griggs sat up. "Okay."

"The note just said, 'This is what happens when you cross the mob.'"

"Right."

"So maybe this was written by a person who was not in the mob, but wanted to make a statement about the mob."

Griggs squinted. "Okay?"

"That's really all I had."

"So…we haven't really learned anything from this conversation."

"Nope." Charlie looked back down at the transcript. Murmured, "A difference that makes no difference *is* no difference."

"What was that?"

"What?"

"What did you just mumble?"

"Oh. *A difference that makes no difference* is *no difference.* I read it in a *Star Trek* novel."

"Uh-huh."

They didn't speak again for a long time. Finally, Griggs needed a break, ordered a pizza. The kid asked for pepperoni, but Griggs was placing the order, so they got sausage and black olive.

As soon as it arrived, Griggs opened the box on his desk. The smell of sausage poured out. "Have a slice?"

Charlie looked up from the folder, rubbed his eyes. "Sure." As they were chomping, Charlie got that geek sparkle in his eye. Griggs braced himself for whatever it was.

"I was thinking about Carl Kolchak."

"Who's that?"

"He's a newspaper reporter."

"Here in Kansas City?"

"No, on TV. He worked for a small news service in Chicago, and every week he seemed to run across monsters."

"What, psychos? Serial killers?"

"No, monsters—you know, vampires, wolfmen, stuff like that."

"Oh." Griggs took another bite of pizza. Chewing, he said, "It figures."

"And then I was also thinking about Jack McGee."

"Was he one of the monsters?"

"No, he was a reporter for the *National Register*."

"Here in Kansas City?"

"No, on *The Incredible Hulk*."

"I should have known."

"And I was just thinking how here were these two hard-luck newspaper reporters chasing after monster stories, one never actually catching up to his monster, the other always catching the monster, but they never let him print the story."

"Yeah?"

"Yeah."

Griggs finished off one slice. Wiped grease and sauce off his mouth. "And?"

"And what?"

"And why were you thinking about this?"

"Well, I was also thinking how the Hulk series was produced by the same guy who produced *The Six Million Dollar Man*."

"What, the show with Lee Majors?"

"Right."

"Okay..."

"And so you have this story about this scientist who is traveling around the country, trying to find some big scientific cure for his condition, and you have this show about this bionic man who goes out on these missions for this science agency…"

"Okay."

"And then you also have two reporters who both chase after these unusual stories."

"Right."

"So it seems really easy to sort of connect the dots and have them all cross paths. Kolchak stumbles on some government project, which involves the bionic man, which is a government secret, and then the Hulk is there, which brings McGee…" Charlie broke off. Shrugged. "The idea has not actually crystallized yet. But I feel like it's right there on the edge of my mind." Took a bite of pizza. "You know, like a dream when you first wake up."

"How do you come up with this stuff?"

"Well, those were all in the '70s. They were all on TV within a few years of each other."

"Why stop there? You might as well add *Star Trek*."

"*Star Trek* was the '60s."

"Are you sure?" Griggs noticed Charlie's dark look. "Sorry. Of course you're sure." The two fell silent, munching their pizza. Finally, Griggs said, "You got all these stories bottled up inside you, don't you?"

"Yeah, I guess."

"I thought your friend told you to stop writing other people's stories. You know, write a story of your own."

Charlie thought over his partner's words. Nodded. "Yeah. Maybe that is the best way. I just gotta come up with some ideas, I guess."

Griggs wiped his fingers off on a handkerchief. "Hey, I have something for you." He started sorting through the stacks of papers on his desk. Found a particular sheet and, grinning, handed it over to Charlie. "I saw this online and printed it out for you."

Charlie wiped his hands on his pants and read it:

Bible Scholar Solves Mystery of the Great Pyramid, Riddle of the Sphinx

Throughout the ages, scholars have pondered the mysteries of Ancient Egypt, including the mysterious Great Pyramid and the riddle of the enigmatic Sphinx. Who built the Pyramid? Who carved the Sphinx? And, even more puzzling, for what purpose? Archeologist and Bible scholar Lester Helman shares his controversial answers in his new book, *Bible Prophecy and the Mysteries of Ancient Egypt*—in which he unlocks the secret calendar that counts down to the return of Christ.

"Oh, great." Charlie looked up from the paper and snorted. "Another crackpot."

"Just keep reading."

Based on the extensive research conducted by the late Reverend Daniel Glory, Helman unlocks the secret numbers found in the earliest books of the Bible, as well as the Great Pyramid and Sphinx. These secret numbers foretell the First and Second Coming of Christ.

Helman reveals the meaning behind the numbers in Genesis, Exodus, and Numbers, explaining many of the Bible's stories as scientific parables, linked to secret codes embedded within molecules.

"It's just one more person cashing in." Charlie set the sheet down. "Fabricating some complicated theory about the end times."

"Yeah, but you study that kind of stuff. You're a religious person."

"This guy is a crackpot. Not everybody who claims to quote the Bible is a Christian. In fact, not everybody who claims to quote the Bible is actually quoting the Bible."

Something about the comment made Griggs mad. He spent the rest of the night trying to figure out why.

～ 85 ～

Bailey Andrews, forensic artist, continued her work on the skull. The John Doe. She'd been given the task of helping the sheriff's department make a positive ID. In all, the process took her the better part of two weeks.

She popped a CD in the player—Everett Lester's *Living Water.* She hit "repeat" and let the music just play over and over for hours on end. It was how she got into the zone.

She consulted the full report from the forensic team. Based on the skeleton and other evidence at the crime scene, they had determined it to be a man in his late 60s. About five-foot-ten. On the heavy side. Caucasian.

The skull indicated the man had likely died from a bullet in the back of the head. Buried in what was then an undeveloped vacant plot in the middle of Kansas. The area had grown up in brush, only recently cleared away by an archeology class. However, that group's main focus had been the neighboring lot. They had not gotten permission to dig in this particular lot, so they had left it alone.

Leaving the deceased to be discovered by two boys playing. Digging as part of some game.

Now they just needed to know who the deceased was. *Who are you?* Bailey found herself wondering. *Does your family miss you? Do they lie awake nights wondering what happened to you?*

On a good day, the forensics team had more information to go on. Some leads. A huge stack of printouts, listing all missing persons on file who might match the John Doe. Vital data, name, date of birth, date and place of last contact, race, sex, weight, hair color, eye color, any unique characteristics—any information available about scars, prosthetics, clothing, anything at all that would make this person stand out from a sea of printouts.

Bailey knew that the forensic anthropologist had gone through the whole set of printouts by hand, checking one by one. It had probably taken a couple of days.

But there were no matches with this guy. No matches with any reports filed with missing persons. No matches with any dental records on file. No possibility of checking for fingerprints. Despite what they made it look like on TV, the big databases were still hit-and-miss. Not every person made it into them. And if the John Doe had been a loner, maybe nobody had filled out a missing-persons report.

And since they could not find him on any files, that meant they had to do this the hard way.

Bailey studied the skull. Keeping in mind the anthropologist's findings, she took careful note of unique features, from the jawline to the brow to the nasal cavity.

The first step was to make a cast of the skull. Bailey made small holes to insert vinyl pegs for measuring facial tissue depth. She consulted the chart for standard thickness of skin for a Caucasian male of heavy weight, used modeling clay for muscles and features around the nose, mouth, cheeks, and eyes. A thin layer of clay went over the mold. She shaped facial features, tried different wigs and artificial eyes before choosing the final look. She added makeup, like an embalmer uses to dress up the dead.

Finally, twelve days after she had started, the sculpture was the way she wanted it. It was not perfect—the process did not tell her whether the subject should be wearing glasses, or have some unique hairstyle. All she had was the shape of the face.

When she got to the almost-finished stage, Bailey took some isopropyl alcohol and dripped it into the inside corner of each eye. When enough alcohol was applied, the twin pools would stream down the sides of the face like tears. It was a trick she had picked up from Emily Craig, the noted forensic anthropologist and artist. When a tear falls from a person's eyes, it follows a predictable pattern down the face. These "tears" flowing on the sculpture would determine whether the reconstruction was true to life.

Satisfied, Bailey made a mold out of rubber and fiberglass plaster, and then polished it. The final step was to take a picture. Often, such a photo would show up on flyers, in newspapers, and on television.

In the meantime, of course, the sheriff and his people were following up other clues from the scene. The sheriff had occasionally been in touch with her the past week, but had largely left her to her work. They would put together their efforts as soon as she had this picture ready.

Bailey gazed for a minute at the finished product. Tried to imagine who this poor man was. Hoped they'd be able to figure out his identity. *Then we can contact your family, and bring them some sense of closure.*

⌐ 86 ⌐

A block away from Frozen Futures, Ross Cleaver and Bill Lamb parked in the alley. Cleaver turned to the other man, said, "Okay, here's the plan."

"I'm listening."

"Shut up."

"I was just tellin' you—"

"*Shut up.*" Cleaver turned to stare out the window, gritting his teeth. Wondering whether he could work this to get rid of Lamb too. Maybe blame Mikolaczyk for the stray bullet. He breathed through his nose, forced himself to seem relaxed, turned back to Lamb with a friendly grin. "Just let me say this..."

"I'm listening."

Urk. "I know." *Grr.* "Thank you." Breathe in. Breathe out. There. "We need to send a message that nobody messes in Mr. Massey's business. Right?"

Lamb nodded a dummy nod.

"But we do it in such a way that nobody can pin it on us. Right?"

Lamb paused, like he was waiting for something. As the silence went on, he nodded another dummy nod. "But the boss don't like notes."

"I know. I know. You see, that is exactly why I just said, 'We do it in such a way that nobody can pin it on us.' If I had meant something different than that, I would have used different words."

"I was just agreeing with you."

"No, you were arguing with me."

"No, Ross, I—"

"Shut up." Breathe in. Breathe out. Make sure this guy don't get back to the car. "Okay, here is the thing: We need to draw Mik's attention—"

"Mik?"

"Mikolaczyk."

"Oh."

"The big guy without the neck."

"Right."

Breathe in. Breathe out. "May I proceed?" Another long silence. The dummy musta thought it was a rhetorical question. "Huh?"

"Oh. Right. Go on."

Breathe in. Breathe out. "We need to distract Mik. While he's looking the other way, we take him."

Lamb wrinkled his nose. "You think so?"

"Who's running this operation?"

"But the boss said—"

"Who is running this operation?"

Another long silence. "You, Ross."

"Stop calling me that." Cleaver gripped the steering wheel with white knuckles. It would all be resolved soon. "We watch for Enid to leave the office for lunch. I am going to park in front of Frozen Futures."

"Frozen...?"

"The ice-cream place."

"Oh."

"You go in first, fast. I stop the car, you step out and just walk right on in there and demand to see Mik—Mikolaczyk."

"What if I can't say it?"

"Say it?"

"His name."

Cleaver sighed. There had to be an easier way to whack a guy. "Try it."

"Mickle...Mickey...Mickle-AT-ose..."

"Just ask for 'Mr. Mike.'"

"Who's that?"

"It's the same guy." Breathe in. Breathe out. "People who have trouble pronouncing his name call him 'Mr. Mike.'"

"Why not call him—"

"Shut up!" *Keep it together, Cleaver, you're almost there. Relax.* "That's what they call him. Now, you go in and you demand to see him."

"What if he's already there?"

"Then he'll come when you ask for him."

"No, I mean, what if he's standing right there?"

"Then this will all go much faster."

"Who do I say is calling?"

"When they ask, you say, 'Mr. Massey.'"

"Really?"

"Really." Cleaver grinned. "We are official representatives of Mr. Massey here. So when you go in and you demand to see Mik, you are demanding it in the name of Mr. Massey."

Lamb sat back in the passenger seat, staring at the car ceiling, smiling. "Wow. Imagine that."

"Right. Imagine that."

"And then what do I say?"

"That's it."

"No, I mean, when Mr. Mickle...Mr. Mickelinie..."

"'Mr. Mike.'"

"...when Mr. Mike comes in, what do I tell him?"

"Just call him. I'll handle the rest."

"Seriously?"

"Seriously."

"So you're going to negotiate with him?"

Cleaver thought over the choice of words. Nodded. "Sure. I will negotiate with him."

"And then we, what, make a citizen's arrest?"

Cleaver was somewhere else for moment. "What?"

"You know, because Mike killed the guy. That's what you said, right?"

Cleaver paused again. Thinking. "Sure."

He checked his watch. 10:47 AM. Enid would be leaving for her lunch soon. Every morning at 10:58 AM she left the office to walk two blocks West down to a deli that made her favorite sandwich. It was a pattern from which she never deviated. Reuben, hold the kraut, pickles on the side. She hated pickle juice on her sandwich. Door to door, she would be gone exactly twenty-seven minutes. Enough time to make this work.

Cleaver started the car, inched out onto the road. Parked along the curb, one block east. There would be no reason for her to see them there. He checked his watch again. 10:50. Turned to the other guy, held out his hand. "Gimme your gun."

Lamb looked panicked. "Whaddaya mean?"

"I mean gimme your gun. You do not want to walk in there with a gun. Trust me."

Lamb's eyes flicked out the side window as he considered this. Finally, he tentatively reached into his belt and pulled out the gun. "Okay—if you're sure…"

Cleaver grinned. "Trust me."

Another few minutes passed. At 10:53, the front door to Frozen Futures opened and Enid came out.

Five minutes early.

Mikolaczyk was at the door, too, chatting it up with her. She laughed at something he said. He was grinning, so maybe she was laughing with him and not at him.

Cleaver was worried that both of them were walking to lunch together. But Enid took off down the sidewalk, Mik watched her from behind for a moment, then went back inside.

Somewhere in Cleaver's mind was the twitch—why was she leaving at 10:53?

He shook the question off, shifted the car into drive. "You ready?"

The other man paused, breathed heavy a second, in and out like he was going to hold his breath for the Olympic swimming competition, then answered, "Yep. Ready."

Once Enid was out of sight, Cleaver hit the gas. Entered traffic for the several yards, then double-parked in front of Frozen Futures. "Now!"

The other man threw open his door, slammed it shut, and strode purposefully toward the entrance. Yanked the door open and rocketed inside. He never looked back, never noticed Cleaver a few steps behind him.

Neither man noticed the van across the street.

Inside, Lamb blustered loudly, more loudly than Cleaver expected, "Mr. Mike! I demand to see Mr. Mike!"

The dummy sounded drunk. No matter, it was a diversion.

There was no one at the front desk. The side door opened and Mik came out. "What the—"

He was cut short by two bullets to the chest. Mik clutched his chest a second, gurgled blood, then slumped to the floor.

Lamb turned, horrified, saw Cleaver holding his gun. "What did you do that for?"

Cleaver shrugged. "He might talk." He walked slowly over to the fallen man, started searching for Mik's gun.

"But if he killed the preacher—"

"Are you really that stupid?" Cleaver found the gun. Clicked off the safety.

"But then—who killed the preacher?"

Cleaver grinned at Lamb. "I say you did." Still clutching Lamb's gun in one hand, he raised Mik's gun with the other.

"But he was dead when we got there."

"Not until I stuck that letter opener in him."

"Huh?"

Cleaver squeezed the trigger twice. Barely noticed the front door yanked open. The look on Lamb's face as he fell to the floor was priceless. He came into this world without a clue, was leaving with—

"Ross!" At the door, Enid, holding a brown paper bag. Lunch for two. She screamed.

Cleaver, holding two smoking guns, was mulling his next move when the Feds burst in around her. "Drop it! Now!" Suddenly he was in the sights of what seemed like a dozen weapons. He dropped both guns. He heard them clatter on tile.

But he wasn't looking at the guns. He was watching Enid cradle Mik's head, sobbing.

— 87 —

On a Thursday, Hank Barton, candidate for City Council, Seventh District, broke down and explained himself. Well, tried to. At the last house on the street, an old man peeked out the curtain—he didn't even open the door—and yelled through the glass point-blank, "Why should I vote for a murderer?"

Hank winced. When that reporter, that Ben Carlson, had followed up his headline CANDIDATE LISTENS TO VOICE OF GOD, THE PEOPLE with the equally questionable headline CANDIDATE LISTENS TO ORGANIZED CRIME TOO, Hank had fought savagely to hold his temper. Had struggled valiantly to not take a swing at yet another human being. (And, he had told himself secretly, to not get sucker-punched a second time.)

The previous story that had appeared in that so-called newspaper was damaging enough. At that point, the challenge for Hank was how to avoid the death spiral of negative public opinion. He had the urge to explain he was not some religious nutcase who heard voices. (And yet, there was also the challenge to somehow explain himself in a way that did not offend that percentage of the constituency who thought hearing voices was perfectly normal. He had no wish to make the problem worse.)

But this new story in the Kansas City Blade, this CANDIDATE LISTENS TO ORGANIZED CRIME TOO, presented a now almost-insurmountable challenge: Reverend Daniel Glory's murder was now hanging over his campaign like a black cloud. And candidate Hank Barton was caught without his umbrella.

When Hank had gone in and spoken with the authorities, it had never occurred to him that somehow it would leak to the press. What about a citizen's rights? What about being innocent until proven guilty?

Somehow, this so-called journalist Ben Carlson had gotten wind of the whole thing. Gotten wind of Hank being interviewed by the police. Gotten wind of Hank's subsequent visit to confess that he might have not been entirely forthcoming in his previous remarks. Gotten wind of the curious juxtaposition of events—his visit to the minister on one day, the visit from suspicious figures on a later day, and then the suspicious figures being wanted in connection with the murder.

The article in the Blade connected the dots in a certain—and certainly damaging—way. Damaging to Hank Barton's profession. Damaging to Hank Barton's reputation.

Damaging to Hank Barton's campaign.

His inner circle told him to ignore it. "Just power through," Sven had said. "Just stay on message. These people are just trying to rattle you. Don't let them do it."

Hank was not so sure about that. "When your entire platform is about values, about integrity, about representing the rights of the forgotten," he said, voice rising as his spirit was sinking, "the suggestion that I am in a mobster's pocket and am now also involved in murder is somehow...somehow..."

"What?"

"It just seems *antithetical* to my entire campaign."

— — —

When Hank and his volunteer—a young man this time—had reached yet another closed door, yet another pair of furtive eyes through a curtain, yet another voice telling him to go away, Hank Barton, candidate for City Council, Seventh District, could not just ignore the damage done.

Which is why he finally broke down and tried to explain himself. He got as far as "No, sir, the report in the newspaper was fraudulent—" before his uncaptive audience left the window and went back to his TV to watch Montel Williams.

He glanced at his volunteer, who seemed to be preoccupied with something on his shoes. Hank Barton, candidate for City Council, Seventh District, sighed. Chose to ignore it. Chose to power through. Chose to stay on message. "Let's try the next one."

— 88 —

I finally admitted it to myself: I had lost my way. Had by that point not been back home for several days. How long had it been? Three days? Five? I didn't dare go back. Surely someone would be looking for me there. The police. The Mendels's lawyer. Some big, thick-necked guy named Guido who wanted to pay a visit to my kneecaps.

I had given up on the radio, on the hope of any news about the Antichrist or his evil machinations. Any news that we faithful few were about to be called up into the sky, rescued from our tribulations on earth. And boy, did I have tribulations. I just never thought it would strike as close to home as being a fugitive from a murder rap and owing a lot of money to organized crime.

For the time being, I had pulled into the parking lot of Mister

Bee's Grocery. It was shut down now, but hopefully nobody would think twice about the car parked in front of it. I checked the gauge. The car was almost out of gas. Running on fumes. Leaving town was no longer even an option.

I had spent the past few days in a fuzzy, hazy state of mind. Moving the car from parking lot to parking lot. Nowhere to go. Nowhere to hide. I spent my nights asleep in the car, my days trying to think of a place to stay, a place to crash, a place to stop and think.

I didn't dare go back to the office—not that it was actually even my office anymore. After the way I'd told Sherman off, I certainly would not be welcome there.

I hadn't heard from my wife in a long while. Tried to check my cell phone for messages, but the battery was dead.

I looked at the big, empty parking lot. It was a shame this place had been dark so long. I couldn't even remember when it was operating. It seemed like yesterday when I'd brought the boy out here with his little go-cart and we'd run figure-eights in the empty parking lot.

And now, I remembered, my little boy was in the hospital. There must have been something in the air, because my eyes started to mist up.

Everything was such a mess. My life. My career. My family. My religion. Everything in jeopardy.

The Lord had no business hiding all those secret codes in the Bible. Distracting folks with tantalizing conspiracy theories.

Reverend Daniel Glory had no business leading his people astray like that. Deceiving even the very elect.

The wife had no business spending the last of our money on herself. Spending our life savings on her material lusts, frittering away the kids' college fund.

The mob had no business offering money to an innocent bystander like that. Preying on the unfortunate circumstances of ordinary people's lives.

Then a thought came to me. An idea. (Was it the voice of God? I don't know.)

I saw in my mind two things from the Bible. Two projects. Two stunning examples of engineering: Noah's Ark and the Tower of Babel.

But their results were vastly different from each other. One was enormously successful—it saved the human race from extinction. The other was an enormous failure—it led to the disintegration of civilization.

What was the difference between them? Listen, this is important. It was like, sitting in that parking lot of Mister Bee's, someone had flipped a switch in my mind. Like the light came on.

Noah's Ark was a success because God spoke first. It was God's idea. And man went along with God's plan and was blessed.

The Tower of Babel was a failure because man spoke first. It was all backward. And man was cursed for it.

And I realized I had lived my life like the people building the Tower of Babel. I had come up with the ideas, and expected God to bless them.

Here I was in this horrible, horrible mess, and I was blaming everybody for it but myself. I blamed God. I blamed Reverend Glory. I blamed my wife and kids. I blamed the mob.

No.

It wasn't them.

It was me.

All me.

I had been deceived by my own arrogance. By my own greed. My own lust for material possessions. And I'd ended up here, alone.

And now my boy was in a hospital bed. Who knows how bad off. Who knows how much longer he had to live.

I cried out to God. I owned up to the mess.

I asked the Lord for help to do the right thing—to get me back on track.

That's when I saw the black-and-white police car pull into the parking lot. Did God send it? It was probably just turning around. But when I leaped out of my car and started running toward it, the men inside noticed me quickly. I also realize I should have approached them more calmly, less like a crazy man.

But I was crazy. And I knew how to get better.

And that's how I ended up seeing you, Detective Griggs. I needed to make my statement. I needed to come clean.

So that is my statement. I am prepared to be charged with the murder of Reverend Daniel Glory.

~ 89 ~

Detective Charlie Pasch. Sunday morning. First service. Serving in children's church. And it was going pretty well.

Following the eggs incident of a couple of weeks ago, apparently some of the kids had decided Mr. Charlie was "the funny one." When they first started calling him that, Charlie was embarrassed. But as the morning progressed, he began to realize the kids meant it as a good thing.

During the service itself, there were no major accidents. Charlie did not ignite anything flammable. Drop anything breakable. Splatter anything gloppable.

And the lesson had really seemed to connect. Pastor Wallace had taught on using the Bible as a practical tool in everyday life. "The Bible is not just something you bring to church and then throw aside when you get home. When you're at school, the Bible is a part of your life. When you're out playing with your friends, the Bible is part of your life. At home with your family, the Bible is part of your life."

Charlie liked that. He wondered how he could share it with Detective Griggs without getting his head bitten off.

When the big class broke up into discussion groups, Charlie did not have to field any crazy questions about mature passages from the Bible. He was even able to engage the silent children in discussing the lesson. He was able to draw even the youngest kids in the circle into thinking of everyday ways the Bible could be used as a practical guidebook.

Afterward, the usual mob of parents came to the gym and lined up to check their kids out. To Charlie, the whole atmosphere seemed a lot more polite than in previous weeks.

He also discovered that word had gotten around about how he'd rescued the little boy. It turned out the dad had broken out of jail and had intended to take his son to Mexico with him. Thanks to Charlie, young Jack was safe again with his mom—and the dad was cooling his heels back in jail.

Several parents came up to Charlie and thanked him. Some asked for a play-by-play, but he was too shy for that. Some kids asked to see the bump on the back of his head.

Jack's mother brought Charlie a zip-lock bag of homemade cookies. "It's not much for rescuing my little boy, I know," she said. "But I just wanted you to know how much I appreciated what you did."

After about twenty minutes, the crowd by the door dwindled. Most of the kids had been claimed, their families headed home or to Sunday dinner. Charlie and some of the other helpers started preparing for the next service: re-straightening the rows of red folding chairs, restocking the plastic tub of Kingdom Cash, getting enough cookies to hand out as prizes for the Bible-memory-verse game.

Charlie was hanging out by the soundboard, setting up the music. His attention on the knobs and switches, he heard a voice. "How'd it go?"

He looked up, "Hmm?" It was one of the helpers, Kara. Charlie nodded tentatively. "I think the service went pretty well." He grinned. "At least, nothing was damaged this time."

"Good to hear."

While Charlie was checking sound levels, one last set of parents and children came to find him. "Excuse me, Mr. Charlie?" That was what was on his nametag, so few people here knew his last name. "We want to thank you for setting such a good example for our children."

Charlie looked up to see a pretty Hispanic woman smiling at him, her family just behind her. He felt himself blush, smiled back shyly. "Well, ma'am, I am trained as a cop, so when that man ran off with that little boy—"

She blinked and shook her head. "No, I mean when you spilled the cartons of eggs."

Charlie stopped short. "What?"

The father, holding a little girl in his arms, said, "Julio told us all about it. He said that during one service you smashed some cartons of eggs—and you stopped right in the middle of church to clean it up."

"Oh. That." Charlie blushed. "Well, that was nothing. I just didn't want to let it ruin the gym floor."

The woman grinned. "But you stopped what you were doing to clean up your mess. This week, Julio spilled spaghetti in the kitchen, and I didn't even have to ask him to clean it up. He said, 'Mr. Charlie cleans up,' and he cleaned it up all by himself." She turned and grinned at the little boy holding her hand. "Well, mostly by himself."

She tousled Julio's hair. The boy grinned up at her.

The man said, "So we just wanted to come thank you for setting a good example for our children. And for serving and helping our kids every week."

She nodded. "These are our children. They are important to us."

Charlie grinned at both of them. "It is our pleasure." He reached out and tweaked the little girl's knee. She grinned and squirmed playfully in her father's grip. "These are tomorrow's leaders. We need to build for the future."

The man and woman smiled at him again and left for the exit. Charlie went back to setting up for the second service, whistling a happy tune.

He had a good feeling about this.

— 90 —

Campaign headquarters. Hank Barton, candidate for City Council, Seventh District, sat off to the side, shoulders hunched. He couldn't seem to stop staring in the general direction of the signage tossed in the corner.

Most of his friends and supporters had already left. Of the stragglers remaining, most were either loitering or throwing away the now useless campaign supplies.

Some milled around the office in a daze, chatting quietly, drinking heavily from the now-ironically-named "victory punch." Fighting to keep up their spirits as the TV news wrapped up its report of the special election. His failure.

Over on Hank's desk, a copy of that morning's *Kansas City Blade*. Buried somewhere deep in the back of the paper, *MURDER INVESTIGATION TURNS AWAY FROM CANDIDATE*. The newspaper had finally exonerated Hank Barton, finally declared he was not consorting with organized crime, not a murderer, not a fugitive from justice.

But too late—and too little—to do any good. A few people suggested he could sue the paper. But even that would not repair the damage. It certainly was not going to help tonight.

All told, it had been a long night—waiting by the phone, watching poll results, pacing, pacing, pacing. At first, it was a packed room, electricity and hope in the air. Every eye glued to the set, the phones ringing off the hook.

But as the evening wore on, it became more and more clear he just did not have the votes to make it. Now it was all over but the sweeping.

His eyes down on his shoes, he heard a voice. "Don't let it get you down, Hank." He looked up and saw his friend Sven Surtees. The man offered a reassuring smile. "You gave it a good run."

Hank sighed. Deflated. "Sure." He offered a weak smile back.

Sven shrugged. "Come on, man. Don't let them see you like this."

"Who?" Hank's eyes took in the few people left in the big empty room. He shrugged. "See me like what?"

"Stand up." Sven grabbed Hank by the arm and tugged. "You're the fearless leader. Lead us."

Hank grudgingly stood, knees cracking. "Okay, now what?"

"What do you mean?"

"You got me up, now tell me what you want."

Sven frowned. "What are you doing?"

Hank just didn't have the strength for debate. He just wanted some simple directions to end this night, and then he wanted to go home and sleep. For a week. "No, seriously, just tell me what you want."

Sven leaned in close. Narrowed his eyes. "Hank Barton, you had a vision. Remember? Storm the gates of hell? What about that?"

Hank shook his head. "Gates appeared to be closed." Pointed toward the TV, where somebody was now flipping the channels, looking for sitcom reruns. "The people have spoken." He heard a cracking sound, saw someone stuffing oversized *BETTER WITH BARTON* signs into a metal trash barrel.

"So that's it?"

"What?"

"These people looked up to you. Listened to you. Believed in you." Sven shook his head. "Believed in what you stood for."

"And it was a waste of our time." He motioned to the boxes of unused flyers, the piles of unused signs. Lisa, his wife, was packing up her desk. "All that work we did. What did we get out of it?" He sighed. "Maybe I didn't deserve it."

"With that attitude, maybe you didn't."

Hank furrowed his brow. "Hey!"

Sven frowned. "Prove me wrong."

Hank's eyes flashed. Then he relaxed and smiled at his friend. "I guess I never did give my concession speech." He turned for the front. His friend patted him on the shoulder and Hank turned back. "Thanks."

Hank Barton, candidate for City Council, Seventh District, reached the podium. Stragglers gathered around the staging area. He cleared his throat. He remembered a piece of advice he had gotten one time, from a man named Joe Konrath. *When you don't have the confidence, just pretend—and it will come to you.*

Hank leaned into the microphone. "Friends, the people have spoken tonight—and they have picked the newest member of the City Council." He paused and looked out into the faces of his supporters. "And while they did not put us in office—and I won't lie to you, this is a disappointment—we did not run this race in vain. We have made our case. We have raised our voice. We had our eyes on the goal…and if we have not yet reached that goal, then we have not yet stopped running.

"What we have lost is today. But there is tomorrow—and there is next week, and the next election. As long as we are citizens, it is our duty to live as citizens. It is our duty to participate in the culture. It is our duty to participate in the political arena. It is our duty to make a difference—and that starts with being good neighbors, good churchgoers, and good citizens."

He looked over at Sven, and the two exchanged smiles. That is when Hank finally felt understood.

He turned back to the mic. "We are not broken. We are not in mourning. We ran a good race. As we press forward, we do not look back. Pushing everything aside, we press on. For a better day. No one person can change this city—and that's why we offer our support to the newest member of the City Council. And the entire council. We offer them our support. Because good citizenship requires it."

By the end of the night, Hank Barton had made a point to shake every hand, to look every person in the eye and thank them for their help. To a person, they each said, *Next time.*

As Sven and Wendy and Lisa went out the door, Hank took one last look around the now defunct campaign headquarters. Nodded. Shut the lights out and headed after the others for dinner.

Next time.

— 91 —

It took some navigating through the bright white hospital corridors, but the two men finally found the right hospital room. Mark Hogan shuffled his feet uncertainly, then stepped through the doorway. The officer took up his post out in the hall.

The patient was sleeping. Hogan's wife, Marge, sat at their son's bedside.

When she first saw him enter the room, she rose, face scrunched up, hands clenching. But as Hogan stumbled toward the bed, her face changed. "Mark! What happened?"

He put his arm around her, acutely aware of his smell. "I'm fine," he grunted. "Got a ride from the police."

"The police?" She moved closer, touched his face. Her voice softened. "Are you all right?"

He nodded. "I will be." He swallowed, trying to figure out his words. He'd never admitted to being wrong before. He didn't much like it. "They're only going to charge me with tampering with evidence. And a couple of minor offenses."

"Charge you...?"

He winced as he turned and put one hand on his son's. "How is Clint?"

"It was touch and go when they first brought him in. But he's able to breathe on his own now."

"What happened?"

"He lost control of the truck and flipped over. He hit another car, but the woman is all right, thank the Lord." She put her hand on his arm. "We haven't seen you for days."

Hogan sighed. "Reverend Glory is dead."

Marge wrapped her arms around herself, nodding sadly. "It was on the news." Then she blanched, stared at him. "Y-you didn't...?"

"No, I didn't kill him." He shook his head. "But I thought I had. By the time I turned myself in, the police already had it all figured out."

His knees shaking, he grabbed the back of a chair and sat down. His head was swimming. "Could I have some water?"

Marge grabbed the plastic pitcher, poured water into a Styrofoam cup. Hogan gulped it down. Wiping his mouth with the back of his arm, he grimaced at the taste of grime and sweat.

But she was still waiting for details. He filled her in. The trip to Chicago, the rude awakening, confronting Reverend Glory—every last humiliating thing. As the story went on, Marge's eyes grew wider. Finally, she covered her mouth with her hand.

"I thought I'd killed him," Hogan finished. His eyes started welling up and he wiped them with the back of his arm. The grime and sweat stung them, only making it worse. "I just left him. Ran like a coward."

Marge bent down and put her arms around him. "But you didn't kill him?"

"Apparently I just stunned him. The police say he was probably conscious when the other guy went in there. The guy who…killed him."

"What's the…the evidence they say you tampered with?"

"I panicked. Broke into the video system at church." He wiped his nose on his sleeve. "We may be hearing from the church's lawyer too."

She just nodded.

"They say if I'd left the videos alone, they would have recorded it when the other guy killed Reverend Glory."

After that, they just sat. Neither had much else to say.

Hogan wondered what sort of jail time he might be facing. Wondered about the truck and the boat. Wondered how much it was going to cost to fix the Mendels's garage.

Wondered whether Marge still had the receipts for all those shoes and things.

He almost didn't hear the weak voice from the bed. "Hey, Dad."

Clint, eyes half open, was smiling with everything he had. Mark Hogan pushed himself out of the chair, stumbled to the bed. Tried to think of something to say, anything at all, but words failed him. All he could do was reach through the wires and tubes to hug his son.

⁓ 92 ⁓

Bailey Andrews was not impressed. Out on a double date with her roommate, Julie Lennox, and Julie's boyfriend, Virden. Bailey with her blind date.

"His name is Kurt Wyatt," Julie had said. "He is perfect for you—he's tall, he's really well built, and he's got great teeth."

Anytime a guy was described by looks alone, it always made Bailey nervous. "So, he's as dumb as a post?"

Julie had frowned. Thinking. "I don't think so. Not really. No."

And with that glowing endorsement, Bailey had allowed herself to be roped into the double date. And tonight, on making contact with the gentleman himself at the restaurant, things were not turning out any better than she'd expected.

They had nothing in common. He did not do any reading, except for sports magazines. Did not watch any TV, except for ball games. Did not attend church, except during the church softball season.

Most surprising, though, was that he had no interest in her work. Most guys, upon discovering that Bailey worked with dead people, seemed fascinated with the level of grossness the job required. *What is the worst thing you ever saw? What was the worst thing you ever had to do?*

And such.

On the topic of work, Kurt revealed he had "no special plans." He was still in the process of "finding himself." Was working at a coffee shop to save up enough money to go to California and become a surfing instructor.

Somewhere between the main course and dessert, Bailey and Julie went to the ladies' room. As they checked themselves in the big mirror, Julie grinned broadly, practically elbowing Bailey. "So, what do you think? Huh?"

Bailey leaned closer to the mirror, carefully reapplying lipstick. "He's...nice."

"Nice? He's gorgeous!"

"Yeah." *Almost as gorgeous as he thinks he is.* "But don't you think he's sort of...shallow?"

Julie shrugged. "Men are like that."

"I don't know that all men are like that."

"Trust me, girl, all men are like that."

"Virden doesn't seem like that."

Julie leaned closer to the mirror herself, checking her eyebrows. "Virden is different." She licked her pinky and smoothed down an eyebrow hair. "He's a special kind of shallow."

Bailey didn't even know how to answer that sort of statement. Realized she was dreading going back to the table. She primped in front of the mirror a couple more minutes, hoping to think of some escape.

Her reprieve came in the form of a ring on her cell phone. She checked the ID. Sheriff Fletcher. "Hello, this is Bailey."

"Oh." Sheriff Fletcher sounded caught off-guard. "I thought I was going to get your answering machine."

"Well, you got me live." She put a hand over the mouthpiece and, to Julie, mouthed, *The sheriff.* "What can I do for you?"

"Well, we got a positive ID on that body. The one those boys dug up."

"Oh. Great!"

"But I didn't want to interrupt your Saturday night."

"No, it's all right." She put a hand over the mouthpiece and mouthed to Julie, *They made a positive ID.*

Julie mouthed back, *What?*

A positive ID.

A what?

Bailey shook her head and went back to the call. "So what do we have?"

"Really, this can wait until Monday. I was just intending to leave you a message."

"No, sheriff, this is important. Are you at the station tonight?"

"Yeah. The wife is at some charity event, so I thought I would come in and catch up on some work."

"Look," Bailey said, thinking, "I can call you back in about an hour. Can I do that?"

"Sure. If you want to. Again, I didn't mean to—"

"No, sheriff, you did right in calling me. I'll call you in an hour." She snapped the phone shut. Gave Julie her best pouty look. "I'm sorry, Julie, but I'm going to have to cut the evening short."

– 93 –

Griggs and Charlie spent the afternoon at the batting cages. Griggs was hitting pretty strong.

Charlie had already struck out and was glad to be sitting it out, eating his hot dog. "You know, there are ways to authenticate that signature."

Inside the cage, Griggs had his eye on the ball. SMACK! The ball shot up into the net. He glanced over his shoulder toward Charlie. "What?"

Charlie wiped mustard off his mouth. "I said there are ways to authenticate that signature on your baseball."

"Ah." Griggs shook his head. "That again." Another ball rocketed out of the machine. SMACK! It shot up into the net. "That's how you do it!"

"It could be authentic, you know."

"It could be fake."

Griggs hit a few more balls. Charlie watched. Once his time was up, Griggs sat on the bench next to his partner. Together they watched the next man up.

Charlie said, "Not every fake is malicious."

"What are you talking about?"

"Sports autographs. Not every fake is malicious."

"If somebody is trying to make a buck—"

"No," Charlie said, shaking his head. "In the field of sports memorabilia, the reason some sports autographs are not authentic is because the athlete's spouse or manager might have signed it. It was not intended as fraud."

"Fine."

"I'm talking about classic signatures, of course. Remember, sports memorabilia has only become an industry in the past twenty or thirty years."

"Sure." Griggs looked off into the distance. "I don't know what that has to do with my dad."

"I'm just saying, the baseball your father gave you might be authentic. But even if it is not…" Charlie let the sentence drop. The two men sat in silence a while.

Finally, Griggs spoke. "I've been thinking about that man who came in. You know, the one who thought he killed the preacher."

"Hogan?"

"Right." Griggs sat on the bench, thinking about his next words. Charlie did not push. Finally, Griggs reached into his gym bag and pulled out an object. The autographed baseball he had gotten from his father.

Charlie squinted. "You have it with you."

"Yeah." Adjusting his fingers on the ball, Griggs turned to his partner. "This man Hogan—here was a guy so wrapped up in himself, so wrapped up in his own story…"

Charlie waited. "Yeah?"

Griggs shrugged. "He became disconnected. From his wife. From his children. He was blind to them. Blind to their needs. Blind to their…" He trailed off. Finally, he shrugged. "He was blind."

"Uh-huh."

The two were quiet again, watching the others in the batting cages. Finally, the older detective, still fidgeting with the baseball, leaned toward Charlie and grunted. "Do I get like that?"

"What?"

"Like that guy. You know, so wrapped up in my own stuff—"

"You're comparing yourself to a freak who borrowed money from the mob so he could be in a boat for the Rapture?"

"He was so focused. On the wrong stuff. At the expense of... everything else."

"When you put it that way," Charlie nodded, "maybe we all do that."

"No, this is something that goes much deeper."

"So...what are you saying?"

"Just thinking." He tossed the ball to Charlie. "Go ahead." At the younger detective's confused look, Griggs said, "Check it."

— — —

At the end of the workday, Griggs stopped on the way home to get Carla a bag of M&Ms. She was allergic to peanuts, so he got the kind with almonds.

Carla greeted him at the door with a kiss on the nose. "You're home early."

"I thought it was a normal hour."

"For you, that's early."

He handed her the bag. "Got you a present."

"Hey! Great!" Carla took the M&Ms toward the kitchen. "Dinner will be ready in about twenty minutes."

Griggs went to the easy chair in the living room and plopped down in front of the TV. Flipping through the channels, he kept thinking of his conversation with Charlie. Thinking about that man Hogan. About the baseball.

He yelled toward the kitchen. "How much longer?"

"Few more minutes!"

He got up from the easy chair and went to the front closet. Pulled out the box of unopened letters from his father. Set the box on the dining-room table. Braced himself. Muttered, "Let's try this again."

He picked up the most recent envelope, which had arrived just a couple of weeks ago. The postmark was from somewhere in Mexico.

He carefully opened the envelope. Pulled out the folded paper inside. The most recent letter from his father. The man who'd abandoned his family. The man who'd emptied the till and run off with another woman.

Griggs paused, considering whether he was up to reading it. Staring at the postmark, he realized he was holding his breath.

The phone rang. He walked over to the hall and answered. "This is the Griggs residence."

"I am trying to get in touch with a Thomas Griggs."

"This is Tom."

"Is this Detective Griggs, of the Kansas City Police Department?"

"Yes, it is."

"Detective Griggs, this is Sheriff Ray Fletcher, calling from Braxton County, Kansas."

"Yes? If this is official police business—"

"I apologize for calling you at home, sir, but there is no easy way to break something like this." The man's tone was so dramatic.

"Well, what is it?"

"We found the remains of your father just outside the town of Covenant."

"The...remains?" Griggs looked at the envelope in his other hand. "I'm not sure I understand."

"We discovered the remains of Edward Griggs on a tract of land that was being developed. He was murdered."

Griggs had to sit down. "When did this happen?"

"Based on the evidence, your father has been buried there for at least six years."

Griggs looked again at the envelope in his other hand, postmarked only three weeks ago. "But that's impossible..."

— ~ —

ABOUT THE AUTHOR

—

Chris Well is an acclaimed novelist and an award-winning magazine editor. His "laugh-out-loud Christian thrillers" include *Forgiving Solomon Long* (one of *Booklist*'s Top 10 Christian Novels of 2005), *Deliver Us from Evelyn* (#1 on Technorati, and a #2 Christian thriller on Amazon.com), and the semi-apocalyptic *Tribulation House*.

By day, he is the Web Content Manager for Salem Publishing *(CCM* magazine, *Youth Worker Journal, Preaching)* and a contributing editor for *CCM*. He has also contributed to *Thriller Readers Newsletter, 7ball* magazine, *Alfred Hitchcock's Mystery Magazine,* and *Infuze* magazine.

Chris and his wife make their home in Tennessee, where he is hard at work on his next novel.

— ~ —

NEAR THE END.

⌂ ▭ ⑦   ⊠

BLOG

WHERE IS BLAKE #027
whereisblake.blogdroid.com

"Education is a progressive discovery of our own ignorance."
—Will Durant

My fault. My fault. If I had never started this blog, never started spilling company secrets, never come to Kansas City searching for my past, for my future, none of this might have happened.

But now a human being is dead. As dead as if I had aimed the gun myself and pulled the trigger. And now they're coming for me.

They're going to find me any minute. I know it. I must have been crazy, but then, that's how it always is, isn't it? You feel the thrill of secrets, the thrill of sharing from behind an anonymous mask, the power—and then you are caught. Napoléon was caught. "Hubris," I think it's called. Icarus. I would log onto a dictionary site and check the definition but I don't have the time.

Because they're coming for me. When my adoring fans log onto my blog tomorrow morning, I wonder whether my secrets will still be here. I wonder whether my "crazy theories" will have been proven.

I wonder whether I will have paid for my part in the death of Warren Blake.

But they're coming. These are not people who forgive. These are not people who forget.

All I can think is how it must have been for Warren Blake when his time came. Nobody deserves to go like that.

How will it be when my time comes? A shot to the heart? A knife to the back? A push into an open elevator shaft? Can a person ever know how it all ends for them?

~ Chapter 1 ~

NEAR THE BEGINNING.

Sunday night. April 23.

On his last day of this life, the Right Fair Reverend Missionary Bob Mullins checked the party dip. Just stuck his finger right in there, pulled some glop free, stuck it in his mouth, and sucked.

Hmm, good dip.

He wiped his saliva'd finger on his jacket, popped the top on a can of Pringles, shuffled a neat row of curved chips onto a Dixie paper platter.

There.

Setting the can down, he stepped back from the secondhand coffee table in the middle of the shag-carpeted office, looked at what his party planning skills had wrought. And he saw that it was good.

He went to the stereo system across the room, selected a CD. Personally, he would have preferred something by the Rolling Stones, maybe *Exile on Main Street* or *Beggars Banquet*—muscular, honky-tonk rock 'n' roll you can get drunk or stoned to, depending on your mood. He could really go for the bluesy wail of "Tumbling Dice" right now.

But the music library here offered none of that. Besides, his marks—that is, the members of his "flock"—held certain expectations regarding what music was appropriate for a prayer meeting. Especially in a small armpit of a town like Belt Falls, Illinois.

(Who names a town "Belt Falls" anyway?)

The ladies would be here soon. Then Missionary Bob would use his people skills, honed from his years of "ministry," to good effect.

Would lead the group in a spontaneous (but carefully planned) evening following "the Lord's leading"—some Bible, some hymns, some ministry time. A carefully rehearsed prayer, a combination of wails and pleas, which experience had shown to be a very effective prelude to the passing of the offering plate.

Swept up by the rush of maudlin and spiritual emotion, the ladies would cough up plenty.

"Yea, but there are those who do not have it as comfortably as we do," he found himself practicing, fiddling with chair placement in the circle, maneuvering pillows on the couch. "Poor children who do not have the food or clothing or shelter such as we take for granted."

He double-checked the handy photos on the table. The orphanage in Mexico went by a lot of names. It would not do for the Right Fair Reverend Missionary Bob Mullins to get all weepy-eyed over JESÚS AMA LOS NIÑOS PEQUEÑOS and then whip out a photo showing a bunch of tiny brown faces smiling under a banner that said CHILDREN OF HER MERCY ORPHANAGE.

Following the fiasco in the last town, he'd played it cool once he got to Belt Falls. (Really, who brings a wagon train across the frontier, breaks ground on a settlement, and says, "From henceforth, this shall be known as 'Belt Falls'"?)

Ever since Andrea—his partner, his companion, his ray of light—had got Jesus, she'd stopped helping with the scams. Stopped helping him fleece the flock, so to speak. She laid it on thick enough—*It is appointed unto men once to die, but after this the judgment,* and all that.

He tried to smirk it off, tried the face that always brought her around, but it didn't seem to work anymore. Whatever had got hold of her wasn't letting go.

Missionary Bob would never admit it to anyone, least of all himself, that the dividing line between success and failure began and ended with Andrea. When she was working with him, the scams worked like butter.

But then she got religion, and the whole machine went up in flames.

Not that Missionary Bob got the clue. He kept working his games, town to town, each new gambit failing, each new town harder to crack than the last.

Once he set up shop here in Belt Falls (don't get him started again about the name of the town), he took his time getting to know the people. Found them to be a small, close-knit community, smugly going to their church services.

Smug, but not that pious—it did not take much effort to plant sufficient evidence that the only pastor in town was a raving drug user, maybe even a dealer. Not enough evidence to get the man convicted—even the hick sheriff saw it was a weak case—but the hapless pastor had to make only one phone call to the wrong deacon asking for bail money before word of his *unholy lifestyle* rushed through the congregation like wildfire.

In the eyes of God and the law, he was probably an okay guy. But once a congregation chooses to believe the worst, a preacher may as well pack his bags and move on.

Missionary Bob had even heard tell of one particular church, somewhere in the Midwest, where the members had booted the pastor because he'd had the temerity to wear *short pants* to a *church potluck*.

Yep, hell—if it existed—would be packed to the lips with smug, busybody churchgoers who ran their preacher out of town because he had worn shorts to a church potluck. Or, as in this case, had been the victim of circumstantial evidence planted on him by a traveling huckster.

He stood and straightened his dress jacket. Felt a bulge in his left pocket, was surprised to discover a coaster with the face of Jesus on it.

He looked around the office, befuddled. When had he picked this up?

You don't have to lift anything here, he reminded himself. *You've pretty much lifted the whole office already.*

Missionary Bob, in what used to be the hapless pastor's office, heard steps echoing from the foyer, somebody clomping up the stairs. *My, my*, thought the Right Fair Reverend Missionary Bob Mullins, *these ladies do need to lose some weight, don't they?* Whoever this was, she was pounding the stairs to wake the devil.

He stopped fidgeting with pillows and stood up straight, getting into character. Thinking of his plan, his mission, remembering the correct accent and speech patterns of a Right Fair Reverend Missionary, an accent as specific and undeniable as the drawl of New Orleans or the wicked blue-blood of Boston.

There was an insistent pounding on the door, a battering, really, if he had stopped to think about it. But he was too wrapped up in the character of a Right Fair Reverend Missionary. He slapped on a toothy grin and opened the door. "Welcome, child, to—"

It was a man. A. Large. Man. A grizzly bear towering over him, bloated flannel shirt cascading out of pants where they were almost tucked, tractor cap on his head declaring EAT ROADKILL. The grizzly bear pressed his flannelled beer belly against the Right Fair Reverend Missionary, leaned down from on high, and belched, "I'm Darla Mae's husband."

The Right Fair Reverend Missionary Bob Mullins broke character and cursed.

The rest of the confrontation was like a dream, a nightmare of slow motion, the bear smacking him, a freight train to the skull, tossing Missionary Bob across the room. Hitting the coffee table as he went down, elbow in the dip. The grizzly roaring, storming in, Missionary Bob on the floor, scrambling backward, away, fleeing in the only direction he could, farther into the room. The angry husband kicking the table over, party snacks flying, dip spattering across the bookcase.

As Missionary Bob kicked to his feet, always moving backward until the wall stopped his escape, one question kept flashing through his mind: *Is this about the fake antique Cross of James, or is this about the adultery?*

Either way, his back against the wall, this grizzly man bearing down on him, Missionary Bob was out of options. The giant man, his eyes red, had barrel fists clenched and ready to swing like sledgehammers.

There was a noise behind the grizzly, at the open door. "Missionary Bob?"

One of the ladies.

The enraged husband turned at the voice. Missionary Bob took his one and only chance, grabbed the stone head of Molière, clubbed the grizzly across the side of the head. The man stumbled backward and fell.

Missionary Bob, fueled by anger and fear and blind, stupid adrenaline, kept clubbing, again and again. The man on the floor now, blood streaming from his head. Missionary Bob clubbing him with the bust again and again. On his knees, on top of the man, clubbing him again and again and again.

Finally, adrenaline loosening its grip, Missionary Bob became aware the man was not moving. Clutching air in hot, painful gasps, he dropped the bust to the carpet. Felt something wet on the side of his face, wiped it with his sleeve, saw blood smeared on fabric. Not his own blood.

Gasping, wheezing, he looked up and saw the witnesses, ladies pooling in the doorway, staring agape at the Goliath on the floor, downed by the David with his stone.

— — —

Deliver Us from Evelyn
by Chris Well

ISBN-13: 978-0-7369-1406-2
ISBN-10: 0-7369-1406-4

Now available from Harvest House Publishers

An Epic Saga
of the Pursuit of Faith and Honor

Packer Throme longs to bring prosperity back to his fishing village
by discovering the trade secrets of Scat Wilkins, a notorious pirate who

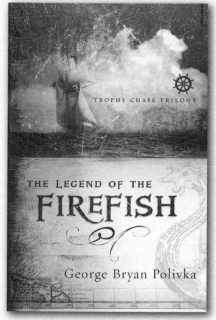

now seeks to hunt the legendary
Firefish and sell its rare meat.

Packer begins his quest by
stowing away aboard Scat's ship,
the *Trophy Chase,* bound for the
open sea. Though he is armed
with the love of a Nearing Vast
priest's daughter, Panna Seline,
and a hard-won mastery of the
sword, many tests of his courage
and resolve follow—beginning
when the young adventurer is discovered by Scat Wilkins himself.

Will belief and vision be
enough for Packer Throme to
survive? And will Talon, the
Drammune warrior woman who
serves as Scat's security officer, be Packer's deliverance…or his death?

And what of Panna Seline? In her determination not to lose Packer,
she leaves home to follow the man she loves, but soon she is swept up
in a perilous adventure of her own.

This epic struggle of faith makes *The Legend of the Firefish* a com-
pelling story that will be enjoyed worldwide by fans of adventure,
fantasy, and visionary tales of honor, conflict, and sacrifice.

Book One of the Trophy Chase Trilogy by author
George Bryan Polivka

Trial by Ordeal
Craig Parshall

✥

Kevin Hastings is ready to stake out his piece of the good life.
The last thing he has in mind is a spot under the Chicago River...
courtesy of the local Mafia.

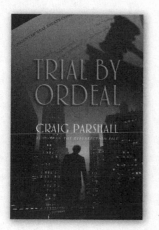

Pursuing a good real-estate investment, the young professor stumbles onto a prime chunk of property in downtown Chicago. It just has an old church building to be cleared away. But the dream deal turns into an ordeal when Kevin discovers he's signed a contract with the Mob—one he can't deliver on.

With death threats coming from the Mob boss and lawsuits piling up, the one bright spot is his new love interest, Tess... until he finds out she's a rabid architectural preservationist.

What else can go wrong? Don't ask. Kevin hires an attorney to untangle the mess, and the guy turns out to be a master of legal intimidation and dirty tricks. When he starts dispensing pain and chaos, Kevin has to run for his life. He ends up finding sanctuary at a local rescue mission.

The lawyers keep ringing the cash register while the bell tolls for Kevin—and he begins to wonder if there's Somebody who can bring justice into all the torment...

"An enjoyable romp for legal thriller aficionados."
Publishers Weekly magazine

From author Brandt Dodson

Mystery and suspense readers are invited to meet Colton Parker, P.I.

Original Sin

Colton Parker was just fired from the FBI, has a teenage daughter who blames him for her mother's death, and now that he's hung out his shingle as a P.I., his first paying client—Angie Howe—has enough money for only one day's worth of investigating. But Angie looks like she could use a friend, so Colton has his first case.

By the time the mystery is resolved, Colton is also resolved—reluctantly—to improve his parenting skills with his daughter. And while the pair still struggle, hope finally gets a chance to grow.

Seventy Times Seven

Lester Cheek had everything a man could want. A beautiful home, a thriving business, and money to burn. But he was alone—very alone. Until he met Claudia.

The attractive and effervescent Claudia was everything Lester could hope for. But then, she mysteriously disappears, and Colton Parker is hired to find her.

The Root of All Evil

Wealthy businessman Berger Hume is dying. And what he wants most is the one thing his millions cannot buy—a relationship with the son he has never met. As Colton Parker, private investigator, searches to locate the son, he finds himself the target of threats from a powerful gang with ties that extend to high levels in the government.

The twists of this case cause Colton to question his own values. Will he risk the one thing that matters most? And will this race against time become a race for his own life?

Suspense...intrigue...drama
in the tradition of Dashiell Hammett and Raymond Chandler